# PRAISE FOR MINDY KLASKY

## Girl's Guide to Witchcraft

"Mindy Klasky's newest work, Girl's Guide to Witchcraft, joins a love story with urban fantasy and just a bit of humor.... Throw in family troubles, a good friend who bakes Triple-Chocolate Madness, a familiar who prefers an alternative lifestyle plus a disturbingly good-looking mentor and you have one very interesting read." *SF Revu*

## Sorcery and the Single Girl

"Klasky emphasizes the importance of being true to yourself and having faith in friends and family in her bewitching second romance.... Readers who identify with Jane's remembered high school social angst will cheer her all the way." *Publishers Weekly*

## Magic and the Modern Girl

"Filled with magic—both of the witch world and the romance world—complicated family relationships and a heavy dose of chick-lit humor, this story is the perfect ending to the series." *RT Book Reviews*

D1447164

# Joy of Witchcraft

### Book Five of the Jane Madison Series

## Mindy Klasky

**Book View Café**
Cedar Crest, New Mexico

Book View Café Publishing Cooperative
P.O. Box 1624
Cedar Crest, NM 87008-1624

Publisher's Note: This is a work of fiction. Names, characters, places, and incidents are a product of the author's imagination. Locales and public names are sometimes used for atmospheric purposes. Any resemblance to actual people, living or dead, or to businesses, companies, events, institutions, or locales is completely coincidental.

Book Layout ©2013 BookDesignTemplates.com
Cover by Lee Jay Stura

Ordering Information.
Quantity sales. Special discounts are available on quantity purchases by corporations, associations, and others. For details, contact the "Special Sales Department" at the address above.

Joy of Witchcraft/Mindy Klasky – 1st ed.
ISBN 978-1-61138-544-1

# Joy of Witchcraft

# Also By Mindy Klasky

### The Jane Madison Series
Girl's Guide to Witchcraft
Sorcery and the Single Girl
Magic and the Modern Girl
Single Witch's Survival Guide
Joy of Witchcraft

### The As You Wish Series
Act One, Wish One
Wishing in the Wings
Wish Upon a Star

### Stand-Alone Novels
Capitol Magic
Fright Court

### The Diamond Brides Series
Perfect Pitch
Catching Hell
Reaching First
Second Thoughts
Third Degree
Stopping Short
From Left Field
Center Stage
Always Right

### The Glasswrights Series
The Glasswrights' Apprentice
The Glasswrights' Progress
The Glasswrights' Journeyman
The Glasswrights' Test
The Glasswrights' Master

*To Kirstin Olsen,*
*who introduced me to a NWTA so many years ago*

# Chapter 1

SOMETIMES A THUNDERSTORM is just a thunderstorm.

Opaque black clouds, torrential rain, and wind whipping across the front yard at hurricane force don't *have* to mean anything arcane. At least, that's what I told myself as I looked out the farmhouse window after sunset on Samhain.

Alas, I knew better. Plenty of people wanted to see the Jane Madison Academy fail, and this was exactly the type of tactic they'd use. Threaten me with direct lightning strikes, and I couldn't very well celebrate the witch's new year. Without a magic ritual, I couldn't officially welcome my first real class of students. No students meant no classes, and then I'd be in violation of my hard-won charter.

And it wasn't just the Academy on the line. My enemies wanted my magical tools—the books and runes and crystals laid out on shelves in the farmhouse basement, painstakingly organized by all the principles I'd mastered as a librarian before I ever knew I was a witch. They wanted Neko too, my familiar.

As another torrent of rain slashed across the front porch, Neko shuddered from the crown of his immaculately coiffed head to the tips of his leather-clad toes. There were times I almost forgot I'd awakened this man out of a magical statue of a cat, that I'd bound him to my service on the night of a full moon. But when he trembled the way he did now, he looked every bit like his feline avatar. I half expected him to lick the side of his palm and use it to smooth down the flawless velvet of his close-cropped hair.

Instead, we both jumped as a vicious fork of lightning struck the main road. I barely had time to brace myself for the crash of thunder that followed. The entire house shook under the assault.

"We've got to get everyone in here," I said, squinting through the glass into the rain-whipped darkness. "They aren't safe in the garage apartment. The barn, either." The school year might not have officially started yet, but I was already responsible for more than a dozen souls out there.

Neko cocked his head, as if he could hear something in the distance. "They're fine," he said.

I gave him a penetrating look. Neko could speak to other familiars; they had some obscure network that was hidden from us witches. I'd asked him to explain it before, but he always ran out of words. Familiars weren't telepathic; they didn't transmit individual words from mind to mind. Rather, they spoke in entire images, in complete concepts. That's how a newly awakened familiar knew details about the world he faced, about how to best serve his witch.

But Neko wasn't above lying if he thought he could spare himself a drenching.

"What?" he asked, the picture of complete innocence. "You don't *trust* me?"

"I didn't get to be magistrix of the Jane Madison Academy by trusting the world's craftiest familiar."

He preened, as if I'd just given him a compliment. "I'm the one who recommended that anti-frizz shampoo, didn't I? And it's worked wonders for your hair." Neko devoted a lot of time to sounding like the most blatant stereotype of a gay man who ever belted out a Broadway anthem. I was convinced he put on the act just to astonish everyone when he proved to be the most attentive familiar a witch could ever ask for. "And I told you your fingernails would stop splitting if you added a tablespoon of protein powder to your smoothies. And just the other day, I distinctly remember telling you to practice your Kegel exercises if you really want to drive—"

A dry cough cut him off, and we both whirled toward the arch that led to the dining room. David Montrose stood there. My warder and I had met on a night much like this one—storm-tossed and chaotic, my then-newly-awakened powers tingling like the aftermath of a too-close lightning strike.

The first time I saw him, I thought he was an egotistical boor. I'm pretty sure he thought I was a naive twit—at best. I've never had the nerve to ask him what he thought, even though he'd stood by me through more arcane adventures than any witch should have in one lifetime. Even though I now wore his diamond engagement ring on my left hand.

"TMI?" Neko asked demurely.

"By half," David said, striding across the room. His black Lab, Spot, stayed close by his heels, whining softly when another flash of lightning gave way to a roll of thunder. David automatically settled a hand on the dog's broad forehead, murmuring a few words before he said to us, "The students *are* safe in their dormitory. Their familiars and warders, too. That barn has withstood worse storms than this."

David came to stand behind me, and heat radiated from his body, all the warmer for the chill coming off the glass. His palm was warm against my nape, and I leaned into the firm touch of his fingers on my scalp. Spot pressed his head under my hand, eager for a comforting pat.

"Fine," Neko said. "Believe your *warder*. Don't trust what your *familiar* has to say."

I smiled serenely, certain he would pick up my reflection in the window. "My warder completed the construction on those buildings. Of course he knows if they're secure against this storm."

Neko spluttered in mock protest as David slipped his hands to my waist. "You should get ready," David told me. "In half an hour, we'll get a break in the rain."

I looked out at the storm savaging the lawn. "I didn't know warders could work the weather."

"We can't. But we can check apps on our phones. According to the National Weather Service, we'll get a break around ten. By midnight, though, we'll be back in the middle of the deluge, so we'll have to move quickly."

I brushed a kiss against my boyfriend's—my *fiancé's*—lips before I headed upstairs to our bedroom. My Samhain finery was spread across the bed. The gown was a new one, carried home by a victorious Neko after a recent shopping foray in nearby Washington DC. Sewn of crushed velvet, the gored skirt rippled like a burgundy tide pool. Its laced bodice was backed with ivory linen and princess sleeves fastened tight, with a row of onyx buttons.

I could use the bolstering effect of onyx. The Jane Madison Academy had gotten off to a rocky start, launching before I was fully ready. We'd barely secured our charter from Hecate's Court by completing a Major Working at the last witch's sabbat, on Mabon in late September.

Even then, we'd only succeeded because of the rather...unconventional style of my witchy powers. With the new year and my new students, I had a chance to prove I could conform to the Court's rigid bureaucracy. I'd have to, or they'd shut me down for good.

And my first test was dressing appropriately for the upcoming working. At least my thoughtful familiar had supplied a Victorian buttonhook made out of tortoiseshell. I fastened the last onyx button with a satisfying tug.

As I smoothed my hands over my luscious skirt, I realized the spatter of rain against the window had died down. The wind had slackened as well; I could no longer hear the starving wolf howling around the corners of the farmhouse. David's weather app had been accurate.

By the time I got back to the living room, my warder had knotted a pewter-colored tie around his throat. The fabric echoed the glint of silver at his temples. A well-worn leather belt sat low across his hips, supporting a matching scabbard. The sword would have looked absurd on most men, a bizarre accompaniment to office attire, but on David it looked *right*. His ease soothed me, even though I had not consciously realized I was nervous.

His ease, and the fact that his eyes widened appreciatively as I entered the room. I indulged in a full-skirted twirl. "You like?" I asked.

"Very much," he said.

I wondered if I'd ever get tired of that *flip* in the pit of my stomach, that sudden awareness that David was looking at me as a woman, not just a witch. I tugged quickly on the bond between us, the magical connection deep within our minds, and I offered up a promise that made the corners of his lips curl in the suggestion of a smile.

"Oh, get a room," Neko snorted.

There'd been a time when his awareness of the bond between David and me would have made me blush. But it wasn't like my familiar stinted with sharing his *own* love life. Gander, meet goose. Spoon up the sauce.

David didn't deign to answer. Instead, he commanded Spot toward his bed in the kitchen and opened the front door, gesturing for Neko to lead the way. My familiar collected a reed basket from the coffee table before he stepped outside with a moue of distaste. That pout turned to outright misery when a fat drop of rain fell from the porch eaves, splashing onto his tight black T-shirt. His pitiful moan would have made a lesser woman consider mercy. Hard-hearted magistrix that I was, I strode past him and headed toward the clearing where we would launch our working.

The sacred space had been my responsibility while David supervised the rapid conversion of the barn and the garage to dormitories. As workmen labored over plumbing and electricity, drywall and flooring, my original pair of witchy students and I had sanctified a clearing for magical workings.

Trimming the grass had been the easy part. We'd erected a centerstone, a marble altar that we washed with mugwort tea. That purifying bath would add to the marble's inherent protective powers, securing our circle against unwelcome invaders.

We'd added to the perimeter, alternating stones and plants known for bolstering defenses. Obsidian for grounding. Vervain to stand against metal weapons. Malachite for safety. Rosemary for protection against the evil eye. Agate for strength. Radish to guard against poison.

I'd combed through the books in my basement horde, searching for the best options, trying to combine magical strengths with the very practical considerations of keeping green, growing things alive in Maryland's variable weather. And I loved everything we'd settled on. Even now, before I'd officially called the Academy into session, this circle felt like a spiritual home.

As we approached the altar, I chalked up another win for the silent communication of familiars. My entire student body was waiting when we arrived at the ritual space—six students, their warders, and familiars, all eyeing me with respect and a healthy dose of nerves. All we had to do was complete our ritual and get the Academy under way by midnight. Then we could rest easy until the end of the semester. We'd have six months to prepare a new Major Working, to show Hecate's Court that we were an academic power to be reckoned with.

I'd been robbed of the opportunity to offer an official welcome to my first students—water under the astral bridge. But I wasn't going to miss out on the opportunity a second time. I took a deep breath, exhaled, and said, "Witches, familiars, and warders, all. Be welcome at the Jane Madison Academy. We'll learn from each other and share our knowledge of the world, arcane and mundane. Our powers together will be greater than our powers apart. So mote it be."

"So mote it be," the witches said together, their voices ranging from soprano to contralto. Shimmers of power echoed across the circle, skeins that tangled and stretched without plan, without design. My pulse picked up at the thought of bringing those strands into order, at sculpting our new future together.

A dull rumble of thunder echoed in the distance, and I shoved down an uneasy mix of fear and excitement. Samhain was the time when the barrier between the arcane world and the mundane was thinnest. Ordinary folk remembered that magic by going out in the darkness, defying their fear with costumes and offerings of sweets. This night was Halloween to most people, All Hallows Eve to some, and Samhain to the witchy few.

I gestured to Neko, bidding him to step forward with his reed basket. As he raised our offerings, David swept his sword from his scabbard.

The other warders reacted to the sound of metal scraping free, becoming more alert, more *present*. Each took a stand outside our sacred circle, automatically spacing themselves along the perimeter that had not yet been defined by magic. My students and their familiars clustered inside the nonexistent boundary, each watching with expressions that ranged from wary to enraptured.

I nodded to David, and he strode to the eastern corner, to the cardinal point dedicated to the element of Air. Neko followed, moving with confidence. He produced a candle from the basket, a fat column of red wax that he set on the small marble plinth at the precise eastern limit of the circle. Passing his hand over the wick, he raised up the twisted fiber, readying the candle for the magical energy that would pass through it, consuming it slowly and steadily for as long as we witches used our powers.

When Neko stepped back, I took his place, raising my palm over the scarlet wax. I could already feel the potential energy in the offering, the power ready to be unleashed. "Guardians of Air, light our way," I cried, and the fresh wick kindled. I collected the light in my cupped hands, carrying it toward my eyes as a gesture of humility toward the entire natural world. As my fingers brushed against my forehead, I felt a breath of air, the softest memory of the storms that had ripped across this clearing not an hour before. We were in the presence of Elementals of Air.

Dropping my hands to my side, I walked with David to the next candle. He traced the tip of his sword just above the grass, and the metal seemed to magnetize the air, raising up a shimmering curtain of steel-grey fire. Power sizzled against the damp lawn, sparking away the sodden remnants of the storm. The energy arched above my head, wavering in time with my pulse.

Neko placed the second candle. "Guardians of Fire," I proclaimed. But before I could entreat, "Light our way," another voice rang out across the circle.

"Hold!"

I grabbed Neko's shoulder, forcing him close to my side. His latent abilities opened before me. His entire being *shifted* to echo my magic, to reflect it back to me like a thousand mirrors casting back the light of a single flame.

Adrenaline jangled my fingers, and my ears were filled with a high-pitched whine. I wanted to fight. I wanted to flee. I waited for the assembled warders to react, for David to step in front of me, offering the physical protection of his body and his sword.

But David didn't move.

"Stop this ritual right now, Jeanette."

And then I understood why David wasn't reacting. There was only one person in this world who called me Jeanette: the woman who'd given me that name on the day I was born. She'd abandoned me a year later, leaving me to be raised by my loving grandmother. I'd grown up believing my mother had died in a car crash. Clara Smythe had only walked back into my life four years ago, the summer I discovered my arcane power.

David didn't move to protect me from my mother because he wasn't just *my* warder. He was Clara's warder too. For that matter, he guarded my grandmother as well, on the relatively rare occasions when she engaged in witchy activities. He'd volunteered for the unusual triple assignment when I first forged my unconventional ideas about witchcraft and community. Hecate's Court hadn't intervened to say he *couldn't* do the job.

I planted my hands on my hips. My fingers still trembled in the aftermath of adrenaline, but I tightened them to hide my annoyance. "Not now, Clara. We're busy with an important working."

"I know, Jeanette. But this is a matter of life and death."

"Life and death," I repeated wryly. Clara could turn a hike in the woods into high drama.

"You cannot cast your circle here," my mother said, striding past my astonished students to stand before our centerstone. "This is a place of danger."

My mother and I often disagreed about arcane matters. She had a soft spot for auras and astrology, for claptrap that had no place in any self-respecting witch's arsenal. I could only imagine what hocus-pocus she intended to fling at us now.

As if she could read my mind, Clara tugged at her silk caftan, drawing herself up to her full height. "You're standing on the edge of a hellmouth that can destroy the entire world. You must not seal the circle, Jane."

Jane.

Clara *never* called me Jane, not without a dozen exasperated reminders that I'd long ago set aside my birth name, that I'd built a life on my own, that I didn't need her, didn't want her interference. If she called me Jane, she wanted me to listen.

But hellmouths were only myths, stories invented in the Middle Ages to keep wayward children in line. There was no such thing as a gaping hole to a different dimension. No one had ever seen a passage between planes of being, a maw that released ill-formed ravening fiends into the world around us.

Nevertheless, my students reacted to Clara's pronouncement by stepping toward their warders. They settled anxious

hands on their familiars, looking around our magical clearing as if they expected demons to spring from the sodden
ground.

If a hellmouth actually existed, I surely would have felt it
as I'd prepared our circle.

Wouldn't I?

Of course I would.

Clara was merely being her usual dramatic, disruptive
self. I nodded tersely to David and said, "Proceed."

"Jane!" Clara cried.

To David's credit, he merely shifted his grip on the quillons of his sword, resuming his stance to carve out the next
protective quarter of our circle. I met his eyes and said,
"There is no hellmouth here." To all who listened, my voice
was as hard as marble. No one would ever know how much
comfort I took from his tight nod of agreement.

Lightning flashed in the distance, illuminating the heavy
clouds that once again covered the sky. Automatically, I
started to count: one Mississippi, two Mississippi, three Mississippi, four. Thunder growled, low and urgent.

I knew a cue when I heard one. Ignoring Clara's whim-
pering, I rushed through casting the rest of the circle. I set a
candle at the southern edge and called on the Guardians of
Water. I lit the last wick on the western point and drew in
the Guardians of Earth. David traced the outline with a
matching urgency, pouring his warder's energy into a steely
arc.

He was three strides away from closing the circle. Two.
One. And then I heard my name again, shouted across the
field, from the direction of the house. "Jane! Jane Madison!"

Even as I gritted my teeth against the new interruption, I
recognized the voice. Teresa Alison Sidney.

Teresa was the Coven Mother for nearby Washington

DC, a woman widely regarded as the most powerful witch in the Eastern Empire—at least until *I'd* come into my own. I'd first met her three and a half years before, when my greatest magical dream had been to join her prestigious coven. When I'd watched her lead a ritual in her classic black cocktail sheath, with her perfect strand of pearls across the pulse points in her throat, I'd felt as if I were watching the ghost of Jacqueline Kennedy Onassis or Grace Kelley, as if Kate Middleton herself shared a bit of magic she'd never quite admitted to the British royal family.

Teresa Alison Sidney's veil of sophistication was so strong that virtually everyone called her by all three names, the way people referred to certain movie stars. Or serial killers. But always contrary where authority was concerned, I'd made myself the exception to that rule.

She'd never forgiven me for walking away from her coven. And she'd never stopped lusting after the Osgood collection, the arcane library I hoarded in the farmhouse. Only two months ago, I'd discovered her magical powers bound up in a document meant to destroy me.

She was my enemy, and now she stood on my lawn, accompanied by her warder and her familiar.

Clara might have interrupted our working out of a misguided fear of a hellmouth. But Teresa certainly had a more selfish motive. All she had to do was distract me for a few minutes, a quarter of an hour at most, and the rapidly returning thunderstorm would do the rest. My untried students could never complete a ritual in the midst of a downpour like the one we'd already seen that evening. Without a proper opening to our academic year, my magicarium would stand in violation of its charter, and my magical belongings would be fair game for any witch daring enough to pluck them from my grasp.

Teresa would finally get the magical goods she'd craved from the moment we first met.

I nodded tersely to David. He slashed with his sword, closing the circle before the Washington Coven Mother could make herself heard. Through the shimmering cordon of warder's magic, I could see the rigid lines of David's back. If I squinted, I could just make out other figures beyond the curtain of power—four robed and hooded forms on the very edge of darkness.

Hecate's Court, then. As expected, they'd arrived to witness my working, to verify the operational status of the Jane Madison Academy. The Court had jurisdiction over all witches in good standing. But I didn't have to like being put under their microscope.

Gritting my teeth, I turned to face my students. "Sisters," I said. "We are gathered beneath the sky, above the earth, between the fire and the rain. Be welcome and at peace."

Right. Like any of them would relax during a ritual that began like this one had. Clara fretted beside me, working her hands inside the sleeves of her caftan as if she were auditioning for the role of Lady Macbeth. Emma, the calmer of my first-term students, looked wary but determined. Raven, a firebrand who could give lightning bolts a run for their money, seemed invigorated by the opportunity for something to go awry.

At least Raven had chosen to wear a black robe for our working, forgoing her usual preference for working skyclad, naked to the elements. I was strangely heartened by the violet sash that closed her midnight garment. Its vibrant purple matched the stripe in her hair, underscoring all the ways she and I were different. We disagreed on almost everything, but we'd found a way to work together.

And I would find a way to work with all my new students,

to build the bonds of a healthy magicarium. I was their mentor, their magistrix. I could do this.

With Neko at my back, I extended my arms to either side. Emma understood immediately. She stepped forward and placed her fingers against mine, automatically reaching for her sister. Raven followed suit, bringing one of the new students into the chain. One by one, they all matched hands, until Clara closed the circuit to my left.

"Jane," she whispered, her voice low and demanding.

I merely shook my head. I was committed to this path, and Clara's imagined hellmouth wasn't going to stop me. Not when Teresa paced outside, waiting for me to fail. Not when new rain had set up a steady beat against the steely dome above us. The wind had picked up as well; gusts buffeted the sloping sides of our shielding cordon.

We were running out of time.

"Well met, sisters," I said, faking a confident tone. "Here at the Jane Madison Academy, you'll be asked to set aside much of what you think you know about magic. You'll view the world through new lenses, from angles that will make your old practice seem limiting and strange. For tonight, though, all I ask is that you join with me to complete a simple, familiar spell."

Moving slowly enough that each of my students could follow suit, I touched my fingertips to my forehead, offering up the power of my pure thoughts. I touched my throat, adding the power of pure speech. I brushed my fingers against my chest, giving my pure belief. Raising my voice to counter the steady hiss of rain against the cordon, I chanted, *"Join me, sisters, near the loom."*

It was the first line of an old spell, an easy one. While mundane little girls were making their first elastic potholders on a plastic frame, young witches learned to weave their fledgling powers into a similar magic fabric. At this launch of the school year, my students and I would weave our powers in and out, creating a cloth unique to the Jane Madison Academy. Down the road, when I taught everyone how to create a *true* merged power, we'd laugh at the simplicity of this working.

As I spoke the first words, I lobbed a golden globe of power into the center of our circle. I nudged the physical manifestation of my astral abilities until a rectangular shape shimmered in the night-time air. When it was stable, I sent a mental invitation to the witches I knew best—to Emma and Raven to add their energy to the uprights of the loom, to Clara to feed her power to the horizontal struts. Purple, silver, and emerald light wrapped around my golden glow, each strand pulsing with unique power.

When I was certain the astral loom's structure was stable, I drew a deep breath and recited the second line of the spell. *"Set the warp threads, leaving room."*

I nudged Neko along our arcane bond, urging him to send a message to my new students' familiars. Cassandra Finch responded first. *Cassie*, I reminded myself. She'd made it clear she preferred the nickname. Her magic was pale green, the soft shade of new leaves unfolding beneath a spring sky. It made me think of young things, fragile things, like the spray of freckles that spotted her cheeks, like her twin braids of unruly blond hair. She bit her lip and fluttered her hand against the shoulder of her familiar, Tupa. I was no expert on the animal roots of familiars, but I was willing to bet the curly-haired, obliviously awkward young man had begun life as a lamb. In fact, Cassie herself had a somewhat disturbing resemblance to Little Bo Peep.

Reaching out to her familiar, Cassie gathered the grounding she needed. Tupa leaned in, actually butting his head against her arm, and the tendril of green strengthened, winding its way toward the centerstone and the waiting frame. Green light wrapped our structure from top to bottom, again and again, until a dozen strands formed a warp suitable for weaving.

*"Lift the shuttle, feel its weight,"* I continued, my voice warming with approval. Neko did his part again, thinking an invitation to another familiar, and a sturdy russet strand of energy flowed from the next student, Bree Carter. Working quickly to increase our momentum, I chanted the next line: *"Wrap the new thread, figure eight."* Neko pulled another student into the working, Alex Warner, who offered up a skein of indigo energy. *"Now the shed stick, straight and true,"* I intoned, raising my voice to do battle against the storm outside our protective arch. Skyler Winthrop and her cobalt blue magic came into our circle.

All that was left was bringing our concentration together, gathering the energy of all eight witches. Working together, we could create a fabric of light, passing Bree's thread-filled shuttle along the straight line created by Skyler's shed stick, tamping down Alex's first thread in our weaving and preparing the warp for another pass at the loom.

Even though we remained separate, each strand of magic apart from every other, we were working toward a common goal. This wasn't the true power I would ultimately offer my students, the true melding I knew we could achieve. But it was a start. I took a deep breath and cried, *"All our powers, cloth imbue!"*

There was the expected flash of darkness, the moment when the physical world shifted out of existence, overwhelmed by magic's force. For one timeless instant, my heart ceased to beat, my lungs stopped breathing. I couldn't worry about my students, couldn't fear the consequences when David sliced open the cordon, when my magicarium emerged to face Hecate's Court and Teresa Alison Sidney and the increasing rage of the storm.

As quickly as the world disappeared, it returned. Every witch's eye was trained on the altar. We all waited to see the cloth we had crafted with our effort.

But there was no cloth.

Instead, there was a shadow, darker than the stormy night outside our shield. The *absence* swirled above the altar, seething, reaching out with clinging tentacles.

"The hellmouth!" Clara shouted, and adrenaline fired through my body.

Somehow, the shadow deepened, becoming a darker shade of black. It contracted, sucking in its outer edges, swirling tighter and tighter, like a tornado determined to bore its way through the centerstone. A blast of rain battered the steely shield above us, a sudden downdraft strong enough to dent the protective dome. At the same time, lightning forked directly overhead, shattering across the cordon as if it sought the heart of the altar.

The warders' arch vanished beneath the direct hit.

Before I could blink, my burgundy gown was drenched. The thunder was literally deafening. The silver lightning afterglow bleached my vision.

But none of that mattered, because the shadow had disappeared above the altar. And in its place, very real and very mad, was a full-grown satyr, tossing his head and looking like he was ready to murder every single witch who had called him into existence.

# Chapter 2

YOU PROBABLY KNOW your mythology: satyrs have the top half of a man and the bottom half of a goat, with the goat's horns firmly placed on the human head, just for good measure. If you grew up reading children's books like *The Lion, The Witch, and the Wardrobe*, you might be thinking of a faun—a sweet, somewhat absent-minded creature with the same man/goat blend.

Satyrs aren't fauns. There's nothing sweet about a satyr. Nothing absent-minded, either. Satyrs have one thing on their mind, and because they don't wear pants, that thing is pretty obvious.

Our magical visitor was no exception. Engorged, erect, he scraped his hooves against the altar as he hunched his shoulders, snorting and tossing his head like a bull maddened by a red cape. But there was no red cape in our Samhain circle, only innocent women. The satyr cackled as he searched for his victim, and the crazed sound made the hair rise on the back of my neck.

He chose Cassie.

Maybe she made some noise, a shout or a whimper, something the rest of us couldn't make out above the chaos of the storm. She might have been the first to move, to recover from the paralyzing effect of the warders' broken shield. Perhaps the beast was drawn to her child-like innocence, her wide eyes, her fresh, freckled face.

Whatever the creature's reasoning, he lost no time in his pursuit. He leaped from the altar and landed on the drenched grass with the legendary sure-footedness of his hircine half. The downpour did nothing to slake his lust; he fell on Cassie with a craven howl.

Cassie's protector, Zach Spencer, lunged for the creature's shoulders, tugging at the human torso in an effort to free his witch. I leaped forward, determined to help my student, but my progress was checked by a strong arm across my belly. Caleb was there, Emma's stalwart warder. I'd known him four months; I'd already trusted him to protect me in dozens of other workings. Now, I wanted him out of my way.

But before I could snap a command, I realized the warders had formed a wall with their bodies. All of us witches and our familiars—everyone but Cassie—were safe behind the bulk of their bodies, protected by their brawn and bared swords. At least three of the men faced out, in case the satyr wasn't the only magical manifestation attacking this night.

Caleb had me, because David had joined forces with Cassie's warder. The two men were struggling to get a grip on the satyr in the rain. The space was too tight for swordplay; they were forced to grapple with their bare hands, lest they harm Cassie in their effort to free her.

The satyr was not so far gone in lust that he forgot to butt at them with his sharp-pointed horns. He forced both men back whenever they seemed close to dragging him to the ground. His hooves landed half a dozen blows as well; I heard David's curses above the roar of the storm as he took a direct kick to his ribs.

Raven's warder, Tony, launched into the fray, using his sword where Zach and David had hesitated. He timed his thrust perfectly, employing a two-handed grip to slam the edge of his blade against the satyr's spine. Bronze sparks flew as if the sword were being held to a grindstone, but the blade made no meaningful impact. The satyr snarled and kicked back with another fierce hoof, but was otherwise unaffected.

Cassie put up her own fight, shoving the heel of her hand into the beast's face. She smashed his nose with enough power that he was forced to back off. As he shook his stunned head, she tried to follow up with a knee to his groin, but she slipped on the grass, falling beneath the ravenous creature again.

Her hands pushed at his chest, but she couldn't get the leverage she needed. Her fingers wove a pattern in the air before the satyr closed once more, a spell I did not recognize. Whatever it was, it required strength and concentration. She might have been able to gain both from her familiar, but the satyr's sharp hooves kept Tupa from getting anywhere near his mistress.

Cassie could not work her spell. But I could try my own.

I raked my hand through my hair, sluicing rainwater off my face as I planted my feet in the slick grass. I didn't have time to bring my students into the working, couldn't worry about demonstrating my novel approach to spellcraft. Instead, I shot out my hand and gripped Neko's forearm, pulling him out of the scrum of desperate, shouting witches and familiars.

He lapsed into his role immediately, bracing his own feet for a better purchase and stiffening his arm to give me a stronger base for working. I tugged on the astral bond between us, and he was ready, waiting, a reflecting well of power for me to use however I needed.

My eyes closed, and I pictured one of the most obscure books in my collection. It was bound in forest-green Moroccan leather, and the cover was set with a trio of cabochon-cut emeralds. The title was picked out on the spine in gold leaf: *On the Bynding and Banishment of Magickal Creatures.*

It contained spells to counter wayward familiars and ravenous bookworms, rebellious cockatrices and invading dragons. And somewhere toward the end, between rocs and trolls, there was a spell to banish a satyr. I took a deep breath, trying to summon an image of the ancient writing. I exhaled slowly, using the motion to center myself as I once again offered up pure thought, pure speech, and pure belief. I sent tendrils deep into Neko's reserve and drew on his reflective power to bolster my own as I chanted:

*"Half man, half beast, figure of a goat,*
*Sharp of hoof, hard of horn, sleek and shiny coat."*

I was only two lines into the spell, but I knew I didn't have enough power to make it work. Not with this monstrous creature that was shielded against traditional warders' weapons. Not with a beast I'd never seen before, had never completely believed in before. I couldn't master the spell with the battle raging in front of me, with Cassie's warder knocked onto his back, his arm canted at an angle that even in my panic I could diagnose as a fracture.

The satyr tossed his head, butting hard against David's chest before screaming and diving back to Cassie. I scraped more power from Neko. Knowing I was doomed to fail but needing to try, I shouted the next two lines of the spell:

*"Wise fool, wild child, scrambling to be free,*
*Hear my voice, know my words, banishéd you'll be."*

As I got to that word, though, to *be*, I realized another voice was raised with mine. Teresa Alison Sidney stood across from me, ignoring the rain and the wind. She rested one hand on the shoulder of her familiar, the other on her warder's forearm. She stared across the line that had marked my magicarium's arcane shield, smiling serenely.

She was certain I didn't have the power to finish the working on my own. But she knew the rest of the spell. She stood ready and willing to help.

She understood what it would cost me to accept her aid, how I longed to shake my head, to refuse her offer of assistance. But I didn't have that luxury. I needed Teresa. And so I nodded, matching her smile with my own grim twisted lips. Her eyes flashed in victory as I raised my arms, letting a wash of golden light ripple to my fingertips and flow toward Cassie and the satyr. Teresa matched me, wave for wave, the ruby glow of her own prodigious powers meeting mine in a fiery line.

Together, we chanted the final couplet of the spell:

*"Satyr leave us, go your way, back from whence you came.*

*Stay away until the day our powers call your name."*

Simultaneously, we changed the last line of the spell, making it plural, making it match the magic we wove. The flash of darkness was immediate, that power-filled absence of everything—the storm, the circle, the weight of my body. And when the world lurched back into being, the satyr was gone.

Half-moon hoofprints quickly filled with rain. David sucked in his breath as he pressed his hand against his ribs. Cassie's warder gritted his teeth, trying to support his broken arm with his good one. Cassie herself collapsed against the ground, her ribcage rising and falling as if she were a salmon plucked from a spawning stream.

David recovered first, snapping out commands to the other warders, ordering everyone back to the farmhouse. The building was warded, protected from all types of marauders, magical and mundane. As my shocked students started to move, David helped Cassie to her feet. Gingerly, he handed her over to the combined attention of Tupa and Zach. At his repeated urging, all of the student witches, their familiars, and their warders began the short trek back to the house.

Only then did David turn to Teresa. Not quite able to bury a lifetime of respect for Teresa's title, David said, "You too, Coven Mother. To the house, for grounding."

Her eyes narrowed, and she stiffened her spine. The defiant gesture helped to mask her rapid breathing, but I was willing to bet her pulse was pounding as hard as mine, harder maybe, because she wasn't on her home turf. "I'll stay to clean up," she said.

David's gaze didn't waver. He didn't even look for the tiny shake of my head. He knew I didn't want Teresa anywhere near the circle we'd created for magical workings. She was not my friend. There'd been no legitimate reason for her to attend our Samhain working. She'd only been present to help banish the satyr because she'd wanted me to fail.

David turned to her warder. "Get her out of here, Ethan."

Warders had their own rules, their own hierarchies, separate from witchy politics and aspirations. We stood on David's property. His wards protected this land. His witch had initiated the Samhain working. Therefore, David's word controlled. Ethan slipped his fingers beneath Teresa's elbow and guided her toward the farmhouse. Her familiar trailed behind, looking lost in the dim light.

"You," David said, jutting his head toward Neko. "Get everyone into dry clothes. Make sure the witches eat."

Ordinarily, Neko would have pressed for David's permission to gut the refrigerator, to devour whatever fine cheese we might have on hand and to plunder the pantry for high-end delicacies he'd previously conned us into buying for his snacking pleasure. I realized exactly how serious things were when my familiar merely nodded and disappeared into the night.

That left David, Clara, and me.

"You're okay?" David asked, taking in both of us with a glance.

I nodded. "What happened to Hecate's Court?"

David's jaw tightened. "They left as soon as the satyr manifested."

"What?" I was shocked.

"Their purpose was to make sure the magicarium completed a working. Calling the satyr sufficed."

"He could have killed us! He nearly raped Cassie!"

"That's not the Court's problem."

Technically, he was right. But the Court should have felt *some* obligation to aid their fellow witches. That was only human nature.

Right. Like the Court was bound by common human decency. Somewhere, some time, some member of Hecate's Court might slip up and show a hint of emotion. But I'd never seen a hint of ordinary human feeling from any of them in the past. They had one job: keeping peace among all recognized witches. Their word was final in all disputes. Beyond that, they refused to become involved.

"They left that behind," David said. He nodded toward the marble altar. A single sheet of parchment was plastered to the stone.

"What the—" I pried it loose. The document was clearly ensorcelled—it didn't tear, even though it was soaked through. And the ornate lettering was cast in some magical ink, a formula that didn't run in the rain. I skimmed through the formal language to find the key phrase at the bottom: "All magicarium classes must be conducted on a regular schedule throughout said academic term, or said charter shall be immediately and permanently revoked."

More interference from the Court. More intimidation directed at the Jane Madison Academy.

It hardly mattered, though. I fully intended to conduct my classes on a regular basis. I didn't need dictates from Hecate's Court to do what was right. I handed the document to David, who folded it in three parts and tucked it into his pocket.

Shaking my head, I rested my hand against the marble altar. It felt absolutely ordinary—like any other rain-washed stone. There wasn't a hint of malevolence, not a whisper of the evil that had burst through with the satyr. Suddenly exhausted, I asked, "Where did that thing come from?"

"I told you," Clara answered before David could. "A hellmouth. That's what I learned in the course I'm auditing."

"Course?" I asked.

"*Urban Planning and the Ancient World*. At the University of Maryland."

I shook my head. "Why are you taking classes at the University of Maryland?"

"Now that you've officially launched the magicarium, Jeanette, I want to be close by. In case you need help with your more esoteric courses. And as long as I'm on the east coast, I figured I'd take a class to help me plan Oak Canyon Coven's nootuh."

"New what?" Obviously, the banishing spell had taken more out of me than I thought. I seemed to be losing my hearing. I glanced at David for clarification, but he only shrugged.

"Nootuh," Clara enunciated. "N-W-T-A. Nucleus with tentacles attached. It's a form of planned community. We'll have a central building for communal activities—meals and entertainment and rituals—that's the nucleus. But each of us will have our own living quarters, our own private spaces."

"The tentacles. Got it." I turned to David and faked a sweet voice. "Did you know Clara was studying nearby?"

His scowl told me he'd known. And Clara's adult education campaign fell squarely in the category of things where he refused to act as middleman between my mother and me. With a brittle smile, I turned back to my Clara. "So, your professor at the University of Maryland just happened to feature local hellmouths in his class?"

"Professor Kipperman didn't *feature* hellmouths. This week's lecture was about necropolises, cities of the dead built near ancient settlements. The lost necropolis of Epidauros in ancient Greece was built around a perfect circle of cleared earth. Scholars theorize the villagers excavated a hellmouth, a way for heroes to banish creatures back to Hades."

I shook my head, unable to link mundane archeology with modern witchcraft. "And that relates to my ritual circle how?"

"We had a homework assignment, choosing a modern town and comparing its plan to an ancient one. I chose Parkersville."

Everything became clear. "And let me guess. When you map Epidauros onto Parkersville, you end up with a hellmouth right here."

"Oh Jeanette! I *knew* you'd be receptive once I explained! That's what the turquoise means on the edge of your aura."

David finally came to my rescue after my mother folded me into a sodden embrace. "Come on, Clara," he said with a weary shrug. "You need to ground yourself too. Head back to the house, and fill everyone else in on Epidauros and the hellmouth. We'll catch up in a minute."

I barely waited until Clara was out of earshot before I hissed, "You don't actually believe her!"

"Of course not." He spread his hands above the center-stone, not quite touching the marble. "But I didn't want her to worry."

"Worry about what?"

"The real source of the satyr."

"Which is?"

"Norville Pitt."

The name sliced a greasy spiral into my belly. The Head Clerk of Hecate's Court had been a thorn in my side since I'd founded my magicarium. More than just a thorn, actual-ly—Pitt's manipulation had nearly brought down the Acad-emy not two months earlier.

Pitt and David had a tortured history together; each man had vowed to destroy the other. David and I had alerted Hecate's Court to Pitt's unlawful activities, including his tak-ing countless bribes. But we'd only succeeded after David had been driven to the trembling edge of madness, building the case.

I tried to swallow a nasty taste in my mouth before I croaked, "What about Pitt?"

"He had something to do with that satyr. No," he said to my frantic look around the circle. "He wasn't here. He wouldn't dare set foot on this land now, not with the inquest pending before Hecate's Court."

The inquest. The official inquiry into Pitt's crimes. The investigation was set to begin in three days, the first Monday of the witches' new year.

David said, "He couldn't make the satyr materialize on his own. He's a failed warder and a washed-up clerk, not a witch. But for just a moment, when the lightning struck, when the cordon broke... I sensed him here."

"Was he working through Teresa?" The Washington Coven Mother and Pitt had teamed up before. That was all part of the case the Court would take up next week.

David shook his head tightly. "I don't think so. She had her own reasons to keep you from succeeding. But I saw the look on her face when the satyr manifested. She and Ethan were as surprised as everyone else."

"And she stepped forward," I said grudgingly. "She helped me banish the thing when no one else could." I extended my hands over the altar yet again, struggling to capture the signature David had sensed. I closed my eyes to better center myself, taking three deep breaths as I reached out with my powers.

Nothing. Nothing at all, not even when I forced myself to drag up old memories of Pitt, to hold his oily presence in my mind as I searched for the faintest sign that he'd been involved with the satyr.

I sighed and let my power dissipate. I knew my next question wouldn't go over well, but I had to ask it. "Are you absolutely certain—?"

"Yes," David interrupted.

"It's just that with the inquest starting on Monday... With your history—"

"I said I'm certain!" David slammed his fist down on the altar, even angrier than I'd feared he would be. He winced at the sudden movement, though, and pressed his palm against his ribs.

"You're hurt!" I said.

"I'm fine."

"David—"

"I'm *fine*," he repeated. "I'm a hell of a lot better than

Pitt will be when I get my hands on him."

"Let the Court handle it," I warned.

"He brought that thing onto *my* property."

I knew better than to start with *if he did.* Instead, I said, "He's trying to provoke you. He wants you to break the injunction. He wants the Court to find against you before they ever get close to deciding his case."

"He could have killed—"

I shook my head and settled a finger against his lips. "He didn't." David started to protest again, but I pressed harder. "He didn't," I repeated. "We're safe. Pitt failed." When David showed no sign of relaxing, I leaned in to brush a kiss against his cheek. "Besides," I said, purposely making my voice light. "You have *much* more important things to worry about."

"What could be more important than—"

"Clara," I said, squeezing his hand. "Clara back in town." Another squeeze. "Clara taking classes at the University of Maryland, practically in our own back yard." One more clutch of my fingers. "Clara jabbering on and on and on, until my only choice is to go crazy or turn her into a toad."

I felt the moment he made the conscious decision to set aside his tension. His shimmering anger crumbled, releasing his shoulders, relaxing his spine. After all, the satyr *was* gone. We'd defeated Pitt. Again.

David curled a finger beneath my chin, tilting my lips toward his. "She only makes you crazy because you let her."

I pulled back enough to protest. "What am I supposed to say when she starts raving about ancient Greek *hellmouths*?"

"How about, 'I'll keep that in mind.'"

"Like that would work!"

"Try it," he said.

I laughed and tightened my arms around his waist. I was surprised when he sucked in a sharp breath between his teeth. "You *are* hurt!" I said.

"I'll live. That thing probably cracked a rib or two."

"Let's go," I said, setting a fast pace across the grass. "I want Neko to take a look at you. He can tape you up, at least." The fact that David didn't protest made me realize just how injured he was.

I only started to relax as we approached the house. The curtains were open in the front room, and warm light splashed onto the porch. Inside, Neko was skirting the coffee table, balancing a tray that looked like it held enough food to feed a football team. "Looks like a trip to the grocery store is at the top of tomorrow's agenda," I said to David.

"But first, you have something more important to do," a voice said. A shadow rose from the top of the porch steps, sleek and graceful as a panther in the night.

David's hand tightened on mine, but he didn't try to edge in front of me. I blinked hard, and the shadow resolved into a human shape, a woman's body. Teresa.

"And what might that be?" I asked, edging my words with defiance. "What's more important than caring for my magicarium?"

Teresa took the steps slowly, like she was sizing me up for a fight. "Paying your debts," she said, closing the distance between us. "Jane Madison. Magistrix and witch. I hereby claim the right of benefaction."

# Chapter 3

"FOR THE EVERLASTING love of Hecate," I swore, not entirely succeeding in keeping my curse under my breath. I planted my hands on my hips and said to Teresa, "You have got to be kidding."

"I never 'kid' about witchcraft."

Of course she didn't. Not when she was the strongest Coven Mother in the Eastern Empire. Not when she'd held that position since she was freaking ten years old. Not when she had me over an astral barrel.

"Fine," I said. "But not until after I've checked on my students. And had a chance to change."

"Of course," she answered, her lips compressed into a superior smile. I couldn't help but notice her dress was dry and every hair sat in perfect place on her head. She'd used magic to pull herself together, blatantly grandstanding that she had power to burn even after our near-disastrous working in the circle.

I brushed past her, barely resisting the urge to toss my dripping hair over my shoulder, to leave a trail of fresh raindrops across her immaculate handiwork. David followed close behind, guarding my back as Teresa, Ethan, and Connie also came inside.

Neko glanced up the instant we passed over the threshold. He'd been setting out food, piling treats high on the coffee table, but as soon as I entered the room he ceded all of his attention to me. I shook my head at his silent question. I didn't need him to serve me. Not yet.

I was more concerned about Cassie.

She crouched on a wooden chair that had obviously been dragged in from the kitchen, pressed into service because Cassie's soaked clothes were covered with mud. Her head was buried in her arms, and she slowly rocked back and forth. Tupa huddled beside her, one small hand balanced on her knee. Zach stood over both of them, his face drawn as he supported his broken arm with his good one.

Everyone else in the room studiously avoided looking at them, giving them some semblance of privacy in the crowded space. But I crossed over to my student, ignoring the fact that my dress left a wet trail on the hardwood floor, on the well-placed throw rug. "Cassie," I said, kneeling before her and reaching for her shoulder.

She flinched before I could touch her. But she stopped rocking.

"Cassie," I said again, dropping my hand. "I'm so sorry. Let's get you to a doctor. There's a hospital in Pine Ridge."

"No," she said, and her voice was thick, clogged with tears.

I wasn't sure how to respond. Even if she looked like a naive little girl, she was a full-grown witch. She had autonomy over her body, just as she had the right to control her magic. She could decide if she wanted medical attention.

"You have to eat something," I said. And Neko manifested by my side, holding a laden plate in one hand and a mug of fresh apple cider in the other. I glanced at the food—treats from the Cake Walk bakery, sent along by my best friend Melissa to celebrate the official launch of the Jane Madison Academy.

When she'd prepared the pasteboard box of goodies, Melissa couldn't have predicted how welcome her Butterscotch Blessings and Lemon Grenades would be. How *necessary* they'd be. When witches stretched themselves to accomplish prodigious magic, they needed something to anchor them back in the mundane world—food and drink, consumed immediately after the effort. Given the horror Cassie had experienced, she needed the grounding even more than the rest of us.

"Cassie," I whispered, edging the plate closer. "Please."

When I got no response, Tupa took the mug of cider from Neko. "Cass," he bleated, touching the rim to his mistress's fingers.

The attention seemed to reach her when nothing else would. Her entire back tensed, and her neck grew stiff. But she raised her head enough to take the mug, to hold it in trembling hands. I barely squelched the urge to rub a streak of mud from her forehead, to smooth the spikes of blond hair that had worked loose from her braids.

"Drink, Cass," Tupa urged.

Like a child swallowing from a sippy cup, Cassie complied, gulping once, twice, three times. I passed the plate of food to Tupa, hoping he could work additional familiar magic there. He selected a morsel of blondie and held it under his witch's lips. Cassie hesitated, swallowing hard, tightening her fingers around the mug.

But then she opened her mouth and let her familiar feed her, bite by painful bite. I waited until she'd finished the entire Blessing before I spoke again. "Please, Cassie. Let us help you. Let us take you into Pine Ridge."

She shook her head. "I don't need that. He didn't—" A

sobbing breath shut her throat, and she gulped noisily. "He didn't do anything."

The satyr might not have succeeded in raping her. But he'd done plenty. All of us could see that.

Still, she was allowed to refuse treatment.

"Come upstairs, then," I said. "Lie down in the guest room. Just for a little while."

Her arms tightened close to her sides, and I thought she was going to refuse. But Tupa cupped her near elbow with one small hand, rubbing the side of his face against her biceps. I couldn't feel the specific tug of their magical bond, but I knew what Neko would have done in a similar situation. I wasn't surprised when Cassie staggered to her feet.

She sucked in her breath as she straightened. Bruises were already coming out on her pale arms. I was certain her back was mottled black and blue from where she'd writhed against the ground. But Tupa leaned close on one side, and Zach closed in on the other.

"There you go," I said. "Up the stairs. First room on the right. There's a change of clothes in the closet." Feeling helpless, I watched them shuffle toward the landing, supporting each other, step by painful step.

"The rest of you," I said when they'd completed their climb. "Eat. Drink. Take care of yourselves. I'll be back in a moment."

I brushed past Teresa as I crossed to the stairs. I was grateful for David's presence at my back, even when he pushed past me into our bedroom, barely waiting for me to close the door before he exploded. "You can't let Teresa Alison Sidney claim a benefaction."

"Hush," I said. "Cassie will hear you." He paced three steps away as I continued. "What choice do I have?"

He whirled and marked three paces back. "You realize

what benefaction means, don't you? She can take any magical possession of yours, anything equal in value to the assistance she lent."

I met David's dark brown eyes, refusing to quail when I saw the green glints that meant he was furious. "What do you want me to do, David? She matched her powers to mine and we succeeded in a working I couldn't complete alone. I admitted as much in front of witnesses."

"What if she claims me? If she demands Neko?"

"She can't," I said flatly. "A witch can only lose her warder or familiar if her life was at stake. The satyr wasn't after me."

"But Cassie is your student. She's under your protection."

"I know that!" My exclamation was all the sharper for the fact that I couldn't shout, couldn't alarm Cassie down the hall. I hated when David acted like I was a child, like I was too young or naive to understand the consequences of my actions. I knew exactly what I'd done in that circle; I'd weighed everything to within a gram in the desperate heartbeat before I'd nodded to Teresa.

David filled the spiky silence, backtracking to a subject where he knew he could prevail. "I want you to eat something."

"And I want you to get your ribs wrapped," I countered. "Looks like we'll both be disappointed until we get Teresa out of this house. And the fastest way to do that is to yield to her claim."

David's face set in stone. I reached out a hand to his jaw, cupping the familiar stubborn line with my palm. "You're right, of course. Cassie's under my protection. But that's not enough for Teresa to claim you. Or Neko."

"I don't want her claiming anything at all," David said,

his voice barely registering above a sigh.

"That makes two of us. But I won't let her bring this before the Court. Not with…" *Not with the Pitt inquest starting on Monday.*

I didn't say it. I didn't need to.

David sighed. "Let's get you out of that dress."

It took all our combined concentration to unfasten the rows of onyx buttons, to peel away the clinging bodice and wrestle the heavy folds of velvet into submission. I would have given a pretty substantial claim of benefaction to anyone who helped me slip into the soft fleece of a sweatshirt, into the warm flannel of pajama bottoms.

But I was a magistrix. That was the crux of everything that had happened this Samhain night. And a magistrix didn't retreat into comfort, not with an enemy on the premises. I forced myself to pull on a black pencil skirt, to add a crimson shell and a respectable jacket. To hell with heels, though. My ballet flats would have to do.

By the time I'd towel-dried my hair, David wore a fresh shirt and the clean, dry slacks of another dark suit. I suspected he'd changed quickly so I couldn't see the damage left by the satyr's hooves. At my accusing look, he held out his hands, as if to prove his innocence. I chose to ignore the fact that he winced as he gestured.

Back in the living room, battle lines had been drawn. My students, their familiars, and Clara all stood close to the fireplace, where some enterprising person—my money was on Caleb—had lit a cheerful fire. The warders were gathered on the far side of the coffee table, spread in a carefully casual line, feet planted with deceptive attention to angles, to lines of attack.

Sporting a patronizing smile, Teresa stood near the foot of the stairs. Connie, her familiar, twitched as she looked at the far side of the room, at the plates and mugs, at the patent simulation of good cheer. Ethan didn't bother with pretense. He was clearly on alert, his back to Teresa, his hands flexed by his sides as if he'd throw the first person who made a false step.

"All right," I said from the small landing, a few steps above the living room floor. I'd admit I took some pleasure in making Teresa and her entourage turn around, in forcing everyone to look up at me. "Let's get this over with."

I looked across at my confused students. "Teresa Alison Sidney made a claim of benefaction after assisting us this evening. Of course, the Jane Madison Academy follows all the strictures of Hecate's Court. Therefore, we yield to the claim, and offer up our dearest possessions in eternal gratitude for the risk our sister took on our behalf."

The words made perfect sense, following a long-time formula. But I made sure no one would hear a drop of gratitude—eternal or otherwise—in my tone. I pushed past the unflappable Teresa and led the way to the basement, palming on the overhead fluorescent lights as I stalked down the stairs.

I could still remember the first time I'd seen the Osgood collection of magical goods. They'd also been housed in a basement then, in a groundskeeper's cottage in the garden of the library where I'd worked. The vast array of books had made my librarian's heart beat fast. I'd hardly noticed the other items—runes and crystals and wands, cauldrons and casks and a host of hand-held knives made sacred to Hecate. Neko had been there too, in the form of a giant statue of a cat.

I hadn't known it on that dark and stormy night, but I'd been looking at one of the greatest hordes of arcana ever assembled.

Now, I swept my hand toward the shelves, inviting everyone to look around. I'd intended to wait a while before showing the collection to my new students. I wanted them to build confidence in their own magical abilities, to explore their unique relationships to the witchy world we shared. But Teresa had forced my hand, and now I had to make the best of things.

The collection could have been used for a graduate seminar on the history of bookmaking. The oldest works were on scrolls, vellum or sheepskin wrapped onto rowan rollers, onto yew. Titles hung from tags on the ends of wooden bars, dangling testimony to ancient wisdom. There weren't many scrolls in sight, though, none of the truly ancient texts, the obscure ephemera of the magical world.

I'd arranged all the books by topic, then by author. There were hundreds of handwritten books, copied out long before the invention of the printing press. Many of the books were simply pages bound between heavy cardboard covers, with slips of paper pasted to the spine to identify the treasures within. Leather bindings were reserved for rare titles. Some sported gold leaf on the cover and on the spine. A handful had semi-precious stones bonded to the leather—turquoise and amber, even a garnet or two.

Teresa studied the shelves as if she were a customer in an exclusive organic market, tracking down the latest in gluten-free, cruelty-free, non-GMO, paleo-certified foods.

I studied her as she shopped. Had she plotted with Pitt to release the satyr? If so, it had been a risky plan. She'd had no way of knowing I knew the banishing spell. She could have been the satyr's next victim, as easily as any of my students.

Besides, Teresa had to keep her distance from Norville Pitt. The inquest was a serious matter. Teresa was already on the hook to explain payments she'd made to Pitt, bribes intended to cripple the Jane Madison Academy. No sane witch—and whatever else she was, Teresa was coolly, coldly sane—would purposely draw even closer scrutiny from Hecate's Court by intentionally sabotaging my magicarium's Samhain working.

I had to believe Teresa's only goal had been to delay me, to gain access to the Osgood collection.

But even *that* wasn't entirely accurate. She longed for the riches of my arcane holdings. But she also disliked me. She disliked my warder.

*Dislike* was too soft a word. Teresa wanted to torment David. He had once been tied to her coven, warding a Washington witch. He'd challenged his witch's ethics, questioned her use of the Shadowed Path. Ultimately, David had been cashiered, detailed to work in Hecate's Court. But not before he'd brooked Teresa's authority. And for that, she'd never forgive him.

"Ah!" Teresa breathed when she reached a particular section on the far wall.

Of course. I should have known. She stood in front of the section about warders. I watched her finger a dozen titles, all classics in the field: *Warders' Ways: What Works for Women. Warders and Witches, a Historical Analysis of Successful Pairings. Who Wards the Warders?* And the most valuable book I had on the subject, a first edition bound in ostrich, with hand-colored tipped-in plates: *Warders' Magic: A Complete Guide to Managing Your Protector.*

Teresa slid the book from the shelf. I had to give her credit. She knew her way around rare books. She didn't tug at the top of the spine, didn't stress the binding in any way. Instead, she cradled her prize like the treasure it was, carrying it to the reading stand I always kept prepared at the center of the room. She eased it onto the baize-covered surface, slipping velvet wedges beneath first the front cover, then the back. She carefully turned to the title page.

She was good at hiding her reaction. A casual observer would think she was simply interested in an old book. But I saw the quick flare of her nostrils, the sudden dilation of her pupils as she studied the colophon, the early printer's mark that indicated she held a first edition. *Warders' Magic* excited her. She was thrilled.

She closed it with the same precise care she'd given to taking it from the shelf. "I claim this book as benefaction."

I swallowed hard, not adverse to heightening my role-playing a bit. I let my teeth scrape my bottom lip. I glanced at the empty space in the collection, the darkness that now gaped like a missing tooth. I dripped a little of my real fatigue into my voice, letting my words quaver as I said, "I grant your claim. Let balance be restored between us. May we share perfect trust from this day forward."

"From this day forward," she said, and then she intoned "Ethan." She passed the book to her warder, like a 1950s heiress handing off a hatbox to her chauffeur. She actually snapped her fingers to summon Connie. The nervous familiar jumped as if she'd been shocked with a live electric wire. Then Teresa processed past David, climbing the stairs like Queen Elizabeth taking the throne.

Not to be outdone, I followed her through the kitchen, past the spread of food in the living room, all the way to the front door. I waited for Ethan to reach for the doorknob. Only when he'd recognized the extent of the locking spell David maintained as a matter of course did I reach out a commanding hand. One brush of my fingertip, and the lock shifted back to an ordinary Yale deadbolt.

I nodded once, granting the trio permission to leave. Teresa forced her resentful features into a mask of cool disdain, and then they were gone. I hadn't seen a car on the driveway. Ethan must be transferring them back to Teresa's home using warder's magic.

Before I could summon the strength to restore the lock to its supernatural appearance, Neko reached around me. He set the protective spell, one of the few magic workings a familiar could complete on his own. With the same gesture, he cupped his palm against my elbow, lending me physical support even as he pushed a bolt of pure energy past my tattered defenses. The solicitous gesture reminded me of Tupa and Cassie. I glanced up the stairs, ready to try once more to convince my student to get medical attention.

Neko shook his head, though, offering up a plate with his free hand. Slices of apple and pear were spread in a sweet fan, alternating with wedges of sharp Cheddar. A trio of Bunny Bites set off the healthy snack. I gulped down the first miniature carrot cake like a starving woman, barely taking time to chew. I managed a little more restraint with the second, and by the time I devoured the third I barely resembled a starved prisoner.

Neko grinned and passed me a mug. The smell of fresh cider was so intense I thought I might faint. Instead, I held the cup with two hands and forced myself to take careful sips to the end.

When I looked up, Clara was standing in the arch that led to the dining room. It took me a moment to parse the expression on her face: Concern.

I couldn't remember my mother *ever* being concerned for my welfare. In my exhausted state, I thought I might cry. Instead, I let Neko pass me a chunk of sourdough bread, spread thick with butter.

Clara said, "She was sending a message, you know."

*Do you think?* My sarcasm reflex was automatic, but she didn't deserve that reaction. Not when she'd come to check up on me, to make sure I was still standing after banishing our enemy from the premises. So I said, "Most of what she had to say was for David."

"That's why I told him to stay downstairs. To sit down and catch his breath and let someone else carry the water for a few minutes."

I looked at Clara with new respect. She *was* a witch. And David *was* her warder. He'd been required to listen to her command, so long as her life wasn't directly threatened. Her life, or mine, or Gran's. And her instructions had been exactly what he needed. That, and a tight bandage around his ribs. I turned to Neko, automatically taking a tall glass of water from his hand. "David needs—"

My familiar interrupted me. "He needs to know you're grounded. That you're taking care of yourself."

Clara lifted a plate of cucumber sandwiches from the table, shoving them toward me as if they were medicine. She directed her words to Neko. "Then you can tell him she is, the entire time you're taking care of him." She glanced at me. "What is it? His ribs?" When I nodded, she jutted her chin toward the basement stairs. "Go," she commanded Neko. "And if he gives you any trouble, tell him we'll call my mother. He'll have to take orders from three witches, then."

Neko gave a mock shudder of terror.

"Please," I said, resting a hand on his shoulder. I wanted him to know I was serious, but I also wanted to give him incontrovertible proof that I *was* grounded, that I was recovering from my extraordinary expense of astral energy. "Take care of him."

My familiar straightened with alacrity. "Your wish is my command," he said with a smart bow, clicking his heels together.

I rolled my eyes. "That's the last time I'll ever hear that from you."

He shrugged, grinning, and headed downstairs. Clara gestured toward one of the overstuffed couches. She waited until I sat before she joined me. "I'm sorry," she said. "I know how much your collection means to you. I can only imagine how difficult it was to see Teresa Alison Sidney carry off one of your treasures."

"It wasn't as bad as it could have been."

"I couldn't see perfectly from where I was standing. But wasn't that a first edition?" I raised my eyebrows in surprise, never expecting her to pay attention to a book's credentials. "What?" she asked. "I've listened to you over the past few years. I've learned a bit. Not as much as a real librarian, but enough to know the value of that book."

"It *was* a first edition," I agreed. "But it's not the best specimen of the title in my collection. I have one signed by the author, a gift presentation to the founding Coven Mother of the Seattle coven."

"And Teresa Alison Sidney missed it?" She sounded incredulous.

"She never saw it," I said with satisfaction. "Last month, David and I had some renovations done on the basement. As long as we were investing in the work on the garage and the barn, we hired a couple of specialists for a more challenging…project. We converted David's basement office into a climate-controlled vault for the most valuable books in the Osgood collection."

"Why didn't Teresa Alison Sidney see it? What sort of shields did you put on it?" Clara's voice ratcheted up in disbelief. She wasn't the strongest witch in the world, but she was quite capable of sensing magical wards left lying around.

"We didn't add *magical* protection," I said. "The house is already as secure as we could make it. The vault is state of the art. Climate-controlled, relative humidity of forty-seven percent, steady temperature of sixty-seven degrees. There are ultra-violet filters on the overhead lights, and high-efficiency air-handling filters. We installed mold- and mildew-resistant metal shelves coated in baked enamel. The whole thing is fire-proof."

Clara looked impressed. "It sounds like Fort Knox!"

I shrugged. "My witchcraft collection is worth its weight in gold. More, maybe. But right about now, I'm glad we didn't add any extra spells. Teresa would have detected them for sure. As it was, she never thought to ask if I had anything that wasn't in plain sight."

"And if she'd asked…"

"I would have been honor-bound to tell her the truth." I might not be a member of the Washington Coven, but some rules went deeper than social clubs. Some rules went to the heart of being a witch.

Clara sat back on the couch. "So you still have a copy of *Warders' Magic*."

"Along with several other books that are worth a thousand times more. The precious stones on some of those bindings would pay for the vault several times over."

Clara shook her head. "You played a dangerous game, Jeanette." She caught herself and shook her head. "Jane."

I nodded. "But we won this round. And now it's time to go downstairs and reassure my students that victory was ours."

Clara stood as I did. "You go," she said. "I'm heading home."

"Afraid of seeing David, after you ordered him to submit?" I couldn't help but smile.

"Not afraid," she said. "Just being…practical. We should all get some sleep."

"Where are you staying, anyway?"

"In DC. With Mother and George," she said, like I should have known she was at Gran's apartment all along. "I'm sharing your old room with Nuri." I felt a flicker of pity for my grandmother's familiar. That flicker swelled into a wave when Clara said, "The pink paint on the wall creates *fascinating* vibrations with my aura. I'm attuned to deeper power wells than I've sensed in years."

My mother and her auras… I was truly grateful for everything Clara had done that night, but I had to admit to a wave of relief when I watched the red eyes of her tail-lights turn onto the county road at the end of our driveway.

Moderation in all things. And moderation in maternal things the most of all. I headed downstairs to deal with edgy students, a smart-aleck familiar, and a warder who still needed to be forced into submitting to urgently needed medical care.

For that matter, we needed to get Zach Spencer to the emergency room. And I'd have another try at getting Cassie to see a doctor. All immediate threats might be safely put away, but my evening was just beginning.

The tall case clock struck midnight as I headed down the stairs. Samhain was over. The new year had begun. And the Jane Madison Academy was officially open for business.

# Chapter 4

SATURDAY, I SLEPT until noon, only coming to my senses when David brought me a tray with hot buttered toast, crisp sliced apples, and a giant pot of pear oolong tea. I struggled to sit upright, to reach for my clothes so I could check on my students. I needed to know how they were handling the aftermath of our disastrous working.

David assured me, though, that everyone was fine. He'd conferred with their warders. The witches were resting, restoring the health of their bodies, preparing their minds for Monday's classes.

"What about Cassie?" I asked. "Did she go to Pine Ridge?"

"She went with Zach to have his arm set. Tony drove them."

"Did she see a doctor?"

He shook his head tightly. "She refused. But she was calm enough to make up a story. She told the doctors she was knocked down by a goat in the barn. She said Zach came to help her, but the billy turned on him."

There were enough farms in the countryside that her story *might* have been true. And Cassie *had* escaped without any physical damage, beyond a few scrapes and bruises.

David said, "Zach helped her to sleep when they got back."

Warder's magic. It was better than nothing. Better than a lot of things, actually.

"I don't get it," I said. "Why would Pitt send a satyr to interrupt our first working? It's not like he gets any benefit if the magicarium shuts down. He's not a witch. He can't stake a claim to the Osgood collection."

David's jaw was tight. "He doesn't care about the Osgood collection. He's trying to punish me."

"You?"

"I'm the one who's made his life difficult. I reported him to the Court. I caused the inquest to convene. I've cut off the flow of his income and his power—no witch would be stupid enough to bribe him now that Hecate's Court is involved."

"But isn't that a little indirect, bringing a satyr into my working to get at you?"

David's gaze was steady as he reached over to brush a lock of hair behind my ear. "He knows what matters most to me. Hurting you is the worst thing he could ever do to me."

The admission melted something deep inside me. I turned my head and kissed David's palm. "How *are* you doing?" I asked. "How are your ribs?"

"Broken," he confessed. "But Neko taped them up."

I swung my legs over the side of the bed.

"Where do you think you're going?"

"To the basement. I'm getting my aventurine. You need the healing power of a crystal."

"I *need* you to get some rest." David looked exasperated.

"Fine. We'll compromise. I'll stay up here, but I'll have Neko bring me the crystal."

"I don't need—"

But it was too late. I'd already summoned my familiar.

Neko stuck around to help me energize the healing stone, to focus the power that I poured into the green crystal. The spell was enough to send me back to sleep for the rest of the afternoon.

On Sunday, I had to roll out of bed a lot earlier. It was time for my monthly brunch with Gran and Clara.

My grandmother had instituted Mother-Daughter Brunch when Clara first came back into my life. It was Gran's blatant attempt to make me like my mother. I think she thought I'd come to associate great food with positive family emotions. Clara still assaulted my nerves like lemon juice on a paper cut, but I'd consumed an awful lot of comfort-food calories with her. Today's target was the Original Pancake House.

Our accommodating waitress set plates in front of Clara and me. "Dutch Apple Baby," she said. "We split it back in the kitchen."

"Thank you," I said automatically, leaning over to breathe in the sweet scent of cinnamon and Granny Smiths, all baked into the top of a fluffy pancake. I couldn't imagine making it through even half of what was on my plate; I was pleased Clara had agreed to split the awesome indulgence.

"And the Works for you," the waitress said, beginning to offload plates in front of Gran. One dish held a mountain of scrambled eggs crowned by the cheddar cheese Gran had added to the order. A continent of hash browns balanced out the platter, plump shreds of potato glistening beneath a crispy brown crust. A smaller plate held three of the meatiest strips of bacon I'd ever seen, centered between a trio of sausages and three patties that fragrantly broadcast their sage and fennel spices. Gran had debated between the breakfast meats for long enough that she'd decided to get all three.

And then, there were the pancakes that the restaurant was known for. A tower of five plate-sized rounds groaned beneath a scoop of melting butter. Powdered sugar and an entire gallon of fresh strawberries—deep red despite the November date—rounded out the dish.

"Can I get you anything else?" the waitress asked.

"Some blueberry syrup please," Gran said. And she held up the pitcher of maple that already rested on the table. "And we'll need more of this, dear."

The waitress was too well-trained to react, but I'm sure she wondered if Gran was putting her on. I hastened to add, "And some more hot water for my tea, when you get a chance."

The woman shook her head as she hurried back to the kitchen. Gran devoted her energy to constructing a perfect bite, balancing egg and potato with a chunk of sausage. Clara and I had a much easier time, digging in to the sweet confection we were pleased to call brunch.

Gran then demanded that Clara and I fill her in on the entire Samhain working. She fussed over me, and she fretted about the state of David's ribs. She exclaimed about how well the aventurine crystal had worked for her, when I'd charged the stone to help heal her lungs from double pneumonia. She clicked her tongue about Cassie, nodding knowingly when I said Zach had urged her into a healing sleep.

"Enough!" Clara said after swallowing a cinnamon-laced forkful of pancake. "We *have* to talk about something else." She rounded on me. "Have you settled on a wedding date yet?"

"Mabon," I said. "The autumn equinox next year."

"So long!" Gran almost covered her surprise by spearing a monster strawberry.

"The magicarium will be well-settled by then. This year's

students will be wrapping up their studies, and we won't be dealing with new ones yet. And the equinox coincides with a full moon. David and I are facing enough criticism from Hecate's Court. The least we can do is choose an auspicious day to make our wedding official."

Clara nodded contentedly. "I'm so pleased you're considering the astrological implications. I'll draw up a complete chart for you. You want to pay particular attention to your rising sign and the position of Venus."

As a witch, I was fully aware of the natural world around me—the phases of the moon, the passing of the seasons. But Clara went a whole lot further into astrology than I did. She charted just about everything, and the vast amount of her star-reading added up to gibberish in my book. Tension screwed its hooks into my shoulders. A dozen different arguments fought to come front and center on my tongue. I wanted Clara to know that she made me embarrassed to be a witch, embarrassed to be her daughter.

But then I remembered David's suggestion. I heard his calm voice at the back of my mind, and I mimicked the words he'd given me, just two nights before. I looked at Clara and said, "I'll keep that in mind."

My mother beamed, and I silently saluted David for his detente formula.

In fact, David and I were thinking of Mabon for another reason, one I wouldn't share with Clara and Gran. The equinox meant that day and night were exactly the same length. David and I needed that equality in our relationship, in our lives. If forced to make an honest admission, he would certainly say I was the most headstrong witch he'd ever known, and I'd counter that he was an overbearing warder. For the rest of our lives together, we'd be able to remember at least one time when we'd been in perfect, harmonious balance.

"And have you chosen a place, dear?" Gran asked around a mouthful of bacon.

I had. But I needed to get her permission. And I was surprised by how nervous the thought made me. "The Farm," I said.

"That makes sense," Clara chimed in readily. "It's always easiest to plan something where you're already living."

I shook my head. "Not that farm. Gran's property. Up in Connecticut."

Clara's lips pursed into a surprised O. The Farm had been in Gran's family for centuries. I'd visited for family gatherings throughout my childhood. Clara, of course, had missed decades of trips to the Farm, when she'd been living her own life, far from responsibility and tradition.

But I hadn't chosen the Farm because I wanted to rub Clara's nose in her absence. I'd chosen it because I'd always loved the place. Now that I understood my magical heritage, I knew I'd been primed for witchcraft on the Connecticut property. I'd learned to pour power into the marble stone on the ancient farmhouse's threshold, reciting a "tradition" (not a spell, never a spell) that Gran had taught me when I was just a little girl. I'd absorbed the placement of the woods, the planting of protective herbs and flowers—all the details that made the Farm a perfect refuge for witches, even when I hadn't known I was one.

"But, dear, you haven't been up there since..." Gran trailed off, apparently deciding it might not be a good idea to remind me about one of my famously disastrous romantic relationships. But I was prepared for that argument.

"That's exactly why I *do* want to go back. I've loved the Farm since I was a little girl. I want to build new memories there, good ones. And I want David to understand more about our family."

Gran rushed to reassure me. "That's sounds perfect, dear. How many people are you thinking of inviting? We can host a lot at the house, and there are always bed and breakfasts nearby for overflow."

"I haven't added up the list yet. Between family, and people from the Peabridge, and now the magicarium…"

"Just make sure it's a prime number," Clara asserted, reaching across to spear one of Gran's sausage patties.

"A prime?" Even as I asked the question, I knew I'd regret the answer.

"Absolutely. Everyone knows that a prime number of guests reflects the unique nature of your relationship. If you get married with a prime, then you'll never get divorced."

I wanted to know how many guests had attended Clara's wedding to my long-fled father, but I knew that would only open an entire cargo ship of worms. Nevertheless, I couldn't keep from asking a single honeyed question. "Is it the number of people you invite that matters? Or the number of people who actually show up?"

I must have hit the perfect pitch of curiosity and respect, because neither my mother nor my grandmother bristled. Instead, Clara said with absolute certainty, "The number of people who show up, of course. What matters is who witnesses the actual union."

Great. According to Clara's batty concept of magic, I should keep a cadre of second-tier guests in reserve, in case I needed people to round out the ranks to a sacred prime number at the last moment. "I'll keep that in mind," I said again. The words came more easily the second time.

David's paternoster continued to work its magic, because Clara didn't miss a beat when she asked, "Have you decided on the wedding party?"

"Melissa will be my matron of honor, of course."

"Of course," Gran and Clara agreed at the same time. My grandmother subdued another strawberry before she asked, "Where *is* Melissa? I thought she was joining us for brunch today."

"She was. But Rob's been tied up on a huge litigation matter ever since they got married. This is the first weekend day he's had off in a month, so she texted me this morning and begged off." And I understood that. Really, I did. But a part of me had wanted to type back that *I* hadn't seen *her* in every bit as long.

Married life had done strange things to my relationship with my best friend. I was happy for her; of course I was. But we had yet to celebrate Melissa's wedding—no Mojito Therapy in the six weeks since she and Rob had run off and tied the knot. Not that a marriage should require *therapy*. What I really meant was that I longed to toast Melissa's marriage—just like we'd toasted a million things in the past. Strong drinks, good food, and talking until we'd both gone hoarse. Was that too much to ask of a best friend?

It wasn't Melissa's fault, not at all. And it certainly wasn't Rob's. I'd been every bit as busy as they had been. But there was something wrong when I'd been wearing an engagement ring for six weeks, and my best friend still hadn't seen the diamond.

Gran must have sensed my disturbance, because she offered up the best salve around—a slice of bacon from her plate. It was salty and thick and chewy and smoky all at the same time, a bite of meaty heaven. Gran nodded in complete understanding of my groaned bliss before she asked, "And David's best man?"

"I don't know," I said, struck by the oddness of that statement. "He's got two younger brothers, but I haven't actually met them. There are the other warders at the Academy, but they're more co-workers than friends. I don't know," I said again, and I shoved down a queasy roll of my belly.

No, that wasn't a warning sign that anything was wrong between David and me. It was simply a statement that orange juice and Dutch Apple Baby and bacon were a little too much to eat for breakfast. Really. That was the only problem.

Gran breezed past my uncertainty. "Well, let me know when he's made up his mind. I have a little something I'd like to do for the wedding."

My grandmother had been my support system for years; she'd nurtured me through my tortured teens, through all those college years when I couldn't decide what I wanted to be when I grew up. Gran had the proverbial determination of a bulldog and the legendary patience of a saint.

But she made some terrible choices when it came to wedding festivities. Witness the orange and silver bridesmaid dress I'd worn to her own wedding, the one with a gigantic lamé bow across my butt, with dyed-to-match Gatorade-colored shoes. And *that* crime against the senses had been accomplished with Neko at her side, offering the best of his fashion guidance. I trembled to think of what Gran might come up with on her own. Offering a sickly smile, I said, "I'll keep that in mind."

"Keep what in mind?" Clara asked. "You don't even know what your grandmother is planning."

So much for David's panacea.

I shook my head, as if I'd just been momentarily distracted. Bride's prerogative and all that. "I'm sorry, Gran. What 'little something' were you talking about?"

She wiped her fingers off on her napkin and reached for

her handbag. "Just a little something I came across in a knitting magazine."

"I didn't know you knit!"

"I haven't done it in years," Gran said, producing a sheaf of papers. "But Uncle George's hair is awfully thin on top… I couldn't bear the idea of him shivering through another winter so I knitted him a hat. And I had yarn left over, so I made him a matching scarf, even though I needed to buy more yarn to finish it. And then I started in on gloves to use up the extra, but I miscalculated and only had enough for one. So I bought more yarn and made mittens too. And, well, I've been having so much fun!" I wondered how much money she'd spent on yarn. She unfolded the magazine pages and passed them across the table with a proud smile.

A hat, scarf, gloves, mittens—we probably wouldn't need any of that stuff in September. Gran could choose whatever colors she wanted, and I could pretend to be thrilled. I'd never have to wear the resulting horror.

But Gran was proudly passing me a pattern for a… Well, a… For something that… "I'm sorry, Gran. What *is* that?"

"Why it's a cummerbund, dear. See? There are little knotted buttons at the back; they slip into the holes just so. I found the perfect yarn—it has an amazing sheen. When it knits up, it practically *sparkles*. You'll have to let me know, as soon as you settle on colors for the wedding." As a terrifying afterthought, she added, "I think I'll stick with clear crystals on the edges. Anything else might look a little tacky."

Tacky. That was one word for it. My mind immediately supplied a few others: Horrific, godawful, atrocious.

I was still floundering for an appropriate response when Clara said, "How wonderful! What a shame, though, that Jane and Melissa won't have anything to match. But there are only so many things one woman can knit!"

"Nonsense!" Gran said. "There's plenty of time between now and Mabon."

"I don't want you working too hard, Gran," I rushed to assure her. "The last thing you need is for your arthritis to flare up."

"My doctor says knitting is *good* for my bones! Keeps 'em moving, anyway. And counting the pattern keeps my mind sharp." She stared over my shoulder, as if she were studying the knitting library of the gods. "I do believe I've seen patterns for some knitted jewelry that could be stupendous. A choker for each of you girls. And matching bracelets. No rings of course, that wouldn't work. Not for a *wedding.*"

"No," I sad weakly. "Not for a wedding."

Gran clapped her hands together. "This will be perfect! I can't wait!"

The waitress chose that moment to return, and I could have kissed her for sparing me the need to summon a more credible level of enthusiasm. "Can I box that up for you?" she asked, looking at our half-empty plates.

"Oh no!" Gran exclaimed. "We're still eating!"

At least, *she* was. I couldn't imagine touching food again for a week. That was fine, because Gran kept me busy, peppering me with more questions about the wedding.

No, I hadn't looked at bridesmaid dresses yet. I'd only seen Melissa *in* a dress a handful of times in all the years I'd known her. She was much more of an overalls sort of girl. At least I knew I wouldn't curse her with a bow on her behind. (No. I didn't say that last bit to Gran. But I thought it very loudly.)

I hadn't looked at invitations either. I knew I should send out save-the-date cards, because autumn was a busy time for most people, with kids starting school and adults getting back to work after summer vacations. But designing invitations raised a whole raft of difficult questions. Would I include Uncle George's name along with Gran's? Clara's? (No. I didn't say that last bit to anyone. I was only brave enough to think it to myself, to ask the questions about who I was, who was family, what it meant to be abandoned by my mother for decades.)

I was up in the air about colors, too. Traditional Mabon hues reflected the harvest—red and orange and yellow, the colors of changing leaves. But my favorite color was purple; I'd loved it since I was a little girl. Every time I thought of combining purple with the standard Mabon shades, I had twitchy flashbacks to my days as a bridesmaid for Gran. Orange and purple might be worse than orange and silver. (What sort of idiot do you think I am? Of course, I didn't say that.)

Ring-bearer, flower girls, ushers, readers... I hadn't focused on any of those.

Gran leaned across the table, pushing aside her ravaged plate, with its lone surviving strawberry weeping in a pool of blueberry syrup. "Jane, dear, you know you don't have to do this if you don't want to. I know Melissa's family put ridiculous pressure on her for *her* wedding. We certainly don't mean to do the same thing to you. Even if it means forgetting about knitting the cummerbunds, I'll do whatever you want me to do."

Ah, the temptation...

But I told Gran the truth. Almost all of it, anyway. "I'm not Melissa. And you're not insane like her family, like Rob's. I *want* a traditional wedding. I'm having fun thinking about all of this. But it all seems so far away. And with the new semester officially starting last Friday... All my energy has been devoted to that. Now that classes are under way, I'll have a little more time. I learned a lot about how to teach with Emma and Raven."

Clara swelled with pride. She was the one who had sent my first students to me, even though I hadn't expected them, even though I hadn't been prepared. "How *are* those two?" "Fine," I said. "Better than fine, actually. Emma's still dating Rick Hanson, that firefighter she met over the summer. And Raven…" I trailed off, trying to come up with something positive about the flashy witch.

"I just *knew* they were what you needed! I follow your horoscope every day, you know. And when I read, 'Now is the time to try something new. You're stronger than you think you are,' I knew it was a sign to send you students."

It couldn't have been a sign to start a weight-lifting class at the local gym? Before I could patch together an appropriately snark-free response, my phone rang with the special tone I'd set for Neko. I scrambled for it, relieved to escape the current conversation. "Hey," I said. "What's up?"

"You need to come home," Neko said.

My throat turned into a desert. "Is the satyr back?" I didn't care if any mundanes heard me. They'd never believe I was talking about a real satyr.

"No," Neko said hurriedly. "It's David."

"What about him?"

"He's moving things. Into the vault. Into his old office."

I heard Neko's warning, loud and clear in what he didn't say. David had used that office when we were first under attack by Pitt. At the time, I hadn't understood the depth of hatred between the men. I hadn't seen the warning signs that David was obsessed with his old enemy, spending hour after hour in his office, tracking transactions and plotting out data. I'd almost been too late at discovering David's compulsions. He'd almost gone mad.

"What things, Neko?" My voice was tight.

"The entire Osgood collection. And he won't let anyone help."

I winced, picturing the deep purple bruises on his torso. He shouldn't be moving books. He shouldn't be out of bed. "Tell him to wait until I get there. Make him stop, Neko."

"I'll do my best. Just hurry."

Gran and Clara were already waving me toward the restaurant's door by the time I hung up the phone. It was my turn to pay for brunch, but that didn't matter. They were witches. They understood that our warder needed me. And I might already be too late.

# Chapter 5

HECATE MUST HAVE had a soft spot for me. That's the only way I could explain how I drove from Bethesda to the farm-house in under an hour without getting a traffic ticket.

Gravel flew as I braked to a stop in the driveway. Clambering out of the car, I was struck by how deceptive sights could be. The garage dormitory looked absolutely peaceful, its cheery curtains safe and secure behind double-paned glass. I could barely make out the roofline of the barn over the hill. I could imagine the warders and familiars just starting to stir on a lazy Sunday morning.

But signs of danger were clear, because I knew where to look. Spot stood on the top step of the porch, a low whine rising in his throat. The newspaper leaned against the door where I'd placed it when I left for brunch. Inside, the kitchen was a mess; our dinner dishes from the previous night were still stacked in the sink.

David always washed up, first thing in the morning, as his coffee brewed. He settled at the center island to read the paper, cover to cover. He never failed to let Spot out, waiting for the Lab to do his business, then welcoming the lumbering animal back to the kitchen with a teeth-cleaning bone.

Neko flung open the basement door as I tallied up the evidence. "Hurry," he said.

A corner of my mind screamed that I'd been here before. This wasn't the vague disconnect of déjà vu. It was the bellowing the brute force of learned terror that told me I needed to turn on my heel, get out of the house, leave the farm forever and head back to my safe and quiet life as a librarian. I'd be safe in a world without Neko and witchcraft and warders.

Because I *had* done this before. I'd flipped on the basement lights. I'd walked down the stairs, stepping wide on the fourth one to avoid its groaning creak. I'd opened the door to David's basement office, and I'd seen insanity, the physical manifestation of pure obsession as my warder fought to control a bureaucracy bigger and stronger and more determined than even he could be.

Only a few months ago, I thought I'd lost him—as my warder and as the man I loved.

We'd made it through that. We'd survived. But I was terrified I didn't have the strength to face David's compulsions again. Not to face them and win.

I startled when I felt smooth velvet beneath my palm. Spot had followed me into the house. Now, he leaned his head against my thigh, and he *woofed* a breath of canine concern. I glanced back at Neko, only to catch the same look of worry on his face.

Spot and Neko. David. They needed me. I licked my lips and went downstairs.

Empty shelves gaped on the basement walls, stretches of polished wood that had been filled with orderly volumes only two nights before. A quick survey showed that many of my artifacts were missing as well—a case of crystals here, a stash of wands there. All the runes were gone.

Furtive noises came from David's former office, from the vault. Sweat slicked my palms, but I forced myself to cross to the doorway.

I barely recognized the room. We'd wanted to maximize the storage space, so we'd abandoned classifying the books by subject matter. Instead, they were organized by height, miniatures grouped together, duodecimos on shelves below, giant elephant folios protected on the lowest ranks. We'd talked about adding double-sided bookshelves in the center of the room, but that would have created a challenge in navigating the small space.

Navigation wasn't a concern now. It was downright impossible.

David had stacked boxes against the shelves, filling every cubic inch of space. Some of the containers were small—bankers boxes with neat labels, the ones that had held his warder's papers in his office. Others, though, were cavernous, left over from the appliances we'd recently purchased to outfit the garage apartment and the kitchenette in the barn. The vault looked like a playroom for children with very indulgent parents, children who reveled in a make-believe fort made entirely of cardboard.

David was leaning over a box that had formerly held an oven, lining up the twenty-three volumes of Hoskin's *Crystals, Stones, and Lapidary Magic Around the World.*

"Hey," I said softly. "I thought you'd agreed to take it easy until your ribs heal."

I braced for his response. I told myself I could stand anything—madness, obsession, rage at being interrupted. But I still wasn't prepared for what I saw on his face. I hadn't expected to see *shame.*

Shame, or remorse, or abject apology—the specifics were

lost in the hollows beneath his eyes, in the resigned twist of his lips.

"What?" I asked, moving into the room. Spot shifted with me, and Neko too, but I cast a look at my familiar, a quick shake of my head. He clicked his tongue to get the dog's attention, and they both retreated to the main basement room. "What are you doing here, David?"

He braced his arms on the edge of the box. "I need to protect these things," he said. "The books, the crystals, the runes, all of it."

"They're safe," I said. "The whole house is safe."

He shook his head. "I failed you on Samhain. I couldn't stop the satyr, couldn't keep Teresa Alison Sidney from claiming her benefaction. I didn't keep you safe."

"*No one* could have kept me safe. You saw the other warders. They did their best, too. Some things are stronger than we are."

He shook his head. "That's not good enough. That's not who I am."

"It's *exactly* who you are! You're not a god, David Montrose. You don't get to change natural law, to upend the supernatural, just because you want to."

"You could have been killed!"

I started to interrupt him, but I bit back my protest. This all made sense, in some crazy way. This vault was something he had built, something he had mastered. He could control it, control its contents. And Teresa hadn't discovered it. She hadn't plundered our treasures. Now David was intent on making everything a treasure. He'd gather together my entire collection; he'd watch over it in the only way he could.

I wanted to make him stop. He couldn't swaddle me or my possessions in cotton. He couldn't keep the world from reaching me, keep me from reaching the world.

But I held my tongue. Because part of being a witch was knowing what my warder needed. And part of being a woman was knowing what my man needed, my partner, the one I was going to live my life with forever. So, instead of protesting that he was locking the proverbial barn after the horse had fled, I took another tack.

"All right," I said.

"All right?" He didn't understand. He didn't have faith in my acceptance.

"We'll move the collection. As much of it as we can fit in here. It would be better if we had time for custom-built shelves, but we can make do with the boxes for now. Maybe we should bring down the coffee table from the living room. We can stack books under it and on top. The end tables from the living room, too."

David straightened. "There's a 'but' there. What aren't you telling me?"

He knew me too well. "But *you* aren't doing any more of the work." I glanced over my shoulder. "Neko? Head over to the barn, please. Tell Caleb and Tony we need their help."

"I don't want strangers doing this," David said.

"They're not strangers. They stood by us at the Mabon working. And we can trust them now."

It was hard for him to give in.

But this time I knew I was right. I said, "I'm not asking you to trust strangers. I understand that you don't know the new students, you don't trust their warders. But Caleb and Tony are safe." I looked back at my hesitating familiar. "Neko," I said, and I bolstered my command with a nudge along the magical bond between us. He nodded at last and headed for the stairs, snapping his fingers for Spot to come along.

I took advantage of the privacy to skirt the giant cardboard box. Settling my hand on David's chest, I spread my fingers to feel the steady beat of his heart. "Thank you," I said.

He looked away, but I pressed my free palm against the hard line of his jaw, forcing his gaze back to me. "I mean it," I said. "Thank you for protecting me. Thank you for keeping me safe."

"I didn't—"

"You did, though. I'm here, aren't I? We're here together."

It took a long moment, but he finally shifted his stance, edging away from the box. As his frantic energy waned, the jangle of madness easing away, and I slipped my arms down his torso. I took care to skim over the bruises I knew had to be throbbing. I nestled my head against his chest, and I sighed when I felt his fingers slip through my hair. We stood there until Neko returned with the warders.

By the time Monday morning rolled around, it actually felt like a *relief* to face the first day of class with my new students. There was nothing like concrete magical workings to force away all my lingering concerns—about Pitt somehow bringing a magical beast into the center of our opening ritual, about Teresa trying to cut me off before I even got started, about David's mania to secure every last remnant of the Osgood collection in the basement vault.

I woke about an hour before sunrise. After showering and dressing, I met David in the kitchen and fortified myself with a simple breakfast of steel-cut oatmeal and hot tea. I swallowed the last of my pear oolong and reached out to straighten his tie. "You know I'd go to the inquest if I could."

"You'd just waste your day sitting on a bench in the hallway."

I growled and was rewarded with Spot raising his head from his bed in the corner. As David told the dog to lie back down, I said, "Confidential proceedings. I get it." And I quoted, "The Court shall preserve the privacy of the accused by conducting all inquiries in a secured facility, closed to all but testifying witnesses."

David nodded. His fingers closed around my waist. "I'm the one who shouldn't be leaving you."

"I have six warders at my beck and call."

"But—"

I shook my head. "And every one of them is armed with a sword. I'm not postponing class. You saw the parchment from Hecate's Court. We have to stay in session continuously, or we'll break our charter." I settled my palm over his heart. "We'll be fine. Just tell me there's no way Pitt is getting off."

Alas, it wasn't that simple. Pitt stood accused of using his position in the Court for personal profit. He'd skimmed funds from hundreds of witches, taken bribes and sold favors. And now he faced legal sanctions because David and I had turned him in.

But years earlier, David had tried to take matters into his own hands. He'd falsified documents and forged papers, all in the interest of bringing Pitt's violations to light. David might be called as a witness in this proceeding, but his testimony was suspect for bias. And he could very well be investigated as a criminal himself.

"We'll be fine," I repeated when David didn't tell a lie to reassure me. "It's you I'm worried about."

"Then I'm not doing my job right. You should never worry about me."

I set my left hand on his chest, letting my engagement ring catch the light. "That ship sailed the day you proposed."

For answer, he leaned forward for a kiss. I broke it off first and retreated to the safety of my chair, where neither of us could be further distracted from our busy days. I said, "Let's have dinner in the city tonight."

"There's no reason for you to come all the way down there."

"I'm already driving down. Remember? I'm getting together with Melissa after class. I still need to officially con her into being my matron of honor."

"Sorry, I forgot. Sure. Let's grab dinner. I'll meet you at the bakery."

"Perfect."

But it wasn't perfect. David never forgot my schedule. He never forgot anything. He was more worried about the inquest than he'd ever admit.

But so-called *perfect* was better than panic. I wished him luck and hurried out of the kitchen, determined not to add to his concerns.

I used the walk through the woods to center myself. The driving storm of Samhain had been caused by a strong cold front. In its wake, the sky shone with the sharp blue of lapis. Only the heartiest of leaves still clung to the trees, their bright autumn shades faded to brown. I was grateful for my heavy wool coat.

As always, my spirits were revived by the time I found myself on the crescent beach by the lake. My students waited with their warders and familiars, feet planted on the sand.

Automatically, I looked across the water to a shattered oak and the massive osprey nest that filled its jagged branches. Some time in the past week, the raptors had migrated south for the winter. I found myself missing their sharp cries, waiting for the shadow of their wings as they headed out to snatch fish from the center of the lake.

A distant rumble came from the far edge of the water. I fought a frown; I'd hoped not to hear the commotion. Trees were being cut down on the southern point of David's property, old growth pine that he'd sold for a small fortune. The clearing was the first stage; next would be development of the property into high-end condos and trendy retail establishments.

Compromise. That's what made the world go round. The Jane Madison Academy required money to operate, and David had generated that money by selling timber and land. I'd hated letting him make the sale, but I hadn't been able to figure out an alternative.

So it was up to me to make sure the sacrifice paid off.

"Good morning," I said to my assembled students, taking a moment to look at each of them.

Automatically, I sought out the women I knew best. Raven matched my greeting, raking a hand through her violet-striped hair and knocking a hip out at an enticing angle. A couple of months ago, I would have been angered by the gesture, resenting the way the warders eyed her, furious with her for upsetting the balance of our distaff group.

Now, though, I was accustomed to her harmless habits. I nodded easily, just like I smiled when Emma piped up with her fake British accent: "It's right parky today, isn't it?"

Looking at the others, I was concerned about Cassie. Her face was drawn. The ghost of a bruise stood out on her cheekbone. But her feet were planted firmly, and her hands were shoved deep into her pockets, giving her a look of stoic defiance.

Skyler Winthrop stood close to her. I'd seen the women

talking as I approached. I was pleased to see the gesture of support, even though I was a bit surprised to find Skyler in the role of caretaker. She was the last student I'd selected for the semester and I would never admit publicly how much her sculpted face and patrician airs intimidated me. Her cultivated accent of Boston's Back Bay made me want to check for stains on my workaday clothes, for dirt ingrained under my fingernails.

Her warder was similarly aloof. He reminded me of a banker or a businessman, someone who wore a three-piece suit and sat behind a gigantic desk. He was older than the other warders by nearly a generation, and I wondered how he'd come to serve a young witch like Skyler.

In the end, I'd admitted the Boston Brahmin because of her familiar. Siga was a heavyset woman with short arms and legs. Her stubby fingers reminded me of hooves, but there was a smile in her porcine eyes. Skyler distanced herself from that grin, setting up the same frosty barrier she applied to me. But I liked Siga. I wanted to work with her in my own brand of communal magic. And so I'd invited Skyler into our midst.

And now she was serving as Cassie's confidante, a role I couldn't play. Cassie was holding herself aloof from me, from her magistrix. And while it hurt me to admit it, I needed to maintain some distance from my charges. That was one of the lessons I'd learned the previous term, before we completed the Academy's first Major Working. I'd been too wrapped up in my students' lives when I launched the magicarium, and I intended to do things differently going forward. I would let them support each other, while I did what I should have done all along, serving as their mentor, their teacher, their guide. I would be their magistrix.

"All right," I said. "We all got a taste of formal ritual

magic on Samhain. Obviously, that working didn't go as planned, but I'm proud of all of you for sticking with us. Thank you for trusting the Academy."

I glanced at Cassie, just long enough to catch her nod of cooperation.

"In light of what happened, I've decided to postpone any additional spellcraft for a few weeks."

*I* hadn't decided anything of the sort. David had insisted. But I had agreed that my students needed to regain some confidence before we ventured back into a ritual circle.

"We'll focus on other aspects of your education. As you know, most of our magic isn't used in formal rites. There's power in the entire world around us, in the balance of nature, in the twining of animals and plants, in the bedrock of our fields." A breeze skipped across the lake, ruffling the sand with scalloped waves. A fish jumped, giving me the cue I hadn't known I needed.

"Let's start on the dock today," I said. Confident that my students would follow, I turned toward the weathered grey planks.

Ordinarily, we would have completed a classroom session with only one warder in attendance. That was standard Academy policy, basic common sense. But these were hardly ordinary times for my magicarium. In an attempt to assuage any lingering anxiety from my students, I'd asked all their warders to keep watch, even Zach, whose arm was suspended in a sling.

I wasn't entirely surprised when Tony brushed past me. He was good at his job, scouting out danger and protecting his witch, Raven. He guarded the rest of us as an afterthought, but I wasn't complaining. He took up his post on the end of the dock, his back to us witches as he scoured the distant shoreline for threats.

Neko walked toward the end of the pier as well. I couldn't tell if he was truly trying to support me, or if he was just getting closer to his boyfriend. Even though I'd had months to get used to the idea, I still had trouble adjusting to the notion of my familiar and Tony as a couple. Where Neko presented himself as the essence of frivolity, a fashion maven, a makeup guru, Tony was dour—pugnacious even. I suspected he wouldn't recognize a designer garment if the label choked him in his sleep, and I couldn't imagine him pulling together a costume for even the wildest party.

Opposites attract. At least sometimes. Neko seemed happier than I'd ever seen him, and Tony had lost his feral edge. I couldn't ask for more.

My witches followed me onto the dock, accompanied by their familiars. Their warders took up stations along the beach. It might be overkill to have six armed warders watching over the most basic of witchcraft lessons. But we were gathered. We were safe. We were ready to start the fall semester.

I sank onto the wooden planks and gestured for my students to join me. Neko leaned in close on one side, but I wasn't sure if he was offering astral support or taking refuge from the breeze. I pulled my knees up to my chin as if we were all gathered around a campfire, and I started to tell a story.

"In a standard magicarium, we'd begin by working the Rota, repeating a single spell for days. But you aren't here for that type of education. Instead, our goal is to integrate our magic into the world around us. We'll start by studying the magical potential of natural world. We'll study its balance. Its harmony."

I watched them as I spoke. They nodded. They got it. At least, they didn't want the mindless repetition of the Rota.

"So," I continued. "Let's consider where we are in the cycle of nature. It's autumn, November, a time when most things rest and recover from the exuberant growth of summer. Many birds have migrated. Mammals are hibernating. We've had one hard freeze, an early one, so insects and plants have died off.

"But even in November, there are plenty of animals around us. We just have to train ourselves to sense them. So I want you to start by taking three deep breaths. Center yourself. Then focus on the animals you sense—in the lake and on the shore. When you're ready, let's go around the circle. Everyone will name one living creature. We'll keep going until we've found them all. I'll start."

I closed my eyes and concentrated on my breathing. In. Out. In. Out. In. Out. I was only a little distracted by Raven's theatrical gasps, as showy as a wine connoisseur slurping a fine vintage. Some day, her dramatic ways might even become endearing. After a moment, I said, "Largemouth bass."

Raven waited a beat before she said, "Carp."

Skyler was next. I could tell she was hesitant. I suspected she might guess.

I eased my eyes open and wove my voice into the nervous silence. "Don't make up an answer. Extend your senses. Measure the world around you. Reach out to *feel* that world."

Skyler scrunched her forehead into a frown, but she said, "Minnow." I nodded, still not sure if she'd used magic to find her answer.

Cassie contributed "Canada geese," and my other students followed in rapid order with mallard, trout, and box turtle. I relaxed a little as we began our second round. To remind my students they could venture past the dock, I said, "raccoon."

We went two more rounds before Raven came up dry. She simply said, "Pass", and Alex gave us "squirrel." Bree passed. Cassie was deep in thought, her face smooth, her lips barely parted. She was taking the exercise more seriously than any of the others. She seemed to be in a trance, hypnotized as she sought another animal presence. She took one breath, another, and then she swallowed hard.

Before she could speak, though, a commotion exploded onto the beach. We all looked up, just in time to see a magnificent stag crash onto the sand. Zach stumbled back, falling three full steps closer to the dock before he pulled himself upright.

The buck was broad-chested and regal. His antlers spread like tree branches. As we gaped, he turned a tight circle, cutting away at the beach with his cloven hooves. His hind quarters bunched as he lowered his head, and he swept those incredible antlers back and forth, challenging the forest from which he'd sprung.

No.

Not challenging the forest.

A snarling sound ripped across the beach. Branches crashed and undergrowth was torn up as a creature leaped out of the woods.

Partly blocked by the stag, I could only take in the new animal's haunches, huge and muscled like a gladiator's. Its brindle coat glistened in the bright sunshine. I could make out four massive paws digging into the sand, black claws leaving streaks half an arm in length. A long furred tail lashed back and forth, a weapon in its own right.

The stag broke to the left, toward Caleb. It panicked and leaped back to the right. The predator lunged forward, and the buck sprang for the woodland path, the one we witches had walked to begin our now-abandoned exercise.

Frustrated at the potential escape of its prey, the brindled beast began to howl. The sound was deafening—the bay of a hound amplified by the deep chest of a dire wolf. I wanted to cover my ears, but the cacophony froze me; I lost all power to move. The thing seemed to sense my vulnerability. It swung its head around to glare at me with crimson eyes.

And that was when I realized why the creature was so loud.

The animal on the beach, the largest dog I'd ever seen, the largest *wolf* I'd ever imagined, had two heads. And both of them were slavering, with a forest of teeth ready to rip out the throat out of the first creature it reached. It bunched its hind quarters and prepared to launch at me.

# Chapter 6

CALEB LUNGED FOR the creature, swinging his sword with both hands. The weapon clanged as it struck the dog-thing, and pewter sparks flew. Sparks flew, but the animal did not yield. In fact, it lifted one massive paw and swiped at the sword as if it were a lawn dart. The polished blade snapped at the hilt.

Tossing away the fractured stub of metal, Caleb leaped toward safety, rolling beyond the reach of teeth and claws. His maneuver, though, did not take into account the beast's second pair of jaws. He paid for the miscalculation with a sleeve from his shirt. The toll would have been a lot higher if Zach hadn't shouted to draw the monster's attention, waving his good arm to draw an attack.

Jeffrey stepped up then, wielding his own heavy blade to slice through the creature's thick, brindled neck. Once again, though, the sword bounced off flesh harmlessly, as if the animal wore a massive iron collar. Or as if it were charmed, protected from warders' steel.

As Jeffrey reeled, Caleb lunged toward the woods. He grabbed a massive tree limb that lay half on the sand, half in the underbrush. Judging from its raw wooden end, the branch must have come down in the Samhain storm. It was as long as a baseball bat and twice as thick.

Caleb didn't hesitate. He swung at the dog's left head, putting all his considerable muscle behind the blow, as if he were hoping for a home run. The wood connected with a sickening thud, and the dog yelped, leaping a man's length back on the beach.

The left head dipped toward the sand, shuddering like a cartoon character fighting off swirling stars and tweeting birds. The right head, though, was unharmed. Rather, the beast threw back that snout and howled again, as if it were calling up all the demons of hell.

The sound melted my bones. I could not stand, could not brace myself to offer up my mind, my words, my heart. There was evil magic in that creature's voice. Every canine snarl ripped away a little more of my powers. My magic drained with each guttural growl, with every slashing challenge.

The left head was recovering. The beast's tongue swept out of its mouth, flinging foam toward Caleb, who still held the branch as he circled for another blow. The right teeth clashed, scraping against each other, and both heads bayed at once.

All the spells I had ever known were nothing more than silly rhymes. I couldn't imagine harnessing the power of crystals, of herbs, of the natural world around me.

Caleb took another swing, but the animal reared up on its hind legs. Its massive forepaws came crashing down, sweeping the branch from the warder's grasp. Emma cried out, a wordless wail as lonely and stricken as a loon's. Caleb rolled away, narrowly escaping the double pair of slashing jaws.

Jeffrey harried at the monster, hacking with his sword until the beast hooked the weapon with one massive paw, toss-

ing the blade toward the water. Zach was shouting, still trying to distract the animal, but his voice had gone hoarse.
Tony was trapped behind us witches, and Alex's warder,
Garth had planted himself as a final barrier at the foot of the
pier.

The animal howled again, stripping my power completely. I wasn't a magistrix, proud leader of the Jane Madison
Academy. I wasn't a witch.

The beast pawed the ground, churning up a mountain of
sand. Its hindquarters wound like a catapult, and Caleb
flung a futile hand across his throat, as if he could protect his
jugular, his carotid, his windpipe that would all be ground to
meat between double teeth.

The animal bayed victory, and I was lost, so helpless that
I could not look away, could not close my eyes.

And so I saw Bree's warder, Luke, leap from the sand to
the thing's broad back. He gripped our attacker's scruff like
a circus rider, tangling his fingers in the rough mat at the
back of its neck.

Luke kept one hand flung behind him as if were riding a
bucking bronco in the world's most hideous rodeo. Part of
me gibbered, wanting to tell him to hold on, to grasp a
handhold, to anchor himself in any way he could. This
wasn't a time for showmanship; he'd gain no points for style.

But Luke wasn't showing off a roper's winning form.
Sunlight glinted on his hand, on the extension of a blade *in*
his hand. He held a knife as long as his forearm, unadorned
metal sharpened to a killing edge. He tilted his wrist and
shifted his angle, and then he drove deep into the neck beneath him.

The creature froze, as if a switch had been turned off
deep inside its hulk of living muscle. Its hind legs slipped on
the sand, splaying to either side. Luke rocked forward, and

the front legs spread as well, driving both snouts into the sand. The warder twisted his blade, sawing first to the left, then to the right.

The beast shuddered once, an earthquake that rippled from the end of its tufted tail to the drippings tips of its tongues. A massive sigh rose like the groaning of a mountain, and there was a tumbling sound like an avalanche coming to rest in a valley.

And then the dog, the wolf, the whatever-it-was disappeared.

One heartbeat, it was a slaughterhouse of dead meat. The next, it was gone, not even a fog, a mist, a breath of air remaining to show it had ever existed.

Luke was left kneeling on the beach, his knife winking in the sun, as clean as if it were newly forged. Only the gouges on the sand testified that the animal had ever been there. The gouges, and the harsh gasps of all my witches and their familiars. Warders' angry shouts echoed as men kicked at the empty beach.

I still could not feel my powers, could barely remember I'd ever had them. Panic scrabbled at the corners of my mind, but I knew I needed to maintain an appearance of calm for my students. They were here because of me. I needed to serve as a role model.

Tony, stranded on the end of the pier, helped each of us witches to our feet. He reached for Raven last, keeping hold of her hand until he was convinced she was unharmed. Even as he steadied her, his eyes raked over the rest of us, seething until he found Neko at my side, until my familiar offered up the tiniest of nods, confirming he was safe.

I wanted to shout that we might be safe, physically, but there was something more amiss. The other women all looked stunned. They seemed as stricken as I was. Their magic had also been ripped from their minds. That was why no one had helped the warders, no one had offered up a drop of magic in our defense.

Jeffrey helped Caleb stand, and they both checked on Luke, who was still turning his knife in his hand, marveling at the pristine blade. "Titanium," he said. "Not steel. Used it for castrating bulls back home." He flashed a rancher's grin at all of us, as if he'd just told a thigh-slapping joke.

His witch, Bree Carter, caught on first. The Montana native wiped her palms on her blue jeans, shrugging her broad shoulders in her heavy flannel shirt. She settled an easy hand on the forearm of her horse-faced familiar, Perd, almost as if she wasn't seeking support from the man. Narrowing her dark eyes, she tossed her cap of mahogany curls and said, "If you were going for castration, you started at the wrong end."

"Can't blame a man for trying," Luke said, and he shoved his survival knife back into its sheath, in the side of his disreputable cowboy boots.

"Trying like a steer," Bree said. She won an approving nod from her warder and a ragged chuckle from the other men. No one could blame them if their amusement sounded a little strained. Especially not Zach, who was easing his arm back in his sling and doing his best to shield Cassie from whatever unknown danger might linger on the beach or in the woods.

Still reeling, I acknowledged that Luke and Bree were doing their best to ground us. We witches hadn't spent any magical power—we didn't have any power *to* spend. We didn't need food and drink to restore us to our senses. But we had to be reminded that we were alive, that the beast had not won.

"Let's go," Tony said, eyeing the lake as if a kraken might rear up out of the water. "Back to the house."

He was right. We shouldn't stay out here. Not when we had no idea where the dog-thing had come from. Not when something else—anything else?—could attack. Not when we witches were powerless to do so much as light a candle.

The warders sorted themselves automatically, surrounding us in a tight phalanx. I let them make the decisions, allowed them to keep us safe.

One hundred steps into the woods, I began to sense my magic again, a hum of awareness at the very edge of my consciousness. Five hundred steps in, I could remember every spell I'd ever mastered. A thousand steps toward home, and I sensed the interwoven energy of the world around me, the balance, the give and take I'd hoped my students would learn that morning. My powers were restored as if the beast had never taken them, as if I'd never been stripped bare.

We marched through the clearing like an army of Spartans, skirting the ritual circle where the satyr had spawned. Back at the house, the warders split forces. Luke and Jeffrey, Zach and Garth, they all followed Caleb's lead, collecting my students and securing them with their familiars in the garage dormitory.

Tony nodded as Jeffrey took up a guard post at the single door that led into that building. The other men began a slow walk around the structure. From their extended hands and their gradually widening circles, I knew they were checking the wards they'd previously set. They were testing their magic, bolstering their protective spells.

Tony gave me a chance to see that everyone was safe before he hustled me into the farmhouse. "Stay here," he said. "Both of you," he added, when Neko took a half-step toward him.

"I want—" my familiar said.

"Not gonna happen," the warder said, with enough finality that even Neko gave up the fight. "Stay inside while I double-check the wards. And lock that thing up."

He jutted his chin toward Spot. The Lab had slunk into the living room, belly low to the ground, lips pulled back over his teeth. He was making a sound I'd never heard before, a cross between a whine and a growl, as he traced a tight half-circle around us.

Neko recovered faster than I did. He grabbed a dog treat from the jar in the kitchen and lured Spot upstairs. I was relieved to hear the bedroom door latch closed.

After that, Neko and I sat at the kitchen table. I tried to call David, but I got his voicemail. No surprise; he'd never be allowed to have his phone on during the Court's inquest. I left a message, trying to sound neutral. "Something came up here at the farm. Come straight home, and I'll fill you in on the details."

That's all he needed to know. Especially when there wasn't a damn thing he could do, not now, not from DC. After I hung up, I waited with Neko, both of us straining our ears as we imagined Tony pacing off the perimeter of the farmhouse, checking the protective measures David constantly maintained. One circle, I counted in my mind. A second. A third.

When Tony finally walked through the front door, Neko was a trembling mess. Both of us leaped from our chairs, rushing toward the living room. The door clicked closed, and the warder said, "Everything will hold. For now."

Neko launched himself around the couch, folding Tony into his arms. The warder clutched him just as close, lowering his lips to hair that my familiar would never admit was thoroughly mussed.

I headed down to the basement, to the vault and my books. I wanted to give the men some privacy. And I wanted to figure out what the hell that animal had been, the one that had almost killed us on the beach.

Delving into my books proved more of a challenge than I'd anticipated. David's insistence on consolidating the collection in the vault had destroyed my careful organization. I had computer records telling me which books I owned, careful notations about rank and shelf, but neither of us had taken the time to update those files with "Frigidaire crate" or "microwave box" when David shifted everything into storage.

My frustration only grew when I realized that my best resources on magical creatures were stacked nine layers deep, in the very back corner of the reinforced room. Given the fragile incunabula stored in the front rows, it would take at least an hour to get to what I needed.

Maybe I'd better take another tack. I could focus on magical warfare. *Someone* had to have written a treatise about how to wage battle with animals. No. I remembered stacking those books on the back wall. They were buried under the facsimile copies of the Washington Coven's record books, the forty-one volume cloth-bound set.

Fine. I could research warders' weaponry. I had to have a reference volume that listed all creatures that could be banished by titanium. But the warders' books were the first ones David had brought into the vault after Teresa claimed her benefaction. I couldn't even remember where they'd ended up in the clutter.

If I shifted *that* stack *there*... If I balanced *these* boxes against *those*. If...

My phone rang, startling me out of my hopeless game of real-life Tetris. I barely glanced at the screen as I answered. "Hey, Melissa."

"Thank God I caught you before you left."

"Left?" I craned my neck, trying to identify a cochineal-dyed copy of Reed's *Magical Beasts and the Nightmares They Breed*, going solely by the bottom edge of the volumes stacked behind the haphazard pile of cauldrons.

"You're going to kill me."

I shook my head and sank to the floor cross-legged, giving up on my impossible task. "Why would I kill you?"

"I have to cancel."

Cancel.

That's right. I was supposed to meet Melissa at the bakery that evening. I should have wrapped up an easy lesson with my students about an hour ago. I would have had plenty of time to come up to the house, heat up a nice bowl of soup for lunch, and change into clean clothes before I made the drive down to DC.

"You must hate me," Melissa said.

This probably wasn't the best time to tell her I had forgotten about her completely. "Of course I don't hate you."

"Rob just got invited to dinner tonight with the chairman of his firm, and it's a command performance for me. We're going to a *country club*. I have to wear a *dress!*"

"'What fashion, madam, shall I make your breeches?'" I took a strange comfort that the words came to mind easily. Even if my magical life was in shambles, I could remember my Shakespeare. If worse came to worst, I could give up on the magicarium and get a job teaching high school English. Actually, right about now, that career shift sounded like heaven.

Melissa's aggravated shriek told me she recognized the quotation, even if she wasn't amused. "*Two Gentlemen of Verona*," she said. "And I *hate* that play. I cannot wait until Rob's stupid partnership vote is over. I don't care if he ever makes partner—I just want to be done with the dog and pony shows!"

The panic in her voice almost made me feel guilty for taking pleasure in the Bard. "It's okay," I soothed. "You'll do fine. And we'll reschedule my coming down to the city. I've actually got a lot going on here today." I was *not* going to tell my best friend that I'd been attacked by a two-headed dog on the beach, my powers had temporarily been stripped, and the monster's corpse had disappeared without leaving a single hair behind. She'd make time for me if I told her that. She'd make time all the way to the psych ward.

"Friday night," she said. "Mojito Therapy. I'll come out there, since I'm the one wimping out tonight."

"Friday," I agreed. "Can't wait."

And that wasn't a lie. I desperately wanted to retreat to the early days of our friendship—to the easy times when we lived a few blocks apart, when we were both looking for the loves of our lives, when our greatest dilemma was whether we had enough lime juice for another round of well-muddled tropical drinks.

I heard a bell jangle in the background on Melissa's end, followed by the clamor of kids begging for enough sugar to wire all of DC for a year. "I'm sorry," Melissa said.

"Don't be. Go. I'll see you on Friday."

Melissa's call served one valuable purpose: it broke the hopeless cycle of my searching in the vault. I wasn't going to reach the materials I needed, not without help. I might as well backtrack and try a little mundane research. I headed upstairs.

Tony had rearranged the living room furniture, dragging one of the heavy armchairs so he had a clear view of both the front and back doors. His unsheathed sword rested on the coffee table, in easy reach, and the largest butcher knife from our kitchen lay on the floor by his right foot. Neko sat next to the knife, leaning his head on Tony's left knee. The warder's fingers worked Neko's nape, as if he could smooth away the horrors of the morning as easily as he could work out a muscle kink.

"Did you find anything?" Neko asked, starting to stir, but I waved him back to his place.

"Nothing useful. I'm going to check a few things upstairs."

"Pull the window shades up there," Tony said.

"You don't think—"

"I'm not taking any chances. Pull the shades."

I pulled the shades.

I didn't want to imagine what sort of enemy magic could get at me through a second story window. I collapsed onto my bed and picked up my tablet from my nightstand. My fingers flew over the surface, keying in search terms. Someone had written a song called "Two-Headed Dog" and half a dozen musicians had covered it. A Russian scientist had done freak transplant experiments, creating a two-headed puppy.

Then I hit pay-dirt. Orthros. A two-headed dog. An ancient Greek monster, litter-mate of the three-headed Cerberus that guarded the gates of the underworld.

I followed up on the entries, digging deeper into Greek mythology. Orthros was part of a family of monsters. He was owned by a giant who had three bodies; the dog was supposed to guard a special herd of red cattle. Heracles worked his labors and stole the cows, killing Orthros.

Well, Heracles hadn't quite gotten the job done, had he?

There were references to *The Iliad* and images of Greek pottery, black lines incised on red clay.

I tried to tell myself that myths were just that—stories

passed down through the ages. They often had some seed of truth. Maybe some ancient cowherd had a bitch that whelped deformed puppies. Maybe a man stole cattle and had to explain how he was a good guy and not a common thief.

But someone had taken those stories and turned them into reality. Someone had worked magic, building on the foundation of legend. Someone had launched a horror on the beach, a deadly threat greater than any dusty tale I could read about online. And someone had inured that monster against steel, against warder's magic, honing its ability to strip away witches' power.

Suddenly, the front door of the farmhouse crashed open. I heard a shout, and then my name, bellowed from the landing: "Jane!"

David took the stairs two at a time. I only had time to set aside my tablet, to stand beside the bed, and then he barreled into the room. His hands crushed me as he tested my arms, my shoulders, the back of my head, checking to see that I was there, that I was alive. His eyes were wild, and he said my name over and over as I clutched him, held him close, trying to tell him with the press of my body against his that I was fine, I was safe, I was his.

When I could speak, when he could hear me, I managed, "I didn't hear your car on the driveway."

"I used warder's magic. As soon as I left the inquest, the instant I heard Tony's message."

Of course. My carefully non-alarmist voicemail had been for naught.

David led me over to the edge of the bed. He sat beside me and folded my hands between his. "Tell me what happened."

I did, starting with our lesson on the dock, the reaching

for balance, for harmony in the animal world. I told him about the stag, and then the dog. Orthros. I explained what I'd found in my research so far.

David nodded, as if he were memorizing every word. When I finished, he said, "Again."

I obliged, because I didn't know what else to do. Our lesson, the stag, the dog, Greek legend.

"One more time."

"David—"

"Please."

Lesson. Stag. Dog. Orthros.

When he stood, it seemed as if we'd been sitting for hours. But I understood why he'd made me repeat myself, why he'd forced me to go over the horror again and again. By the time I finished the third repetition, the morning was something I'd read about in a book, a story that had happened to another person ages past. The beast had lost the power to terrify me. I could study it, question my knowledge, live with what I'd seen.

David stalked to the closet. His sword banged softly against the bed as he settled the scabbard around his waist.

"Where are you going?" I asked

"To the beach."

"None of us saw—"

"You weren't in any shape to see anything. Not after that thing attacked."

"Let me go with you?"

Right. Well I had to ask, even though I'd been certain of his answer. I followed him downstairs and watched as he strode down the porch steps, hand firmly placed on the grip of his sword.

It seemed like he was gone for days. It was less than thirty minutes, according to the clock on the mantel. When I saw him crossing the field, no one could keep me from running out of the house—not Tony, not Neko, not the ghosts of a hundred Greek monsters.

David settled his arm around my shoulders, pulling me close as we returned to the house. His face was grave, and he kept his free hand on his sword until the door was locked behind us.

"What?" I asked, my curiosity echoed by Tony and Neko.

David reached into his pocket and pulled out a perfect snowy handkerchief. Unfolding the cotton with care, he peeled back three layers before he extended his palm.

Neko hissed at the item in David's hand, taking a full step back before he could control himself. Tony started to swear under his breath, a steady stream of curses that linked words I'd never thought of combining.

I leaned close enough to realize that David held a tooth, a great curved incisor as long as my index finger. The surface was sickly white, grooved as if it had been eaten by acid. A rusty stain at the base showed where it had been attached to a massive canine jaw.

Tony was the first to speak. "Caleb must have knocked it out of the dog's jaw when he hit the thing." Except he added an adverb before knocked. And he had another word for dog. And thing.

David nodded. "Standing alone, it didn't have enough magical force to disintegrate with the rest of the body." He sounded clinical. Dispassionate. Anyone listening to him might think he was delivering a lecture to a bored audience, speaking from PowerPoint slides in an overheated, darkened auditorium, where the projector's hum lulled the entire audience to sleep.

But I knew David better than that. I knew his perfect

control masked an anger so hot he feared he might destroy everything around him—the house, Tony, Neko. Me—if he loosened his self-control even a micron.

Because, along with David, I sensed what the other men could not. Along with David, I recognized the faintest arcane residue on the tooth. I never would have suspected, if I hadn't first felt in stolen documents, in records David had no business keeping. But I knew that shimmer, that taint.

The tooth, the orthros, had been sent by Norville Pitt.

# Chapter 7

DAVID FINALLY TURNED to me. "Well. It looks like the Jane Madison Academy will be shutting down for an unexpected break."

"No!"

"Jane, you saw that monster on the beach. This time, the warders were able to fight back, and thank Hecate Luke had a knife. But you know as well as I do, that was a close call. We have no idea what Pitt will send next."

"So you're just going to give him what he wants?" I caught the look Neko shot my way, his blatant surprise that I'd take that tone of voice. I didn't bother looking at Tony; I didn't care what the other man thought. My voice ratcheted higher when I said to David, "You *know* he's just doing this to distract you. To screw up your testimony at the inquest. Shutting down the magicarium would be rewarding him for everything he's done."

Nothing. David wouldn't even acknowledge the possibility that I was right.

I took a wild step toward Neko. "Can I borrow a pen?" I asked him, only to face down his elaborate shrug. He wanted no part of my argument with David. I held out my hand, as if I fully expected someone to produce a Bic from thin air. "I want to write a welcome note to Pitt so he feels right at home when he takes over everything we've worked so hard for. That's the only polite thing to do."

David met my sarcasm with a perfectly even tone. "I'm not doing this lightly."

"You aren't doing it at all! *I'm* the magistrix! *I* decide when the Academy shuts down!"

"You're the magistrix, but I'm your warder. I'm still responsible for keeping you safe. You and every one of your students."

"We *are* safe. The system worked. The warders banished the orthros."

David shook his head. "You're lucky. Not safe."

The worst thing was, he was right. If Caleb hadn't reached that branch, if Jeffrey hadn't leaped into the fray, if Zach hadn't distracted the orthros before it could rip out someone's throat… If Luke hadn't kept a titanium blade in his boot… My memory ripped back to the sound of that two-headed beast, the baying snarl that had turned my belly inside out and stripped away my powers.

Without luck, the orthros would have succeeded. And if he had, Norville Pitt might be pawing through my possessions even now. He and Teresa and every other witch within a five-hour radius.

Still… "He *wants* you to do this, David. He *wants* you to shut us down. You saw the parchment. The Court will disband the magicarium if there's any break in classes. Pitt will waltz in here, and he won't even have to spawn another monster. Don't do that. Don't let him win."

David ran his free hand through his hair. The gesture seemed to remind him he was still holding that hideous tooth. He folded his handkerchief tight around the thing and shoved it deep inside his pants pocket.

After taking a breath on a five-count and exhaling just as slowly, he looked through the arch to the kitchen, to the door that led to the basement and all my arcane possessions. "You can hold your classes," he finally said. "But don't try to work with the natural world. Flora and fauna are strictly off the syllabus."

I twisted my lips but I nodded. I wasn't happy, not by a long shot. My students needed to work with a lot of flora and fauna. That was central to what we did as witches. But David wasn't happy either. There was that annoying, grown-up word again: compromise.

And I had to admit his restriction was reasonable, at least for a while. My students and I had plenty to master without reaching out to plants and animals, without opening any more doors for Pitt's potential beasts. We could learn how to recognize the unique signatures of our individual powers. We could work out how to balance those strands of magic. I'd hoped to vary everyone's education, alternating training on group dynamics with focusing on herbs, on crystals, on the living, breathing world around us. But I could stick to the subjects David considered safe. For now.

"And you'll hold all classes in the basement," he said.

"That's impossible!"

"Take it or leave it."

Far too late, I realized I'd committed a strategic flaw. We shouldn't be having this argument here, in front of Tony and Neko. David was digging in, taking a position more aggressively than he might have done if we were fighting alone.

Who was I kidding? David's determination would be every bit as firm if we were alone.

"I'm not running some sort of factory here," I said. "We need time outside. We need to ground our powers in the natural world around us—even if we're just focusing on group dynamics, on how to work together. We're witches, not widget manufacturers!"

David shook his head. "I've set protections on this house, on the dorm and the barn. With the help of the other warders, we can bolster those safeguards. But we can't keep the entire farm safe. Not now. Not when we don't know the full scale of what Pitt is trying to do. We have to assume he's working with someone else, while the inquest is in session."

"I can't work under these conditions."

"It's these conditions or no conditions. Hold class in the basement or the magicarium shuts down."

I wanted to tell him he was being absurd. I wanted to say we witches would be perfectly safe under the late autumn sky, that we could work our magic in the fields, in the woods.

But in reality I didn't know if he *was* being absurd. We hadn't been safe that afternoon. And from the uneasy way Tony eyed the butcher knife by his foot, we weren't safe yet.

"Fine," I said grudgingly.

"Fine?" David pushed.

"Fine, I'll hold classes indoors. For now."

"Until I decide it's safe for you to work outside."

"Until we decide together!" I lashed out, and I was rewarded with a weary nod. I decided to push my luck. "And we don't have to stay in the basement. We can work here, in the living room. In the barn or the dormitory even. We just have to stay behind your existing wards. For now."

He shook his head, but the faintest hint of a smile curled his lips. "You drive a hard bargain, Jane Madison."

"I have a magicarium to run."

"Yes," he said. "You do." I thought it might be a century before he freed me from his storm-dark gaze. When he finally turned to Tony, he held out his right hand. "Thank you," he said. His glance cut to the side to include Neko in his gratitude.

Tony's shoulders rolled in half a shrug before he shook David's hand. "You'd have done the same for Raven."

"Go on, then. Get back to the barn, both of you."

"I'll check the dormitory first," Tony said, even as Neko clutched his arm. "We'll keep a guard posted there twenty-four hours a day."

"Let me know if you need help."

Tony reached for his sword and shoved the blade home in its sheath. Then he stooped to retrieve the knife he'd kept at his feet. He offered it to David with exaggerated care, grip-first. He glanced at me, but he spoke to my warder. "Be careful."

"We will," David said, and he put a lot more confidence behind the words than I could have done.

Neko led the way to the door, but not by much. The two men stayed close as they stepped onto the porch, as they crossed to the dormitory. Jeffrey rose to greet them when they were still a dozen paces from the door, and all three huddled together in serious conversation.

I closed the door and turned around to find David standing too close.

But he wasn't too close, not really. Not when he twined his fingers between mine, when he guided me over to sit beside him on the couch. He pulled my legs up, swinging them around to cross his lap. I leaned back against the arm of the sofa and let his fingers find the tension points in the arch of my right foot, in my ankle, in my toes.

"Shouldn't I be doing that for *you?*" I asked, when the bliss of released stress faded enough for me to form words. "You were the one trapped at the inquest all day."

He shrugged. "It was fine."

I gave him a questioning look, but it became apparent he

wasn't going to elaborate. It was up to me to press for details. "What happened?"

"Inquest proceedings are confidential."

"I'm your witch!"

"Ah," he said. "*That* clarification makes all the difference."

I started to kick at his thigh, undoing all his hard work,
but he merely trapped my toes against his belly, reaching
across for my left foot. I decided to give in, rather than fight
to prove my point. "Okay," I said. "I know you can't tell me
exactly what happened. But do you think the Court listened?
Were they persuaded by the arguments against Pitt?"

He let his head loll against the back of the couch. "No
one made any arguments today, not really. Each side made
its opening statements. They spent the whole time saying
what they're going to say during the rest of the process."

"And?" I asked, sending out the narrowest tendril on the
magical wavelength between us. I wasn't trying to pressure
him into telling me more than he could, more than he
should. But I wanted to remind him I was there to support
him. I was his witch, and I'd always be with him, no matter
what process and procedure was mandated by Hecate's
Court.

"And the next month will be hell. You and I put together
a strong case against Pitt. We handed over the evidence, literally tied up with a bow. But Pitt's not a fool. He never has
been. His entire strategy is to play rope-a-dope, to look like
he's incompetent, unattractive, not worth the time or effort
or energy to deal with. But there's a serpent close beneath
the surface, cold-blooded, sharp-toothed, and hungry."

I nodded. That was the man I'd seen. The man I despised. "You're going back tomorrow?"

He shook his head, a vicious gesture that let me glimpse a

little more of his true frustration. "They won't let me hear the other witnesses. They don't want to corrupt my testimony. I'm banned from the courtroom until they call me back—probably in a few weeks."

I studied David's face. "What aren't you telling me?"

"About a million things. I've taken oaths, Jane."

"What aren't you telling me about Pitt? About his strategy?"

"Nothing. You already know he's right, in some ways. I did trump up a case against him."

"But that was a long time ago. And you didn't have any other options!"

He held up a hand to stop my argument, a hand that I immediately wished was back on my feet. "I trumped up a case," David slowly agreed. "Because I thought I needed to. Because I had to protect others. Because innocents were going to get hurt. I had my reasons, but he has his evidence. He's going to rebut everything I say, and it won't be pretty."

It took me three tries before I could pretend the casual tone I needed. "What happens if the Court sides with him?"

"Worst case?"

I sat up, pulling my feet away from the calm strength of his fingers and bringing my knees to my chin. I kept my gaze steady as I said, "Worst case."

"They'll bust me as a warder. Strip my powers and break my bonds—with you, and Neko, and every law-abiding witch and warder sworn to Hecate. They'll take back my sword and melt it down. They'll break my ring and cast me out forever."

"And if *that's* not enough for Pitt?" My words were bitter. "If he still come after you with magic? What will the Court do then?"

David's laugh didn't yield a glimpse of humor. "If I'm

cast out as a warder, I'll be beyond the Court's jurisdiction. They only handle matters between witches, warders, and familiars."

"There has to be something! Some way to stop him!"

"In theory, there's the Eastern Empire. But they've got a lot more to do than handle assault claims from a disgraced warder."

I knew about the Eastern Empire. The Empire's Night Court maintained a docket for vampires and shapeshifters, for griffins and sprites. I could well imagine they wouldn't make time for a rejected warder, any more than they would for an ordinary human plaintiff.

I tried to ignore the yawning chasm that opened inside my mind, the spinning horror that threatened to steal away all my words. Instead, I pressed: "But whatever happens, Hecate's Court won't hurt *you*. They won't put you in prison or… or worse."

"They won't have to, Jane. Breaking me as a warder would be worse than any prison they could build. I'd have to watch you with your new warder, whoever he is. I'd know exactly what I had. What I lost."

I wanted to argue that David was wrong. That I would never work with another warder.

But I would, and we both knew it. If David were lost to me, I'd have to. I couldn't lose my own magic, even if his was taken by the Court. I'd had a glimpse of that on the beach this afternoon, and the thought of living that way forever made my heart freeze.

So in the end, there wasn't anything I could say to make it right. There wasn't anything I could do.

Except I could slip my hand behind his neck and pull his lips close to mine. And after he'd given in to that pressure, I could take him by the hand and lead him up the stairs to the bedroom we shared. And if we worked a sort of witchcraft together, body pressed to body, it was nothing we couldn't do after the Court finished its inquest. No matter what the outcome there.

They couldn't take that away from us. Ever. At least that's what I prayed to Hecate.

Tuesday morning, I broke the news to my students about our new training regimen. We certainly made a crowd, with all the witches, warders, and familiars crammed into the farmhouse's living room. But I presented the notion of working inside as a temporary thing. I didn't explicitly say we were staying indoors because of the orthros, but I did mention our safety—as a group and as individuals.

No one complained. But that might have been because it was pouring outside, a slow, soaking rain that no doubt nurtured the land. Another few degrees, though, and the driveway would turn into an ice rink.

I felt grim, bleak. That might have been because I'd spent most of the night tossing and turning. Or, to be more accurate, trying to quell the impulse to toss and turn, so I didn't keep David awake. So I didn't have to tell him what I was thinking. What I was planning. What I knew I had to do.

But first off, I had students to teach. And so we all contented ourselves with our caffeine sources of choice. For our first day of indoor classes, I figured I'd keep things simple. I asked each of my students to work her own spell, apply easy magic to conjure up a ball of light.

The exercise served a number of purposes. First and foremost, it relaxed my witches, restoring their confidence that they could, in fact, work magic in my presence without murderous monsters springing out of the woodwork. Beyond that, though, it gave us a chance to get to know each other, to determine the color of each woman's magic, the *feel* of her powers.

Deferring to my second-semester students' seniority, I asked Emma to start. She barely took the time to stretch her hand toward Kopek, to harness her familiar's reflective assistance before she caught a quick breath and opened her palm, displaying a perfect sphere of silver light. The globe was about the size of a tennis ball, and it hovered above her fingertips. I reached toward it with my own witchy awareness, and I could sense her unique astral signature, the cool feeling of water that plunged to unknown depths.

I gave everyone a chance to sample Emma's light, to understand what she had done and to examine her magic so they'd be able to recognize it again. After each witch nodded her understanding, I gestured for Raven to go next.

I wasn't surprised when she was a bit more dramatic with her working. She opened her palm with the force of a dancer displaying "jazz hands," simultaneously snagging a booster of power from her familiar, Hani. The ball of light she created pulsed in time with her breathing, growing to the size of an orange before shrinking back to a tight, smooth marble. The sphere glowed a deep shade of purple, matching the stripe Raven had refreshed in her hair some time after our working on the beach. Reaching for its energy signature, I recognized the sinewy muscle that was unique to Raven Willowsong, the feeling of a snake's smooth, taut body.

Alex Warner leaned forward next, volunteering to be our next guinea pig. Her hair was cut blunt at the level of her chin and dyed as black as charcoal. She sported half a dozen piercings in each ear and tattoos wrapped around both her arms, writhing masses of multi-colored feathers and scales. A metal tongue stud tapped against her teeth as she tossed a quick glance to Garth, her warder. He nodded once, his bullet head seeming to free her to participate in the group exercise. I got the idea they didn't spend a lot of time focusing on touchy-feely communications exercises.

Alex's familiar, Seta, shifted closer, offering up support to her witch. With her broad-set little eyes and her high forehead, I was willing to bet Seta had begun life as a pit bull. That determination likely served her well with her rebellious witch.

For now, Alex didn't rely on her familiar. Instead, she unfolded her fingers with a defiant flare, as if she dared us to question the value of her working. Her light was indigo, a blue so deep it almost looked black. When I touched her sphere with my powers, I recognized the sensation, but it took me several long breaths to put a name to the feeling. Feathers, but not the fluffy touch of down. Rather, Alex's magic felt like the sharp edge of a raptor's wing, stiff enough to support a predator in flight.

Bree took the challenge next, showing us a russet glow and the feel of sun-warmed granite. Skyler offered up a cobalt sphere, a tight ball of energy that was tinged with silver, like the ice of her magical signature.

I hadn't consciously saved Cassie for last. But as we all turned to her, I realized that I felt protective of my final student. Freckles stood out on her pale face, and she gripped Tupa's shoulder as if she might fall over without his support. I realized that the tip of her braid was damp; she'd chewed on it in her nervousness while she waited to exhibit her skills. I caught my breath, willing her to succeed in the working.

At first, she uncurled her fingers only to display an empty palm. She caught her lower lip between her teeth, and I wanted to comfort her. I wanted to assure her that no satyr would get in this house, no stag was going to burst through the door, followed by a ravening two-headed beast.

I held my tongue, though. I needed Cassie to concentrate. I needed her to find her own balance.

She dug her fingers into Tupa's clavicle, tight enough that the familiar winced. A sphere of light finally coalesced, a tangerine glow that glared bright, then faded almost to nothingness before quickening to a creamy, orange glow. I reached for it with my lightest arcane touch, only to find a dense fog, the vague and shapeless manifestation of Cassie's astral signature.

"Excellent," I said, and Cassie let her light fade. A sheen of perspiration coated her freckles, as if she'd just worked a massive feat of strength or weathered some agonizing pain in silence.

Glancing at the clock on the mantel, I was surprised to see it was well past noon. The grey light outside gave no hint that we'd spent more than three hours at our magical work. But the clock—and the tight expression on David's face—let me know I'd pushed my students as much as I reasonably could.

I took a few moments to praise their work, and I suggested they study what they'd learned, focus on each other's unique magical signatures. When I freed them to return to their dormitory, they reacted like students anywhere, chattering about the day's lessons, shrieking at the cold touch of the rain, laughing at an unexpected gust of wind.

I let David fix me a restorative bowl of chicken noodle soup before I brought up the matter that had kept me awake most of the night. We were both scraping the bottoms of our bowls when I said, "I need to go out this afternoon." Something about my tone alerted him. His eyes became as hard as the walnut table between us. "I need more information on the orthros," I said.

"I'll help you find the appropriate books downstairs."

"Books aren't enough," I said. "I need to know if there've been other appearances of that thing. I need to know if satyrs have been summoned in the past, by other witches, working alone or in unison. Other magicaria. Other covens."

"No."

The finality in his tone would have stopped me years ago, would have ended my mission before it began. But I knew that the Osgood collection, as large as it was, had its limitations. It couldn't match the experience of a community that had worked magic together for centuries. It couldn't equal the information I could glean from a single conversation with the Washington Coven Mother.

David prodded my stubborn silence. "Teresa Alison Sidney isn't your friend. She wants to ruin you. She wants you to fail."

"I'm not an idiot!" My tone was all the sharper because I wondered if I *was* an idiot for even considering walking into my enemy's lair. "But I need to find out what she knows. I need to understand the past, so I can protect the Academy now."

"If you're on her territory, I can't be certain I can protect you."

I heard how much that admission cost him. He didn't want to imagine a future where he might fail. But I had to go. I pushed my chair back from the table.

"Let's do it now," I said. "Before dark."

But first, I headed down to the basement. I could not approach the Coven Mother empty-handed. I needed to bring her a gift. Something worth trading for the key that might save my magicarium from complete destruction. Something that would hurt me to lose, hurt me almost as much as it hurt my warder to escort me into a known danger that he didn't have a prayer of controlling.

In the end, I settled on bringing her an ash wand, one that was inlaid with oak. Ash was known for its feminine power, its ability to aid in communication and to promote curiosity. Oak was the most masculine of woods, supporting bravery and leadership, among many other traits. The ash and oak wand was a symbol of the relationship between a witch and her warder, an acknowledgment that the female gained power from the male.

Regardless of the specific woods the wand was made of, it was gorgeous, a carefully polished masterpiece of intarsia. As I wrapped the gift in velvet, its potential vibrated through my fingertips. I nearly set it aside, opting for a lesser treasure.

But no. I needed Teresa. I needed her encyclopedic knowledge, her memory. And one wand was little enough to pay if I kept my witches safe for the rest of the school term.

David, of course, insisted on driving me. The trip seemed to take hours, the time stretched out by the ribbons of tension that wound around us in the car. But to be fair, he didn't try to change my mind. Not when we passed the wards at the outer limits of Teresa's property, the ones that first alerted her to our approach. Not when we were corralled by the safeguards that emanated from her front door, the ones that confined us to our car until she chose to release us. Not when Teresa banished David to the front room, pointedly telling him to close the door so we witches could talk in private.

He looked to me for permission before he left. I nodded my approval, letting him scrape up some semblance of dignity. At least he was responding to *his* witch's command, not to the order of a known enemy.

Teresa's eyes flared with obvious greed as she unwrapped her gift. My palms itched when she stroked the smooth wood; I folded my fingers so I wouldn't accidentally snatch it back. I tried to take comfort in the fact that she handled it with reverence, treating it like the treasure it was.

"And to what do I owe the pleasure?" she finally asked, nestling the wand in its velvet. She centered the gift—the bribe—on the center island and waited for my response.

"I need information."

She set her expertly manicured hands on her hips. "About?"

"Monsters. Myths. You saw the satyr on Samhain. Three days later, my students and I were attacked by a two-headed dog."

"An orthros?"

She *sounded* shocked. But tendrils of suspicion wrapped around my arms. How did she know the animal's name? I'd needed to conduct research to identify the beast. Did she really know her Greek myths that well?

I tried to shrug away my discomfort. When I was around Teresa, I never knew how to stand, where to put my hands, how to look calm and collected and self-possessed.

It would probably help if I had a perfect wardrobe from Nordstroms, a spotless white blouse and tailored black slacks, ballet flats that seemed molded to my feet and a hair-band the perfect shade of crimson, the ideal accent to set off the rest of the outfit. Right. Like I'd be able to wear any of that stuff with the same aplomb as the Coven Mother. Any-one who came to the farmhouse door unannounced was likely to find me in sweatpants and a torn T-shirt. Maybe I should upgrade my slouch-at-home wardrobe.

I recognized my speculation for what it was—a mindless

attempt to avoid confronting the only witch within miles who could match my power spell for spell. I jammed my hands onto my own hips and raised my chin in defiance. "Did you know about the orthros?"

As I asked the question, I expanded the field of my magical powers. I attempted to be subtle; anyone looking at us would only see the faintest shimmer of gold in the air between us. But my arcane sphere functioned like a lens; it amplified my perception of the world around me.

I was suddenly aware of a single link in the gold chain around Teresa's neck, a solitary bit of metal that refused to lie perfectly flat. I could smell honey and lemon on her breath; she'd been drinking tea before we arrived. I could hear the slight rasp in the back of her throat as she swallowed, and I realized she was nursing the beginning of a cold. If I'd had any doubt about Teresa Alison Sidney's otherworldly abilities, they were tossed out the window—cold or not, she looked as glamorous as ever.

There was no magic spell I could speak that would force Teresa to tell the truth. But when I looked at her through the heightened veil of my power, I could at least have a clearer perception of her physical responses. I became a one-woman lie detector machine, counting on respiration, perspiration, and old-fashioned shifty eyes to tell me if the Coven Mother was lying.

"No," Teresa said. She looked straight at me, obviously aware of how I was using my powers. "I didn't know anything about it."

"It was sent by Norville Pitt."

Her nose flared, just the tiniest amount. Her eyes narrowed during the heartbeat before she caught herself. She licked her lips before she said, "I'm not responsible for Pitt."

"But you've worked with him in the past."

"So you and Montrose claim. There's an entire inquest proceeding to determine that."

"It will determine more than that," I reminded her. But Pitt's legal difficulties weren't what I wanted to talk about. "So, you had nothing to do with the orthros. Have you ever seen one before?"

"No."

"Have you ever heard of one being released in the Washington Coven?"

"No."

"Have you ever heard of one anywhere in the Eastern Empire?"

"No. And to cut short the rest of your questions, I've never heard of one existing in real life. As far as I knew, they were legends."

"Like the satyr." She hesitated, just long enough to spark my attention. I pressed, "Then you *have* seen a satyr before?"

Her mouth tightened. "Not here."

"Where, then?"

"In Kansas City." Teresa sighed, letting the motion tug her shoulders into a more comfortable position. "I was a child, five or six years old. My mother and I were visiting relatives. The coven met in a member's home. The group did a working, trying to raise energy for a new series of protective wards. Instead, they called a satyr."

That was the most Teresa had said to me since I'd stepped inside her home. Perhaps it was the longest speech she'd *ever* made to me. And it resonated even more because of the emotion behind the words. Teresa remembered the satyr. She remembered being afraid.

"What happened?" I asked softly.

"The Coven Mother used a Word of power to stop it dead in its tracks."

I shuddered. The Word would have frozen everyone in the vicinity, removed every drop of volition until the casting witch decided to set people free. I'd used a Word once against a handful of humans who didn't—it turned out—actually mean me true harm. Nevertheless, the experience had nearly drained me. I couldn't imagine using a Word on an active enemy who was determined to get his way. Teresa's face was grim. "The Coven Mother mastered the satyr. But not before…"

Not before he'd raped one of the witches.

I could see the truth on her face. I could picture the attack, understand the horror, because Cassie had come so close to becoming a victim herself. A woman had suffered at the hands of that long-ago satyr, and a child—Teresa—had been forced to witness the savagery.

But there was more to the story than that. Because I knew more about the Kansas City Coven. I'd learned about them over the summer, seen their name written on the wall in David's basement office. I'd read documents and followed paper trails.

The Kansas City Coven built a safehold in 1995. Now I could assume the construction had been in response to the satyr's attack. They'd paid for a centerstone to be brought from Romania, a transaction facilitated by Norville Pitt. Pitt's bank account had flooded with extra payments, with bribes to secure placement of the safehold and the election of a new Coven Mother.

I knew all that, because David had traced the records, detailing the case against the man who had lined his own pockets at the expense of the Kansas City Coven. David had unmasked Norville Pitt's crimes. But not before Pitt had spent decades perfecting those exact same crimes against other witches.

Kansas City had been attacked by a satyr, they'd built a safehold to defend themselves, and Pitt had profited. Pitt's astral signature was on the satyr that attacked my magicarium. How many other witches had been subjected to monsters so Pitt could have his way?

"You know what Pitt is capable of," I said to Teresa. "How can you work with him?"

"I'm not working with Pitt," she said. "Not now. Not with the satyr or the orthros."

Because of the lens that my powers focused on her words, I knew Teresa was telling the truth. She might have chosen her words carefully, she might have excluded the possibility of her working with Pitt in the past, on other matters. But she was innocent of the actions that had nearly derailed the second semester of my magicarium. I believed her.

Just as I believed her when she said, "Don't waste your time accusing me. Any magistrix worth the title could tell you Pitt has help on the inside. In Kansas City he used one of the old witches, a woman who'd been passed over for Coven Mother. Find out who he's using with you. Find out which of your students is a traitor to the Jane Madison Academy."

David drove away from Teresa's house, tracing the winding lane with perfect accuracy. We didn't speak until we were past the wards that marked the edges of her property.

"What did she say back there?" he asked, feeding the car more fuel than was strictly necessary.

I was still reeling from Teresa's disclosure, from her accusation. "This isn't the first time Pitt has used monsters to get what he wanted." I gave David the CliffsNotes version of the Kansas City saga. "But that's not all. She says Pitt must have someone on the inside. One of my students is working with him."

David's jaw clenched in automatic protest. He had reviewed my students' applications with me. He had cleared each of them, reviewing every possible security risk. Now I could see him working through scenarios. The satyr had penetrated the warders' cordon; someone had invited it into our circle. And the orthros had known to find us on the beach.

David's face was grim by the time he reached the freeway. "We'll have to test them."

"Before we do that..." I said, trailing off.

"What?" He was accelerating in the fast lane. I could feel his urgency, his need to get back to the farmhouse before any other disaster could strike. He'd missed something, and he wouldn't rest until he'd corrected his mistake.

I needed to make absolute sure, though. Before I tore the magicarium apart looking for a traitor, I needed to know there was absolutely no other source for the monsters. Because if I accused my students and I was wrong, I would never have authority as a magistrix again.

I said, "The Academy will be destroyed if we're wrong."

"So what do you want to do?"

"Do you remember that woman I met over the summer? Sarah Anderson?"

David shot me a dry look right before he braked to avoid an eighteen-wheeler that was chugging along at forty in the fast lane. Of course he remembered Sarah. As Clerk of Court for the Eastern Empire Night Court, she'd been my first—my only—client when I'd considered a career as a library consultant. Something about getting imprisoned by a raving lunatic of a vampire had made me decide I should follow another career path. Sarah had shared that cell with me, and we'd found our way out together.

"If there's a supernatural creature this side of the Mississippi who's used a satyr or an orthros to break the law, the Empire will have records."

"You're clutching at straws."

"I'm trying to keep from accusing one of my students unnecessarily. I'm trying to keep the magicarium together."

David must have heard the pleading in my voice. "Fine," he said. "We'll go to the courthouse. But you better get started mapping out Plan B."

We didn't talk for the rest of the ride. He was probably focusing on traffic. I was praying to be delivered by a legal clerk.

It was nearly midnight by the time we pulled up in front of the District of Columbia courthouse. David walked around and opened my door for me, and we navigated the court's security together. Things were quiet. The Night Court didn't seem to have a lot of takers.

We walked down an antiseptic hallway, moving beneath the watchful eyes of two dozen judicial portraits. Before long, we stood in the deserted clerk's office. A bell sat on the counter, with a crisply lettered sign: "Please ring for service." David tapped it once, and the chime echoed off the walls.

A woman hurried in from the back office. "May I—Oh." Her auburn hair was a little longer than I remembered, but her green eyes were every bit as bright. She still wore the same coral ring and hematite bracelet. "Jane," she said with a smile. "David. Is everything okay?"

I answered with my own quick grin, even as I shook my head. "Not really. It's a long story, and we don't have time to go into details now, but we're looking for any cases involving a satyr or an orthros. Assaults, batteries, things like that."

"An orthros?" she said, automatically reaching for a slip of paper and scribbling down notes. I spelled the word for her and described the beast. She nodded and said, "Our records aren't really set up that way, but let me see what I can find. Can you give me an hour?"

"Sure," I said.

"There's a cafeteria down the hall. Or you can sneak into the back of Judge DuBois's courtroom. He's hearing an interesting case tonight, a water rights dispute between a dryad and a naiad. I'd bring an umbrella, though, if you're going to spend any time in there."

"Thanks," I said. "The cafeteria sounds fine."

And it was. It looked like every other institutional lunchroom I'd ever seen—rows of plain Formica-topped tables flanked by scads of uncomfortable plastic-and-metal chairs. Half a dozen vending machines hummed against the wall, offering a million calories and nothing nutritional.

David and I knew each other well enough that we didn't need to make small talk. Instead, he sat at one of the tables, his hands folded as he studied the poster about our rights under the Family and Medical Leave Act. I became restless after about fifteen minutes, so I stood to pace.

Every time I reached the end of the room, I hit the reset button on the vicious cycle in my head. The warders had raised a cordon to protect our Samhain working. A satyr appeared on the centerstone before the cordon was broken. Someone must have summoned the satyr from inside the circle. Reset.

After a few hundred repetitions, I was mercifully interrupted by Sarah's appearance, heralded by the click of her heels on the black-and-white tile floor. She was shaking her head before David climbed to his feet.

"I'm sorry," she said. "There was one record of a faun being adopted by a pair of sprites. That gave me some confidence that my search strategy was correct. But I didn't find anything about satyrs. No orthros, either. I checked James Morton's files, too, the Department of Security records. If those creatures had been in the building, we would have needed special safety measures, but I couldn't find anything."

I sighed. "Thanks so much for trying. It was a long shot, anyway."

"This is bad news then?"

I nodded. "The worst."

"I wish I had something to make it easier. Cake Walk cupcakes would be perfect just about now." Sarah and I had met over Melissa's baking. But the clerk was wrong—no baked treat on earth could ease the pain blooming beneath my breastbone.

"Thanks," I said. "Maybe we can meet up at the bakery some time soon." Sarah agreed, and she shook hands with David first, then me. Before I could fully process our failure, I was back in the car, and David was driving us toward home.

I'd fought not to believe Teresa's accusation. I'd searched for an alternative at the Night Court. But it was time to face up to facts. One of my students was working with Norville Pitt to destroy me. And it was only a matter of time before she made her next move.

# Chapter 8

ANALYSIS PARALYSIS WAS a terrible thing. I knew I had to take some action. I had to find the traitor in our midst. But if I took a false step, I would destroy the magicarium I'd worked so hard to build.

It had taken me years to figure out that I wanted to open a school for witches. I'd been afraid of the responsibility, intimidated by the authority I would wield. Now, I was terrified I would destroy the Academy with one misstep, and I'd never be able to teach another witch about the joy of working magic through a true community, through true sharing of powers.

It seemed easier to stand on guard, to view every single interaction with my students through a lens of suspicion. At least I wouldn't make a mistake that way. I wouldn't accuse an innocent woman of a terrible crime.

Of all the witches in the circle on Samhain, I could only *swear* to my innocence and Clara's. But I could not believe Raven or Emma was at fault—if they'd wanted to destroy me, they'd had ample opportunity before we started our second semester together.

That left four suspects: Alex, Bree, Cassie, and Skyler. I forced myself to list them alphabetically. That way, I couldn't show any possible hint of favoritism.

I'd misread one of my students disastrously. I'd invited evil into our midst. And I hadn't even known until Teresa told me. That fact rankled the most. It almost made up for the fact that I'd bribed her with my precious ash-and-oak wand.

By Friday, I was still awash in indecision. My students and I had spent the week getting to know each other better. I don't think anyone suspected the true nature of my inquiry as I gauged their powers, measuring their ability to use the rowan wands I kept safe in the vault. They didn't guess what was truly at stake as we studied different cauldrons, as we calculated the sharpness of various magical knives. They probably thought the most noteworthy thing about the week was my conducting four straight days of classes, without a single ritual going awry, with any mythical beast springing out of nowhere to attack any of us.

We were all ready for a break by the time the weekend rolled around. I begged David to let everyone go into Parkersville. I needed a respite from the tension, from the constant parsing of every glance, every word, every possible message from the traitor in our midst. Besides, if our enemy already lurked behind our wards, what could it hurt to let folks escape their cabin fever?

Emma left the dormitory first—her boyfriend, Rick, swung by after his shift ended at the fire station. Raven and Bree sweet-talked the firefighter into giving everyone a ride into town in the back of his pickup truck. David and I stood on the front porch, waving to the taillights, as they disappeared down the driveway.

Before the lights faded, David sighed with a frustration that sounded bone-deep. "Now's the part where you and I argue about the rest of the evening."

"We don't have anything to argue about," I said, tugging the sleeves of my sweater down to cover my bare hands. The early November evening was bracing. "Melissa's going to be here in about an hour, and you're going out for the evening so we can talk in private."

"You want me to abandon you when any one of those women could double back from town?"

I huffed my annoyance, sending up visible smoke signals in the chilly air. "I'm not in any greater danger than I've been in all week."

"I've been with you all week," he pointed out.

"David, I need some privacy!" I heard the sharpness in my voice and I reversed tactics mid-breath. "Melissa and I want to talk about wedding stuff. Bridesmaids dresses and flowers. Invitations. Whether I should wear a veil. You'd be bored to tears in thirty-seven seconds."

I wasn't *just* trying to manipulate him into leaving us alone. I really wanted to talk about those things with my matron of honor. I wanted to spend a giggly, gossipy evening like an ordinary bride planning an ordinary wedding. But I wasn't above exaggerating the boring, mundane details, if that would get me my way. "I think I've chosen the perfect dress. I just need Melissa's advice on whether I have to wear a corset under it."

David's eyes glinted in the porch light. "And now you've overplayed your hand. Melissa wouldn't know the first thing about whether you need a corset."

He was right, dammit. I should have told him I needed a consultation on the wedding cake. "David, I need time to talk with her. Alone. She's my best friend."

He nodded, and his voice was gentle but firm. "I know that. But I'm not comfortable leaving you alone in the house. I'll stay upstairs. You won't even know I'm here."

I knew an absolute when I heard one. By the time Melissa arrived, David was secure in our bedroom, bolstered by a plate of sandwiches, a bottle of wine, and a book he swore he'd been looking forward to reading for months. Spot had followed him upstairs willingly. Or maybe the dog was just hoping a slice of roast beef would slip out of that sandwich.

I could feel the booster David had given to his warder's spells, the extra tingle of energy that said our protective barrier was cranked to a maximum. But Melissa seemed absolutely unaware of the crackling power as she stepped over the threshold. She held out a white pasteboard box, sealed with a familiar printed sticker. "For me?" I asked, feigning surprise.

"I brought a cup of Dream Puff filling for Neko. And Almond Lust for David. And yes, a few treats for you. I figured I couldn't go wrong with Cinnamon Smiles and Ginger Sequins."

"Thank you," I said, astonished to feel tears pricking at the corners of my eyes. It seemed like years since anyone had done anything so nice for me. For that matter, it seemed like years since I'd had a conversation with anyone that wasn't about witchcraft. I let a little of my gratitude spill into my tone as I said, "And thank you for making the long drive out here."

"Honestly? It's nice to get out of the city. To get away from *lawyers*."

"Having that much fun with Rob's crew, huh?" I led the way into the kitchen, automatically crossing to the pantry to take out a box of crackers. "How was dinner with the big boss last week?"

Melissa hooked her foot around one of the bar stools at the center island, pulling it back so she could settle with a gusty sigh. "The first thing we do, let's kill all the lawyers."

I grinned at the easy reference. "*Henry IV, Part II.* But you know that was the bad guys talking, describing their own version of heaven." Melissa waved off my English-major lesson. "It went that well, huh?" I asked.

"I'm not cut out for this."

"What do you mean?"

"All the *formality*," Melissa said. "All the *rules*. The first question out of everyone's mouth is 'Where do you work?' And when I tell them Cake Walk, they just look confused. Last week, someone actually asked me if that was a British firm."

I laughed, but Melissa didn't laugh with me. I tried to sound sympathetic. "So when do they vote on letting Rob in?"

"The Saturday before Christmas. We'll either have a whole lot to celebrate for the holidays, or we'll be in mourning." She cracked her knuckles and started to chew her bottom lip. From the way she stared across the room, the faucet on the kitchen sink was suddenly the most fascinating thing in the entire house. She took a shuddering breath before she blurted, "The thing is, I'm not sure I *want* him to make partner."

I sat beside her. "What do you mean?"

"I'm a terrible person, I know that. He's been working toward this forever. It's the only thing that matters at the law firm, the only way to define success."

"And I know you want him to succeed," I said gently.

"I do!" But she tugged at her sleeve before she repeated with a lot less vehemence, "I do. But once he's a partner, everything will change. I'll have to go to the firm retreat with him, at the Four Seasons. I'm not a Four Seasons kind of girl!" she wailed.

I could count on one hand the times I'd seen her out of

her work clothes. "You'll fit in," I said loyally.

"Hel*lo*," Melissa said, giving me an exasperated look. "I don't think we've met before. I'm Melissa White, and I don't do dresses. Or heels. Or updos for my hair. And the last time I wore makeup, it was when I dressed as a hobo for Halloween."

I laughed, but I wasn't sure what to say. We weren't kids any more. We had to figure out how to live in the grown-up world.

Melissa accurately read my expression. After all, she'd had years to learn how to interpret my silent communication. She crossed her arms on the center island and hid her face, issuing a sound that was somewhere between a groan and a shout.

Her sheer desperation melted my frustration into concern. "Hey," I asked. "Are you okay?"

She nodded, but then she shook her head. "I just thought it would be easier than this. I mean, when Rob came into the bakery every day, we were in *my* world. *He* fit into *my* life."

"And now you have a new life, together. Don't forget— you fell in love with the whole package. The Rob who's a lawyer and the Rob who comes home after work."

She made a broken attempt at a smile as she twisted her wedding band. "Oh, I don't expect you to understand. Not when everything's perfect with you and David."

I snorted.

"What?" she asked, her voice shrill with accusation. "You two are perfect together!"

"Yeah," I said, unable to resist a frustrated glance at the ceiling. I knew David wouldn't purposely eavesdrop on us, but I couldn't shake my constant awareness that he was up there, that he could overhear every word of my conversation with Melissa if he tried.

"Hey," Melissa said, shifting away from her own misery with the light-speed devotion of a best friend. "What's going on?"

*One of my students was nearly raped by a satyr. We were all attacked by a two-headed dog on the beach. I'm teaching a traitor who could destroy everything I've worked for, everything I've built, and I don't have the first idea who she is. I'm terrified to do anything, and I'm terrified to do nothing, and I keep praying to Hecate that David doesn't break under the pressure like he did last time...*

Right. Like I could tell Melissa any of that. She knew I was a witch. She'd even seen me work a spell or two. But I couldn't expect her to understand the dangers my magicarium faced. There was no way she'd grasp the true terror someone like Norville Pitt could raise inside me. And I could never tell her about the inquest. I couldn't mention it at all.

"So?" Melissa prompted. "What's up?"

"I love him," I said, surprising myself with the defensiveness in my tone. I hadn't realized I needed to say that. I hadn't thought anyone could possibly doubt it.

"Of course you do," she said. The naked concern in her voice was an invitation to share more.

"I love him, and I know he wants what's best for me. But I'm afraid what's best for me will hurt him." I pictured the mottled purple bruises on his torso, left by the satyr's hooves. I saw him stacking books in the vault, desperate to protect me, to protect everything I owned. I forced myself to admit, "I've already hurt him."

"Oh, Jane," Melissa said. She slipped off her stool and folded her arms around me. I hadn't realized how close I was to the edge, to sobbing like a baby. Melissa squeezed me, one quick hug. I caught the smell of vanilla in her hair, of cinnamon and ginger, the spices she folded into the sweets she baked every day. The scent carried me back to Cake Walk, to the long hours we'd spent in the bakery, talking about all the things we'd thought were important. All the things that seemed so silly now.

As I hugged her back, I caught a sob against the back of my throat and said, "What a great pair we make. You're afraid of going to dinner at a fancy hotel, and I'm afraid of…everything."

"I'm not afraid!" And she wasn't. She wasn't frightened. She just didn't want to change. Didn't want to become someone she despised to keep the man she loved.

And I understood that, every single word that neither of us spoke out loud. I understood it in spades.

I squared my shoulders and faced the *real* disaster of the evening. "I'm sorry," I said. "I made you drive all the way out here, and I think these Triscuits are the only food in the house." *David won't let me go shopping in town.* "I didn't have a chance to lay in mojito supplies or anything."

Melissa offered a brave smile. "Then we'll have to make do with Triscuits. Let me guess. There isn't a chance Neko left a rind of cheese in that refrigerator, is there?"

I shook my head. "Not much of one."

But what sort of friend would I be, if I didn't even look? Besides, there might be some wilted celery sticks, a few wrinkled carrots, something too healthy for my conniving familiar to have stolen. Bracing myself for disappointment, I opened the fridge.

A forest of mint filled the top shelf, fenced in by half a dozen limes. Two bottles of club soda nestled in the refrigerator door, flanking a fifth of rum. And on the bottom shelf, wrapped in brown paper, were three wedges that had to be cheese. David's bold scrawl shouted in capital letters: "Touch this, Neko, under pain of death."

Melissa came to stand beside me. "Huh," she said. "I guess things aren't as bad as we thought they were."

I laughed as I started to haul the bounty out of the fridge. David must have used his warder's magic to whisk into town, to lay in supplies. And I'd spent that same time sulking that he'd be lurking upstairs.

Melissa unwrapped the cheese as I dove into making the first pitcher of mojitos. I had a man who could read my mind, who knew what I needed before I knew it myself. I had a best friend who stood by me, even when I wasn't able to share everything with her. I even had a familiar who recognized a dire threat to his bodily integrity when he read one.

Life wasn't that bad. And it got an awful lot better when I doubled the amount of lime juice for the entire batch of mojitos.

I was wrong.

Life sucked.

Exhibit A: Sunday night, the team of advocates who were prosecuting Pitt sent an urgent message to David. They wanted him to come in first thing Monday morning. They were going to study his notes, again. Review his written testimony, again. Prepare him for the inevitably brutal cross-examination he'd face on the stand, again. Both David and I read imminent defeat in their urgent request.

The following morning, I came downstairs to find David standing at the kitchen counter, gulping down a cup of coffee that was steaming like a dragon's breath. "Don't burn yourself!" I said. "Give it time to cool."

"I'm already late," he said. "I should have been out of here half an hour ago."

I heard the warning in his voice. "What's wrong?" I

asked.

He pushed a curl of paper toward me. No. Not paper. Paper didn't roll on itself that way. It was a scroll of parchment, sealed with the crimson wax of Hecate's Court.

"Where did this come from?"

"It was shoved under the windshield wiper on my car. I suspect the wards kept the Court's delivery person from getting any closer to the house."

"At least we know they're good for one thing," I muttered, and I started skimming the words. *Requirements for all magicaria... Demonstration of consistent progress among a majority of students... Ongoing monitoring... In danger of termination prior to the end of the semester... Substantial advancement must be shown by the conclusion of this week or we will be forced to suspend the charter of the Jane Madison Academy.*

I wished there was a way to harness the flash of anger that heated my face. "How many times can they change the rules?"

"As many times as they want. They're the only game in town."

"But how, in the name of Hecate, can they assess the progress of *any* of my students, much less a majority of them? They never took a baseline measurement!"

David shrugged. "You granted them monitoring access when you accepted your charter."

I bit back a harsh reply. He was right, of course. The Court had always monitored the workings of the Jane Madison Academy. That was where I'd first run into conflict with Norville Pitt.

But their requirements were unreasonable. They didn't have a "before" so they couldn't possibly measure an "after." They certainly couldn't take into account the different nature of the magic I taught. My students *always* had a hard time finding their footing—it had taken months before Gran and Clara caught on to what I did. Raven and Emma had studied for weeks before they understood the odd balance I expected, the different exchange of power that my magicarium used. My new students hadn't had a chance to try. And I was pretty sure I didn't want to launch them down that path, not until I'd identified the traitor.

Even without the complication of a student trying to dismantle my entire magicarium, the Court was being unrealistic when they demanded a sign of progress by the end of the *week*. By the end of the term, sure, that was fair. But I couldn't be certain I'd have anything to show in five short days.

"Call Clara," David said. "Ask her and your grandmother to help out with classes, starting this morning."

My immediate reaction was to protest. The house was crowded enough without adding another two witches, another two familiars into the mix. My students needed *fewer* distractions, not more. And while I was sure Gran would lend her fierce support to everything I attempted, I wasn't certain I had the patience to deal with Clara's weird ideas.

"They were the first witches who figured out how to work with you," David said, as if I'd voiced my objections out loud. "They were the first ones to understand the potential of what you do. Let them show your students. Let them help."

He glanced at the parchment scroll, and his worried frown carved even deeper across his face. He had enough on his plate, with Pitt's inquest. It was already killing him to entrust my classes to Caleb's and Tony's protection, when he couldn't invest absolute trust in all of my students. I shouldn't be adding to his troubles.

"Fine," I said. "I'll call them."

"And don't mention the Court's most recent ultimatum to your students. Whoever is trying to shut you down could just skew the results for a week, without ever bothering to summon another monster."

His advice made sense. I just hated that we'd come to that point. I dragged myself to my phone and called Gran and Clara.

They arrived by mid-morning. In keeping with my innovative balance of powers, they instructed their familiars to work with other witches. Nuri perched on the arm of the sofa, closing her fingers around Bree's shoulder like gentle talons sinking into a perch. Majom followed Clara's orders and curled up by my feet. I tried to ignore the sensation as he plucked at the hem of my jeans, teasing at the stitches with his ever-curious fingers.

We worked as a group for over two hours, trying to light a single candle with our pooled powers. Sometimes the wick kindled from the center of the wax column, drowning itself in a few short seconds. Sometimes, the flame leaped high enough to scorch the ceiling, necessitating an immediate banishing spell. Sometimes, the candle tottered back and forth on its plate, tilting first toward one witch and then another before it ended its crazy dance by toppling onto its side. Sometimes—most often—nothing happened at all.

And so I had to consider the option seriously when Clara said, "Jeanette? I have something new we could try."

I was too frustrated by our collective magical failure to bother correcting her about my name. Instead, I used my best magistrix to ask, "What's that, Clara?"

"It's something we were trying at Oak Canyon, before I came out here." She waited for me to nod encouragement. I caught my students' attention swinging from her to me and back again, as if they were watching a tennis match. "We attune our powers to the field of cosmic waves and use those ripples to act *in*directly on the world around us."

I reminded myself that I was the magistrix here. I was in charge. I was responsible for making all of my students feel calm and comfortable in sharing their ideas. I kept my voice completely level as I said, "Cosmic waves... That's a, um, new approach."

Fifteen-love, me, if anyone was keeping score. I glanced over at Gran and was gratified by her nod of approval. I knew she wanted me to find better ways to work with Clara. My keeping an open mind was a present for her, a gift of thanks for all the years she'd put up with my being a ranty teenager.

Clara beamed as she took in my students' rapt attention. "We've been working with waves a lot. They help us to measure power in the world around us, the *ka* of every living thing."

The *ka*. The soul. Riiiiiight.

But Gran gave me a small smile of encouragement. She was right, after all. I wanted my students to understand how we balanced new ideas at the Jane Madison Academy, how we tested theories. We were a regular laboratory for witchy knowledge, applying scientific theory to all sorts of new concepts. Observation. Hypothesis. Experimentation. Conclusion.

Clara had just offered up one of the craziest hypotheses I'd ever heard in my life. It wouldn't take much of an experiment to blow it out of the water. But I owed Clara basic civility. The *Academy* owed her that much. I was a model of calm as I asked, "And how does the *ka* work with unliving things? Like, er, candles."

Thirty-love. Ha!

My students' attention bounced back toward Clara,

whose smile was brilliant. It seemed as if she'd been waiting all day for the question, craving the precise moment when I opened the door for her to share her wisdom with the group. "The candle is woven into the Elemental Vibrations."

"Elemental Vibrations?" I managed a tone of perfect neutrality.

"You know, Jeanette. The souls of inanimate objects."

I glanced at Gran. She sucked air between her teeth, a miniature wince that my students would never have registered. I forced myself to say, "I've never heard of inanimate objects having souls. I thought that was part of the very definition of them being, you know, *inanimate.*"

Forty-love. One more point, and the game was mine.

Clara spoke with the perfect patience saints reserved for idiot children. "Of course inanimate objects have souls. That's what makes a hellmouth so dangerous! Surely you realized that, after seeing the hellmouth in your own front yard!"

*"There wasn't a freaking hellmouth in my own front yard!"* I shouted, before I could look at Gran, before I could remember my role as a magistrix.

I *felt* my students draw back in shock. Their familiars jumped too, reflecting the witches' concern. Tony took a quick step toward Raven, only stopping when she raised a peremptory hand.

Stupid tennis game. I'd never understood how they scored the sport anyway.

Clara sounded hurt. "You saw the evidence, Jeanette, right before your eyes. That satyr had to come from somewhere. I can understand your being tied to tradition, but I hoped you'd have a shred of courage to look beyond classic coven teachings, just this once."

Tied to tradition. Classic. Me. The witch who'd accepted

a triple bond with her warder, who'd launched her own magicarium, who'd built an entire arcane practice on the sharing and exchange of power outside the ordinary bonds of familiar and witch…

I filled my lungs, ready to shout at Clara, ready to drown her ignorance with my volume, even if I had no hope of ever getting a single rational thought through her thick, woo-woo worshipping skull. I didn't care if my students felt shut down. I didn't care if I limited the range of discussion. I didn't care if I destroyed a dozen other lines of scientific inquiry, if I could just eradicate my mother's idiotic, feather-brained, idealistic—

"I could certainly use a break," Gran said, leaning back in her chair and passing a hand in front of her face. "All this hard work certainly builds up an appetite."

"We haven't *done* any—" I started to snap. But I caught myself before I finished the sentence because I understood what Gran was trying to do. She was keeping the peace, the way she'd done from the very first day Clara catapulted back into my life. "Fine," I said. "Let's take a break. Why don't we meet back here at one o'clock."

The class exploded into chatter as the line of our circle broke. Emma crossed the living room and said to Clara, "That sounds quite brilliant, the work you're doing at Oak Canyon. It makes me wish I never left."

I purposely exited the room before I could see which of the new witches gathered around to hear more about my mother's Arizona adventures. It was bad enough to know one of them had betrayed me. If I discovered that anyone else believed Clara's claptrap, I might shut down the entire magicarium—voluntarily—out of unbridled shame for witches everywhere.

Still, the word "NWTA" floated after me into the kitchen. "Nucleus!" Clara shouted. "With *tentacles* attached!"

The tentacles of my own life were tightening around me. I didn't believe my mother's hocus-pocus. I couldn't rely on my grandmother's weakling powers. I dared not trust my students as a group, not until I'd figured out who had released murderous mythological animals into our midst.

I thought about the scroll Hecate's Court had left on the Lexus, and I wondered how much longer I had before my charter was revoked and all of my witchy possessions were at the mercy of Teresa and Pitt and anyone else who wanted to see me destroyed.

# Chapter 9

DESPERATE TIMES. DESPERATE measures.

On Tuesday, I asked Gran to lead our session. I thought she might make headway with the students because her own powers were so weak. She couldn't overwhelm them with the crimson energy she called her own; she couldn't erase their own familiar magic. Once, right after lunch, I saw a spark leap off the end of the candle's wick. Alas, everyone else saw it, and the group's excitement pulled our energy off balance. We didn't repeat the trick all day.

On Wednesday, I put Emma and Raven in charge. They'd worked with me the previous semester. They'd learned the trick I was having so much trouble teaching everyone else. Sadly, they'd only learned to balance the power across a tripod—the two of them and me. Each grew more frustrated as the day went on, as they failed to expand their lesson to the larger student group. I dismissed class in the middle of the afternoon because tempers were frayed. I made a point of staying inside the house, purposely not looking out the windows. Every student I'd ever known who attended boarding school found ways to sneak off campus. I could hardly expect my students to be less enterprising, and I suspected they all needed to blow off some steam.

On Thursday, I decided to practice without anyone leading the group. I let the energy flow, from Cassie to Clara, from Skyler to Gran. Sometimes Raven was in charge, sometimes Emma. Alex took the reins for a while; Bree swept in with her own indomitable style.

By the end of the day, I knew I had to go back to the methods that had worked for me before. *I* was the one who had taught Clara and Gran how to share power. *I* was the one who had finally gotten through to Raven and Emma. I had one day left to make the breakthrough. If I failed at teaching, I'd never need to worry again about which of my students had tried to tear apart the magicarium with the satyr and the orthros.

Friday morning, I woke when David's alarm clock went off. As he headed into the shower, I covered my head with my pillow, willing myself to snag another few minutes of sleep. The winter nights were stretching longer; not a hint of daylight whispered past the window shade into our bedroom.

I couldn't stay in bed forever, though. I finally dragged myself out from under the warm comforter, shivering in the cool air as I hunted up yesterday's jeans. I sprang for a clean sweater—my favorite cable-knit in a blue-green yarn that set off the auburn glints in my hair. Down in the kitchen, I made coffee for both of us.

This was the day when everything had to change. I felt the tension tugging at the witchy bond that connected me to David. I must have transmitted my nerves; when Neko waltzed through the doorway for class, he took one look at both of us and whined, deep at the back of his throat. I gave him a tight shake of my head. I didn't want him to say anything. I didn't want him upsetting my students.

In the end, maybe things would have been better if he *had*

upset the witches. Our morning session was a waste of time. Gran and Clara had declined to join us; after four straight days of driving back and forth to the farm, Gran's sciatica was acting up. Clara claimed she had a field trip at the University of Maryland, some tour of antebellum cemeteries for Professor Kipperman's class. Necropolises, Civil War graveyards—he sounded like one hell of an upbeat guy.

We broke for lunch and came back for a couple of hours in the early afternoon. I finally called another break when I caught *myself* falling asleep; I only jerked awake when Spot started snoring by the fireplace. I suggested that everyone but the dog get a jolt of caffeine, and we'd regroup at half past three. Spot staggered into the kitchen and curled up in his plaid bed.

As soon as we settled into our working circle, I could tell something was off. Emma's eyes were red when she sank onto the couch, and her gusty sigh could have fueled windmills. When I asked how she was doing, she offered up a feeble smile and a shrug. "I'm feeling a bit manky today, to tell the truth."

When Raven walked behind me to take her seat on the couch, she muttered, "Boy trouble." I'd imagine Emma's relationship with Rick was under a fair amount of stress. It had been one thing for the magicarium to adapt to the firefighter's one-day-on, two-days-off schedule when everyone lived in the farmhouse. It was another thing entirely when Emma shared dormitory life with the other students. I couldn't imagine any of the witches was thrilled about a male guest hanging around, especially one with Rick's impressive persistence. And Emma, of course, had barely been allowed to leave the premises.

Not my circus. Not my monkeys. My students' love affairs were none of my business.

Cassie's pale face, on the other hand... That I definitely worried about. "How you doing?" I asked, as she settled back on the ladder-back chair she'd dragged in from the kitchen that morning. She swore the hard seat made her concentrate better. I would have been writhing in agony after the first hour of spellwork sitting on that torture device, but to each her own.

She shrugged and rubbed her hands together, an unconscious gesture I'd caught her repeating hundreds of times since our first working. I couldn't be certain because she never talked about it, but I suspected she twined her fingers together when she thought about the satyr, when she flashed back on the memory of that terrible night. At least that was my speculation, because she usually glanced at Zach as she tugged at her knuckles. Sure enough, she was checking out her warder now, her gaze pinned to the increasingly ragged cast on his arm.

He'd apparently drawn the short stick for this last session of the day. Even though David was taking the lead on watching over all our sessions, the other warders rotated in on a regular basis. I'd done my best to convince my students this was standard operating procedure, although Raven and Emma knew it was not. They'd worked with me last semester, when I hadn't worried about a snake in our midst. They knew that David generally took days off, that he wasn't bound to every single session I led. I wondered if they'd talked about the change back in the dormitory. I worried that our traitor was even more wary than she might otherwise be.

Alex sat apart from the group, her chair pushed back from the imaginary line of our circle. Skyler was on her cell phone. Bree was in the midst of telling some story to her familiar, a dirty joke, from the way she lowered her voice and raised her eyebrows.

No one cared. No one was paying attention. No one thought we could possibly complete our working.

"Ladies!" I said, and my voice was too sharp. I was as tired of the stupid candle-lighting spell as they were.

Alex cleared her throat, immediately snagging my attention. The other witches studiously avoided her, and I realized she'd been appointed their speaker, the one selected to deliver bad news. She rubbed at her tattooed biceps, looking as if she'd rather be anywhere but in my living room, surrounded by her fellow inmates.

"We were talking just now," she announced, her tongue stud tapping her teeth on the "t" sounds.

"About what?" I truly didn't intend to sound like an ice queen. But I felt singled out by their private conversation, as if they'd all gotten together to point at my ugly haircut and call me names behind my back. Not that Neko would let me walk around with bad hair.

"If we're going to spend weeks working on a single spell like this, maybe we should just go ahead and follow the Rota." When I didn't respond, Alex glared at her sister witches, clearly demanding additional support before she brazened on. Her ears blazed scarlet beneath their rows of piercings. "Look. We thought we were going to learn differently here at the Jane Madison Academy. We thought we wouldn't have to do the repetitive stuff. The boring stuff."

Here it was. Open rebellion in the ranks.

I glanced at Neko, hoping he could translate the level of seriousness of this protest. He could at least reach out to the other familiars and gauge their concern.

Except Neko was fascinated by the seam of his jet-black jeans. He stared at the stitching as if it carried a message from the past, as if aliens had used the fabric to convey all the secrets of the universe.

Traitor. Even if he was only expressing the same revulsion for the candle spell that I felt.

Well, it wasn't fair to leave Alex hanging. And I wasn't going to let her take the fall for the group, even if my students had other ideas. "So?" I asked everyone. "Is this the way all of you feel? Is Alex the only one who'd prefer to go back to the Rota?"

I wasn't surprised that Bree had the guts to meet my eyes immediately. Honesty seemed to come as easily to her as snow in the high plains. "She's not saying she wants the Rota. None of us want that. But we don't want to repeat the same four-line spell every day for the rest of the year."

Skyler found her own voice, locking her jaw and drawling her Boston vowels. "We know your method works for small groups. You told us about finding the balance with your mother and grandmother. Raven and Emma said they made it work. But maybe seven is too many. Maybe it's a type of magic that can't be spread that thin."

"Emma?" I asked. "Raven?" Because *I* knew the magic wouldn't be spread thin. If we found the balance, the magic would be deeper than anything my students had ever experienced. The overwhelming harmony of seven witches reflecting their powers off seven different familiars... The sheer energy, echoed from woman to woman, repeated across the circle... I could imagine it, like a color I'd never seen before.

Raven surprised me by answering before her sister. She chose each word with uncharacteristic diplomacy. "It's not that the magic will be too thin. Maybe the balance will be too hard. Maybe we can't do what you're asking of us. Maybe we don't have the skill."

I heard what that admission cost her. I heard the blatant yearning in her voice. She *had* felt the power of a joint work-

ing. She could imagine the new music we'd write, the un-
heard notes we'd discover when we finally reached our
proper pitch. *If* we reached it.

"You do have it," I swore. "Every one of you."

"How can you be sure?" That was Cassie. Her voice was
tiny, folded in on itself. Her freckled face looked pinched, as
if even those four words had cost her too much. Her question hung in the air, a desperate plea that clenched my heart
more than anything else I'd heard. Cassie had paid a higher
price for my new scheme than anyone else sitting in the circle. She'd been threatened in ways the rest of us had only
seen in nightmares.

I understood why they all asked questions. They'd applied to my magicarium, and I'd chosen them. I'd inter-
viewed everyone, of course, selecting the four newcomers
from a pool of two dozen eager witches, all with a tolerance
for quirkiness, all attracted to the Jane Madison Academy's
unheard-of Second Class ranking after only a semester of
existence. They had all been willing to take the chance that
the magicarium would disband at the end of its first or second semester if we failed to complete our scheduled Major
Workings.

They'd thought it would be easy because they were working with the chosen, with the elite. They hadn't signed up for
monsters. And they hadn't expected the academic rug to be
pulled out from under them before the semester ended.

I knew I could teach these women. They just had to have
faith. They only had to find the balance once, and then
they'd be able to work the spells forever—like riding a bike.

But we had to succeed by sunset, or Hecate's Court
would shut us down forever. I glanced at the clock on the
mantel. It was already a few minutes after four. The winter
sky outside was already growing dark.

I finally allowed myself to look at David. After all, he was
the only other person who knew our true deadline. I'd
sensed him listening to my students, plumbing their questions, their protests, as if those words alone would let him
identify the traitor. I'd felt his protective presence, something
solid as I fielded their frustration.

I knew that no matter what happened, even if the Court
shut us down before the weekend, David would be there for
me. He would love me. He would pick me up, comfort me,
convince me I could go on in the world, as a witch, as a
woman.

But I didn't want him to have to do that. I didn't want to
break.

"One more hour," I said. "Give me until sunset tonight.
If we haven't made it work by then, we'll take the weekend
off. On Monday, we'll go with something new. I promise."
Even now, I couldn't tell them what that new thing would
be. I couldn't hint that the entire magicarium was at stake.
The words were too raw. I swallowed hard and said, "All I
ask is that you commit yourself to the process for the rest of
today. Give me every single thing you have. Hold back nothing."

And they did.

For the first time since we'd begun the candle-lighting
spell, I found myself overwhelmed by the energy swirling
across our circle. There was too *much* power, too much astral
force to be contained. More than once, I caught Zach reeling from a stray burst, fighting to keep his feet as we bom-
barded the room with our collective strength.

After one particularly vicious blast, David muttered
something, and he paced the perimeter of our circle. I
sensed what he was doing with his energy—not offering up
protection from exterior forces; the wards around the house

did that. Instead, he was setting up a sort of swaddling, a protective layer. He was cushioning us from the backlash of the forces we were raising. He was protecting us from ourselves.

I tugged on my bond to Neko, even though he crouched by Skyler's feet. I asked him to pull the familiars into a tighter circle, to focus the mirrors they offered up to us witches. I begged him to share how it had felt to work with Nuri and Majom. The familiars' strange communication network seemed perfectly suited to understanding my communal magic. With their whole images, maybe they could finally explain to the witches what we needed.

Neko scowled, but he did as I asked. And the other familiars clearly attempted to convey the information to their witches. Some of those conversations obviously made more sense than others. I could read Bree's face more easily than I could scan any book in the basement. I saw the moment when Perd reached out to her, the instant that she heard his horsey thoughts, that she translated them into something that made sense from a witch's perspective.

Skyler's comprehension was clear as well. At first, though, she resisted the input from Siga. Skyler seemed not to trust her porcine collaborator. Watching the portly woman's s insistence, I wondered how they could possibly work together on regular witchcraft. I'd never seen a witch and a familiar who weren't in perfect sync, who didn't enjoy completely compatible styles of communication. But Siga insisted, pushing through with a repeat of Neko's information again and Skyler finally gave a reluctant nod.

Alex got the message faster, but she shook her head. She didn't see how it would work. I watched Seta reach out to Neko, who shook his head in an unusual display of exasperation. My familiar squared his shoulders, clearly trying another way of explaining the same facts. He sighed when that method failed too, but he tried once more. And somehow, that last image made sense to Alex. She scooted her chair forward so it was in line with the rest of us. She planted her feet on the floor as if she intended to remain engaged.

And that left Cassie. I was captivated by the other witch's hands. She twisted her fingers as she listened to Tupa, contorting them into painful knots. I watched her swallow, and my throat ached in sympathy, as if *my* lips were chapped and dry, as if *my* belly twinged with nerves.

I would have given anything to take back the terrible events of Samhain. If I could have gone back in time, if I could have drawn the satyr to me, I would have spared Cassie the terror. But there was no way to change what had happened. The only thing I could do was build bridges to the future. I had to show Cassie, had to show all of them, that there were better ways to use magic. Better ways to work together.

At last Cassie's twining fingers settled in her lap. She seemed to still them with a conscious effort, with a shake of her shoulders and a firm set to her jaw. She might have been listening to her familiar, but her eyes were locked on Zach. He was her strength. He was her comfort. He had saved her from the satyr, and he would keep her safe no matter what horror our current working released.

Which was absurd of course. Because all we were going to do was light a candle. We weren't working magic in the middle of a hailstorm. We weren't exposed on an open beach. We were merely sitting in a living room, gathered around a coffee table, staring at a column of pure white beeswax.

"Let us begin," I intoned, and then I touched my fingertips against my forehead, my throat, and my chest. I watched each of the witches echo my movements, offering up pure thoughts, pure voice, and pure belief. I could not imagine any one of them a traitor—easygoing Bree, aristocratic Skyler, rebellious Alex, tortured Cassie.

First things first. Meet the Court's demands.

"*Dark shies.*" We said the words together.

"*Light vies.*" I felt energy arc from me to Cassie's Tupa. I measured *something* through my link to Neko, a pulsing power that he sent on to Skyler.

"*Clear eyes.*" There was a possibility hovering in the air, a *potential* for magic.

"*Fire rise.*" I poured myself into those last two words. I pushed my entire magical being into the phrase, into the spell. Tupa captured the energy I poured into our circle. He spun it into something new, something wider and deeper, like a fleece dragged through dew. There was a flash of darkness, and then the magic circled back to me. An arching rainbow spread across the room. Cherry and walnut and lemon, emerald and sapphire and amethyst, gold and silver and bronze. I didn't know which colors came from which witch, who poured any specific shade into our working. But they were all there, gathered together, organized, ordered.

And for just a heartbeat, the wick of the candle lit. I stared at the flame. I saw it appear out of nothing, coalesce into a perfect teardrop of color, indigo at its core, saffron at the edge. I blinked, and it was gone. But we had done it. We had lit the candle.

From the cheers around the room, you would have thought we'd cured world hunger.

We lit the candle again, all six of us, pouring in our power equally. Then, the familiars shifted around the circle, each one teaming with a new witch, and we worked the magic again. Emma started the harvest of power, asking each to offer up a share, until all were brought into the circle. Skyler lit the candle alone and we practiced dimming it with a controlled touch. Alex led us in an illumination, drawing from all of us to kindle the flame before she poured her own unique signature into the fire, darkening the light until it was almost black. She passed control to Cassie, who let the flame flicker into the pale green of new leaves, then to Raven who surged it back to violet.

With each working, I felt a little more power draw from my store. Even with all of our familiars, with seven witches to share the burden, with a simple candle-lighting spell, there was a cost to the work we did.

I knew I should rein in my students. I should congratulate them on a job well done. I should thank them for having held their faith, for having offered up the very best they had to give. I should be grateful they had saved the Jane Madison Academy, pushing back Hecate's Court for a while more.

But it was too much fun. It was too much of a relief to watch the wick kindle again and again, to feel the give and take of our energy soaring across the circle.

"All right," I finally said, fully intending to put a stop to the waste of energy. But I saw the disappointment on their faces, like children who were about to be deprived of a Christmas-morning toy. I glanced at David. I knew he wanted me to wrap things up, but he nodded once, giving me permission. "One last time," I said. "Let's work the spell together, and then we'll break for supper."

I glanced to my right, to where Neko curled by Raven's feet. I settled my hand on Tupa's shoulder. I watched each of the other witches make contact with the familiar closest to her. Everyone was comfortable. Everyone was confident that this spell would be the best.

"*Dark shies,*" I began.

Immediately, I knew this time was different. There was more power here than all the force we'd spent that afternoon. That made sense—my witches were celebrating their success. They were gathering their energy, prepared to let loose one last joyful blaze.

"*Light vies.*" The others felt it too. I saw it in their faces, in the sudden electric lines of their bodies.

"*Clear eyes.*" We were hurtling down a steep hill, rolling in a tire as if we had some death wish. I should stop us. I should bail out. I had to keep us safe, keep us sound.

But we were going too fast. I wasn't in charge any more. We were a collective, working together. We were a tangle of witches, a storm of familiars. We were all of us and none of us and I could no more stop those last two words from ringing out than I could stop the Earth from rotating on its axis.

"*Fire rise.*"

Another flash of darkness, deeper and longer than any we'd seen that afternoon. My heart stopped. My eyes were blind. My ears were deaf. Every muscle in my body was paralyzed, and I knew I could never say anything, never do anything, never take action again.

Out of the darkness, a torch lit. Not a candle flame, not a simple flicker of wick against wax. An inferno. Great gouts of fire roared toward the ceiling.

And born out of the heart of that holocaust, wrapped in burning wings and sheathed in molten robes of pure white heat, was a woman. A woman with the body and wings of an eagle, with vicious talons where her feet should have been. She shrieked a wordless cry of incandescent rage and started to sail around the room.

# Chapter 10

A HARPY.

That was the word my stunned brain supplied, the name for the creature born of fire. I could see it as if I were reading a page from Brighton's *Magickal Beasts and the Spells That Bind Them*. I could make out every letter set in cold, dispassionate ink.

Harpies were ancient beings, sired by the winds upon daughters of hoary kings. Originally, they were handmaidens to women in labor; they brought newborn babes into the world. But as centuries passed and they could not bear their own young, harpies turned bitter and vengeful. They stole infants. They murdered women in the prime of life, women who were capable of giving birth to their own healthy children. And the entire time they worked their vengeance they sang—clear, strong notes that were their birthright from their fathers.

The creature in my living room swooped over our heads, her wicked claws slicing the air with a sharp whistle. She opened her mouth to cry again, a song that broke my heart. It wove together the pride of an eagle surveying her domain and the wail of a devastated mother watching over the shell of her stillborn babe.

I could not tear my eyes from her. I dared not look away, for fear that those vicious talons would rake across my head, would tear through the hopeless, helpless flesh of the students I had placed in mortal danger. But even as I ducked when the harpy completed her next circuit, I recognized the true threat of the beast we had set free.

Because there was one thing Brighton didn't get right in his treatise, one thing the book failed to mention: This harpy was on fire.

In the split second when she burst from the candle flame, I'd thought she was clothed in molten robes. Now, when I stared into her burning heart, I could make out a shimmering image of Norville Pitt. This was an idealized version of the man—taller and slimmer and blessed with better hair than the real Pitt could ever hope to have. I was staring at the harpy's glorified vision of her maker.

Even so, Pitt's body was obscured by a shadow, a dark spot the size and shape of a woman. The harpy had seen someone else when she was created. The harpy had seen a woman. One of my students. I squinted against the heat shimmering off the monstrous creature, but I could not make out any details in the shadow. I could not tell who had betrayed us.

The harpy spread her wings and cried, a shattering wail that made my heart stutter. She was draped in feathers, white-hot plumes that covered her body, all the way down to her cruel, clawed feet. Each of those feathers was a separate burning flame, hot enough to ignite whatever it touched.

The curtains were the first thing to kindle. The harpy launched herself from the table and flew around the room, beating her wings with the fury of an unjustly caged prisoner. Tongues of fire licked their way from ceiling to floor, tasting the wall beside the windows. The harpy completed another circuit, shedding a feather that started to chew its way through the hardwood floor. She swooped low and brushed the couch, starting a slow smolder that was no match for whatever fire-retardant chemicals were supposed to keep us safe.

"Out!" David shouted. "Now!"

And once I heard his voice, I realized everyone was shouting. Witches were calling for their familiars. Zach was bellowing at Cassie. Familiars were bleating, howling, crying to be free. David was trying to usher us all to the front door, through the wards that were designed to keep evil out, to keep us safe.

"Spot!" he called. "Come!" And then to all of us, he repeated, "Now!"

I understood what he was saying. I knew what I was supposed to do. But I could not yield to the harpy without a fight. I could not give up this house I had come to love, this home where David and I had discovered our life together. I could not yield the treasures in my basement, the Osgood collection that had been entrusted to my care by whatever magical forces had set me on this journey years before.

I lunged toward the arch that led to the kitchen. I had to reach the basement. I had to raise some sort of spell, some type of shield, anything, everything to keep my arcane possessions safe.

The harpy screamed again, a terrible, perfect song of devastation. Her claws brushed above my hair, and my skin was immediately parched by the downdraft of her wings. A feather drifted clear of her body, a bright white curl no longer than my thumb, and it burned like lava when it caressed my cheek.

I brushed the feather free, grinding it into the floor so it could wreak no further harm. That action cost me a second, maybe two. But that was enough time for the harpy to round on me. She hovered in the archway, slowly flapping her wings and blocking my way. The motion fanned the flames around her body, feeding them, magnifying them.

Despite the heat, despite the white-hot wall before me, I stumbled forward. One step. Another.

The paint kindled on the smooth walls beside the arch, bubbling up, turning into thousands of gaping black mouths. "No!" I cried, trying to ignore the heat, to push past the pain, but the harpy threw back her wings and thrust forward with her full avian force, nearly knocking me off my feet. My eyes burned and my throat closed on a sob. I realized I was crying, but no tears made their way down my cheeks; they evaporated in the brutal wind of the harpy's wings.

"Jane!" Neko's fingers closed on my arm.

"Help me!" I commanded. He resisted, though, pulling back, trying to drag me toward the front door. I reached out on the channel that bound us together, the tightly linked line of witch to familiar. I had to compel him. I had to force him through the wall of fire, to the basement stairs, to the treasure we had to protect.

"No!" The bellow was loud enough to be heard over the flame. A hand joined Neko's, iron fingers clamping down so hard I could not resist. I was tugged back a full step. Another. One more.

David gripped me with his right hand, biting through muscle to bone.

He was my warder, and we were bound mind to mind. I could have fought him. I could have ripped away, using my witchy power as a lever.

But he was more than my warder. He was the man I loved. He loved me, and he was determined to drag me to safety, even if I was willing to pass through the wall of fire.

I was sobbing in earnest now, fighting for words. I could cast a spell. I could break free from David's grip, hurting him in the process, maybe destroying him, destroying us. I could offer up the power of my mind, my heart, my voice, and I could use it to break everything I valued.

But I already knew the truth. There was no hope on the other side of the harpy. The fire had caught too well. The walls were involved now, and the ceiling too. The couch was a mound of flame.

And the candle, the pillar of wax that we witches had chanted around for days, for weeks on end, it burned too. Part of me knew that was impossible. The candle should have already melted away, sacrificed in the first burst of the harpy's fury. But another part of me understood that all the rules I'd always known were gone now, incinerated like so much else I'd valued.

Neko shoved his shoulder under my left arm. David yanked even harder on my right. Together, the two men pulled me out of the living room, through the warded doorway, into a protective tunnel of safety bolstered by the warder's energy David had poured into the farmhouse for ages.

We were sheltered on that fiery porch. We were protected down the flaming steps. The wards held despite the blazing onslaught, despite the magic that scorched around us. I barely noted the other witches, gathered in a tight circle a scant safe distance from the house. I scarcely took note of their familiars and warders, all pressed close to the women they served. I hardly realized Spot was leaning toward us, straining to break free from Caleb's restraining hand, howling like a black-coated banshee.

I could not tear my attention from the farmhouse.

I saw the moment the fire reached the curtains in David's office. I watched it stalk into our bedroom. I saw the attic kindle, watched the conflagration in the perfect round window that looked out like a solitary eye. The shingles smoked before they burst into flame.

And then the entire house was bathed in a rain of sparks. There was a roar as the roof caved in, and another as the second floor collapsed. Wooden bones reached to the sky, grasping fingers enrobed in fire.

Out of the destruction, out of the fire and heat and utter devastation rose the harpy. Her wings fanned the flames beneath her, and her voice cried out another shriek of perfect victory and loss.

We crouched beneath her, all of us covering our heads, crying, begging, pleading to escape as the harpy climbed into the sky. She flew toward the garage, toward the witches' dormitory, where she circled three times. Each loop brought her closer to the roof, and each passage shed another handful of feathers, flaming teeth that chewed into the building.

One more time she rose, pumping to gain height in the midnight sky. This time, she stroked toward the barn. We could not see her as she circled that structure. We could not see the feathers drop, could not see the roofline kindle. But we watched her rise above the dip in the land, and we saw her head into the stratosphere like a reverse meteor, fading into a distant golden star.

Before I had a chance to speak, I was confronted with yet another disaster. There was a flash of darkness in the center of the driveway, in the precise spot that was halfway between the burning dormitory and the engulfed house. I blinked, and the darkness dissipated. In its place stood three human figures. A crouching woman, shielding her face from the light and heat of the flames. A man, feet planted, already surveying the landscape for threats. And another woman, a witch, standing tall in a crepe wool suit.

This time, Teresa Alison Sidney was too late to save me from the ravenous beast my magicarium had released. This time, she wasn't here to match my powers, to speak a spell that would drain my energy and make me question my very worthiness to serve as magistrix.

This time, Teresa was claiming the spoils of war.

# Chapter 11

DAVID TOOK THREE strides toward Ethan, curling his fingers into fists. "Get the hell off my property!" He raised his voice to be heard over the crackling flames.

Teresa slashed her hand, forbidding Ethan to respond in kind. Before David could follow through on his threat, the Washington Coven Mother turned to me and said, "Curb your warder."

My fury was as hot as the fire raging behind me. She had no right to insult David on his own front lawn. And she certainly had no right to order me to do her dirty work. Neko glided up beside me, quivering as he leaned close, ready to lend support. I settled a hand on his shoulder and prepared to work whatever spell I needed to get Teresa to leave. I started with staring her down and saying, "Get the hell off my property." I matched David's tone precisely.

Teresa laughed, offering up her palms in an elaborate shrug, throwing her head back in an exaggerated gesture that merely emphasized the long line of her neck. "Careful, magistrix," she said. "I come to offer succor. You don't want me to leave now."

I snorted. "Succor? Is that what they're calling total and complete destruction these days?"

"I had nothing to do with the harpy."

"The mere fact that you know—"

With a flash of her accustomed authority, she interrupted me. "Means that I have a familiar. Connie learned the truth from Neko."

I tightened my grip on my own familiar's shoulder.

Teresa's new laugh was a throaty chuckle, her amusement so confident that my blood started to boil as hot as the paint on the remaining farmhouse walls. "Calm yourself, magistrix. Your familiar did not betray you. He issued a challenge to my Connie. He accused us of summoning the harpy."

I sent an apologetic flash to Neko along our shared line of communication. "But that doesn't explain why you came. What do you want from me?"

"I'm here as Coven Mother."

"You're not *my* Coven Mother."

"Not any more," she agreed. "But you laid the centerstone for our safehold. Your power infuses our coven every time we meet. We know you, sister, and we mourn your loss. I, for one, cannot ignore another witch in need as great as yours."

I didn't believe for one moment that Teresa offered me sympathy or support. But she was right. My need was great.

I needed a place to regroup, to gather my thoughts and my astral energy. I needed to identify the traitor who had brought the harpy into our midst. I needed to go after Pitt. But before any of that could happen, I needed a place to shelter my students, to protect them and their familiars and their warders.

A joist burned through behind me, and part of the farmhouse roof collapsed into the conflagration. The fire roared higher, like an angry bear poked out of hibernation.

Teresa raised her voice to close the distance between us. "You need me, magistrix. You need what only I can offer."

"And what is that?"

"A refuge. A place for you to live with your students. Their warders. Their familiars."

"Where?" My voice curled up in incredulity. Who had instant housing for nearly two dozen people?

"Blanton House."

The two words shocked me into silence. Blanton House was a mansion in downtown Washington. Any DC librarian knew that. "How can you offer a treasure like Blanton House?"

"I own it. Or rather, the Washington Coven does. It's mine to use as I see fit."

Of course it was. Some of the richest matrons in Washington had belonged to the Washington Coven at times in the past. I could only imagine the tangle of paperwork that gave Teresa title. "What's your price?" I asked. Because with Teresa, there was *always* a price.

"Ah, ah, ah," she said, waving a finger as if I were a naughty toddler. "I've offered up my property. You make the first bid."

Another joist burned through the ruins at my back, and sparks soared into the night-time sky, creating new constellations before they flickered and died. Despite the blast furnace behind me, a shiver crept down my spine. I had nothing to bid, nothing to trade. There was no way the Osgood collection could survive the conflagration. Its ancient books were already charred to dust, along with all my wands and runes and herbs. Whatever crystals we eventually dug from the ashes would be clouded and cracked. Even the iron cauldrons and silver flasks would turn to slag.

I had a few thousand dollars in a bank account. The

clothes on my back. My skills as a librarian. Nothing of value to the Coven Mother. Nothing worth trading for a home.

Except…

"I'll serve the coven. I'll work whatever spells you desire. You saw me set your centerstone. You know what I can do."

Teresa's pout was pretty as she shook her head. "Our safehold has been built for two full years. The coven can handle its own witchcraft."

David stepped forward. "Then *I'll* serve the coven."

"No!" I cried, even as Teresa's lips curled into a satisfied smile.

*This* was the reason she'd come to the farm, the reason she'd offered up Blanton House. This bid for David was the logical extension of the benefaction she'd demanded the night she banished the satyr. Then, she was satisfied with a book about warders. Now, she wouldn't leave without the man.

"One year of service," she said. "Bound directly to me and—"

"Never," I interrupted, and for one sharp moment, my vehemence soared even hotter than the flames at my back.

"One day," David countered calmly. "For every year the Jane Madison Academy occupies Blanton House."

Teresa shrugged her acceptance.

I clutched at his arm. "You can't agree to this. This is exactly what she wants."

But David had started this mad bidding seven years ago. Seven years ago, he had reported one of Teresa's witches for improper workings, leaving the Coven Mother to answer to Hecate's Court. Certainly he'd been punished for his own role in the fiasco, cashiered from the coven, relegated to working for Pitt. But he'd embarrassed the famed Teresa Alison Sidney. He'd called her power into question.

And she'd waited all this time to make him pay.

David said to me, "This is exactly what we need."

He looked over my shoulder, to the clutch of my students huddling on the driveway. Most were staring at the flames in sick fascination, hypnotized by the fiery dance of destruction. Raven had planted her feet, leaning into her familiar, Hani, as if she intended to blast the fire into submission by the sheer power of her rage. Bree stood tall, shaking her head at the chaos, studying the ruins as if she were already calculating what could be salvaged.

And Cassie huddled on the ground, sobbing against Zach's sling as if her heart would break. Tupa looked on helplessly, only able to offer comfort by petting one of her braids. The poor thing had passed her breaking point—satyr and orthros and harpy had pushed her beyond any endurance.

Zach needed to get her away from here. He needed a roof over her head, a place where she could sleep for days if necessary, for weeks, however long it took for her to heal.

Cassie was only the most vulnerable of my students. *She* had broken, but the others had to be teetering on the edge as well. They'd all been dragged through chaos. They'd all witnessed the brutal attacks. They'd all been exposed to danger, and their bodies, minds, and magic had to be disintegrating under the constant barrage of adrenaline.

David waited for me to look back at him before he asked, "What other option do we have?"

The farmhouse seemed to hear that desperate question. The back wall collapsed forward, falling into the fiery pit that had once been the basement, that had once held the Osgood collection.

I turned back to Teresa. "I choose the day."

"Absolutely not."

I had to challenge her, make the deal hurt her as much as it could hurt us. "Then we'll sign a lease. Ninety-nine years. Rent-free."

Her eyebrows quirked, as if she were questioning David's longevity. But she humored me. "Ninety-nine years. Rent-free."

This was too easy. One day of warder's service in exchange for a year in a mansion? She had to be planning something, plotting something terrible.

I whirled to David. "We'll rent some place. We can take out a loan. We can sell more of the woods, the lake, something…"

But he only shook his head. We weren't going to find a rental property for two dozen people overnight. Our credit history wasn't that good. And there wasn't time to negotiate the destruction of more of the woods, the ripping apart of the natural landscape we'd sworn to protect.

He set his hand against my cheek. "All will be well," he said.

I pulled away. "It won't be!"

"I'm your warder," he said, grabbing for my hand. "And I tell you all will be well."

He couldn't promise me that. I could keep him from sealing the bargain with Teresa. I could restrain him, apply magical bonds, embarrass him in front of my students, Teresa, and Ethan. I could keep him from making himself a sacrificial lamb.

But David wasn't a lamb. He was a warder with decades of experience, swaddled in his own brand of masculine magic. He recognized the danger. He accepted the risk Teresa offered.

I closed my free hand over his. I bowed my head, and whispered, "So mote it be."

As if on cue, a long wail sounded in the distance. For a heartbeat, I thought it was at the harpy, coming back in vengeance and pride, returning to complete the work she'd begun, burning us all to charcoal strips.

But the cry faded away, only to rise again, and I realized I was listening to sirens. Not the ancient Greek monsters, the songstresses who lured sailors onto rocks. Rather, the Parkersville Fire Department was responding. I glanced at Raven, then at Skyler. Either of them could have summoned the rescuers with her phone.

David took his hand from me and knelt before the Coven Mother. He bowed his head, barely shuddering as she set her palms upon his shoulders. "Well met, Warder Montrose," she said. "So mote it be."

After the ritual words, he was free to rise, free to grip my wrist and drag me toward the approaching firefighters. The men were already shaking their heads, patently admitting they could do nothing to save the home I'd loved, the school I'd founded, the burning shell of all my worldly possessions.

When I looked back, Teresa had disappeared, spirited away with Connie, escaped through the power of her own sworn warder.

I sank onto the steps in Blanton House, running both hands through my hair before I shrugged my shoulders up to my ears. Trying to force myself to relax, I said, "I still don't like it." I directed my words to the carpet runner that covered the oak planks beneath my feet.

David sighed. "We've gone over this a hundred times. I don't like it either. But what other option did we have?"

I didn't answer, because there wasn't anything to say. We'd paid to put everyone up at the Parkersville Motor Lodge, but that was obviously a temporary solution. As the sun rose after a sleepless night, we'd agreed to take advantage of the mundane calendar, to announce a week of Thanksgiving vacation for everyone.

They all needed a chance to recover, to shop for everything from aspirin to underwear. And even Hecate's Court couldn't fault us for giving the time off, not when we'd met their most recent deadline. Lighting the candle communally would have been "substantial progress" even if we hadn't raised enough power to burn the farmhouse to the ground.

So now we were alone in Blanton House. The mansion was actually five joined townhouses, occupying a city block in downtown DC. They'd been built by famed architect Henry Blanton. Each had originally been designed as a separate home—one for the avowed bachelor Blanton, another for his widowed mother, a third for his spinster sister. A fourth house had been dedicated to the Thanatopsis Society, one of Blanton's pet projects, bringing together intellectuals of the day to discuss art, literature, and philosophy. The fifth had been reserved for Mimi Breton, Blanton's mistress. The basements and attics of all five buildings were connected. According to Blanton, the arrangement facilitated care for his aging mother. According to social wags of the day, the arrangement facilitated Blanton having his mistress close enough, but not too close.

I could only hope *I'd* be keeping Pitt's traitor close enough. But not too close.

The real reason I'd given my students a break was because I didn't want the mole nipping at my heels as I set up our new home. Once again, my thoughts flashed around the circle of suspects: Alex. Bree. Cassie. Skyler. I'd felt sheer joy from every one of them when we'd successfully lit the candle. Each of my students had thrown herself into that working, offering up her own powers without limitation. How could someone who had shared herself so intimately be a traitor?

I could ask the question all day, but the fact remained: someone *had* done precisely that. And I was left with the haunting Greek chorus: Who? Who? Who?

"We have to make this work," I said, yielding the argument over David's indenture to Teresa, the same way I had every other time we'd fought about it. "We have to catch Pitt's pawn in action."

"Much more action, and we'll all be dead."

I didn't have an answer to that.

Despite our grim expectations upon arriving at our new home that morning, we'd found Blanton House completely clean. Either Teresa knew housekeeping spells I'd never heard of or she'd hired an army of housekeepers to get the place ready overnight. The floors gleamed as if they were newly waxed, and the windows sparkled like sun-struck lakes. Couches, armchairs, beds—all were dust-free and ready for occupation.

But the immaculate physical premises were not our primary concern.

"Ready?" David asked.

I nodded as he took a seat above me on the stairs. His hands settled on my shoulders, a comfort in the wake of the past twenty-four hours of chaos. I closed my eyes and took three deep breaths, exhaling long and slow between each one. The ritual calmed me, almost too much. I felt the physical world tip up around me, threatening to spin out of control, and I wondered if I should be doing this work on no sleep and a gallon of caffeine.

"I've got you," David murmured, pressing his fingertips into my clavicles with just enough force to anchor me. "Take your time."

I wasted a moment, wishing Neko were with us to bolster my fading energy. But he had his own mission—procuring clothes and groceries for all three of us, everything we needed to start life anew. After one more steadying breath, I touched my fingertips to my forehead, my throat, and my heart.

I wasn't working a spell, not precisely. Instead, I spread my fingers wide, offering up my right palm as if someone were reading my lifeline. Slowly, cautiously, I gathered my thoughts, drawing them into a shimmering golden ball. As I breathed, the light grew on my palm, becoming brighter, firmer, a tiny sun nearly bursting with potential.

The sphere was hard but yielding, like skin stretched over a pregnant woman's belly. It pressed against my palm as if it had physical weight. The world around me shrank, thinning and disappearing until everything was the ball. Everything was the power. Everything was the light.

Not everything, though. Because *I* still existed. And a tiny corner of my brain knew that David still existed, that he was sheltering me with his body, ready to protect me against anything that would do me harm.

I measured the energy cradled in my palm, and I offered up a quick prayer to Hecate that it would be enough. In response, the ball flashed brighter, amplifying my bound power, doubling, tripling the force. Before I could lose the balance, I stabbed at the sphere with one Word, a single thought: "Display!"

The energy exploded, hurtling away as if I'd burst a balloon with an atomic ray gun. All of the power I'd poured into the ball shattered as it hit the air, dispersing into billions of microscopic droplets, filling the stairwell with the faintest fog visible only to witchy eyes.

I swayed for a moment, leaning hard against David's

knees, but when I regained my balance, I could see that my working had been successful. The fog wasn't randomly distributed about the stairwell. It condensed in some places, growing thicker, like a forensic scientist's fingerprint powder.

There, by the front door—the distinctive sweep of wards removed in haste. In the center of the foyer, a ghost of a binding spell, as if some former mistress of this home had tamped down the magical powers of all her arcane guests. Around the arch that led to the parlor, the memory of a peacemaking spell, encouraging good will and bonhomie among all who passed into the next room.

Those were all remnants of an older magic than I used, part of a formal social structure from the days when diners expected placecards, when gentlemen took brandy and cigars after supper while segregated ladies gossiped among themselves. They were phantoms of the past.

But my working revealed more than my predecessors' social niceties. Because between the dusty wards and the dissipated binding spell and the crumbling peacemaking spell, there was something else. Something new. Something jangling against my senses.

Not just some*thing*. Some*things*, many of them. One here in the foyer. Another in the parlor. A third in the dining room. More in the kitchen, and up the stairs, in the bedrooms—hard knots of energy that drew in the dust of my display working like cancerous cells lighting up a medical display. They were tiny, small enough that I'd never sense them without the augmenting fog of the magic I'd worked.

I could see the closest one from where I sat, tucked in tight beneath the newel. Indeed, I couldn't lean in for a closer look because David's fingers had tightened into a vise. He wasn't letting me get close to the nugget. He wasn't going to risk my harming myself.

"What is it?" I breathed.

"A bug," he said grimly. "And it hasn't been there long. If I had to guess, I'd say Teresa had a long night, setting all of them. What? Do I sense seven more?"

I nodded and whispered, "What does it transmit? Is she listening to us now?"

David answered in his ordinary voice. "Not by sound. But she's monitoring astral energy. She'll recognize the Display Word. She'll know she's been discovered."

"So do we leave them in place? Use them to feed her false information?"

He shook his head. "That wouldn't work. She knows you've found her out, so she won't trust anything she receives. It's easy enough to destroy them."

"How?" I braced myself, preparing to spend the energy to disinfect my new home.

"I can do it with warder's magic," David said. "And you can save your strength for the rest of this place. You'll have to repeat the Display Word in each townhouse."

I climbed to my feet, grabbing hold of the banister to steady myself when the room began to spin. "Easy," David said, rising to join me. I took a deep breath, and the floor evened out beneath my feet.

"I'm okay," I said. When David narrowed his eyes with skepticism, I set my hands on my hips. "I'm tired, and I'm hungry, and I hope there's a working bathroom in this place, but I'm fine." I shoved a tendril of defiance along the magical bond between us, emphasizing my words.

His set jaw told me he wasn't happy, but he didn't really have a choice. The best way through this thicket was forward, and that meant finding and scouring away every one of Teresa's spying devices.

We started with the one in the foyer. David rested his

hand on top of the banister, settling his palm on the newel post. "Wait," I said, before he could work his magic. "Should you be the one doing this?"

"You think we should call Ghostbusters?"

I grimaced. "Teresa's going to have power over you at some point. You shouldn't upset her now. Let's have one of the other warders wipe these out after Thanksgiving Break."

David dismissed my concern with one tight shake of his head. "She gets me for one night. I won't let her manage me through fear till then."

Before I could acknowledge the logic of his words, David breathed in sharply, clenching his fist above the newel as if he were crushing a nettle. I *heard* his magic, an arpeggio like someone rolling knuckles over the black keys on a piano. The sound grated against my ears, unfamiliar, like Chinese opera.

Even as I registered the discord, I felt the crunch of shattered magic. A puff of golden dust exploded from David's fist, mixing with steel-grey debris. The remnants of my Display Word floated away, and I knew Teresa's bug had been destroyed.

I followed David into the parlor, listening and watching as he destroyed another bug. The dining room was next, then the kitchen. We headed upstairs to the bedrooms, zeroing in on each device.

No matter how many times I heard the musical notes, the sounds never became familiar. There was something *off* about them, something that jangled, separate and apart from my own witchy abilities. Warders' magic had a different foundation from witches' power, a completely different structure.

"Ready for the next section?" David asked, when he'd banished the device in the third-floor bedroom.

"Lead the way."

We headed up to the attic, taking advantage of the passage between the houses, a hallway as immaculate as the rest of the home. The walls were finished with fine grass wallpaper.

In the next townhouse, I spoke my Display Word on the second-floor landing, giving my spell's fine dust a better chance to reach every corner of the building. I knew what to expect this time—the remnants of witchcraft from generations past, the tight knots of power left by our current "benefactor." David destroyed each bug, and we moved on to the next townhouse, and the next, and the next.

Blanton House was an architectural marvel. There were details in every room—ornate chandelier plaques in the centers of the ceilings, carvings of leaves and woodland creatures on the staircases, shimmering glass tiles set in the bathrooms. Mirrors surprised me in unlikely niches, and each townhouse had at least one floor-to-ceiling stained glass window that rippled with Tiffany glass. I felt as if I was walking through a museum, a gorgeous re-creation of a home suitable for Andrew Carnegie or J. Pierpont Morgan.

Room by room, we claimed Blanton House for our own. Floor by floor, we banished Teresa's devices, guaranteeing that my magicarium could function in privacy, except for Pitt's mole. House by house, we took possession of our new lives.

When we were through, I was exhausted, and David didn't look much better off. Dark circles had bled beneath his eyes. The strong set of his jaw merely emphasized the hollows of his cheeks. We both needed food for grounding— simple food and clean water and an unbroken twenty-four hours to sleep.

My phone buzzed as I swayed on the landing. I dug it out

by reflex, frowning when I saw Neko's name. He'd likely felt the drain of the last few hours and was calling to check up on me.

"Hey," I said, answering the phone. "You would not believe—"

"You've got to see this," Neko interrupted.

"Where are you?"

"The farmhouse."

"Is it the harpy?"

"Just get here. Fast." I heard shouting in the background before he hung up.

# Chapter 12

WITH AN ORDER like that, neither David nor I was inclined to waste time driving from Washington up to Parkersville. Instead, David closed his arms around me, pulling me close to his chest. One moment, I was staring at sunshine streaming through century-old windows in a parlor that once belonged to the mistress of one of the most powerful men in Washington. The next, I was *nothing*; there was no time, no space, no place in the entire world for me to be, to breathe, to live.

I couldn't be afraid because I wasn't anything at all.

Then I was standing next to David on the gutted driveway of the farmhouse. Channels gouged the gravel, deep reminders of the firetrucks that had been there less than twenty-four hours before.

The stench hit me first, the reek of burned electrical wires, of melted plastic, of a thousand things that were never meant to go up in smoke. My eyes watered, and my throat closed around a series of convulsive coughs.

Neko stood at the edge of the charred ruins, his feet planted along the soot-stained line that had once been our front porch. The destruction behind him looked like it might collapse at any moment. The chimney still stood, outlining the edge of the living room, but the entire roof had crashed through to the basement.

"Neko, be careful!"

My familiar turned to me, a grin splitting his face. "Took you long enough."

I shrugged off David's restraining fingers and walked to the edge of the destruction. "What are you doing here? You were supposed to be shopping."

Neko fluttered a hand against his hip pocket, presumably gesturing toward the credit card David had dangerously surrendered that morning. "I figured I should be fiscally responsible. I came back to see what I could salvage."

"Since when are *you* fiscally responsible?"

Neko offered up a resigned smile. "Okay, I wasn't all that worried about spending David's money. I just had to see if it was as bad as it seemed last night. I couldn't believe…"

His voice tightened, as if he'd inhaled too much of the fire's sooty remains. He blinked hard, and my own eyes watered in response. "We'll get through this," I said. "It will take time, and we may never have a collection like—"

"But you do," Neko interrupted.

"I do what?"

"You *do* have a collection."

I stared at him as if he were speaking Ancient Phoenician.

"The vault," Neko insisted. "It kept everything safe."

I heard every syllable he uttered. I understood each individual word. But when I put them all together they were nonsense. "Neko," I said. "Look at this." I gestured to the utter destruction behind him. "You can't even walk across there."

"I don't have to. I've been part of the Osgood collection for over a century. I know the feeling of all those things—the books, the wands, the runes and crystals. They're there."

I wanted his words to be true. I wanted everything to have survived. But the entire house was destroyed. The attic had fallen *through* the two floors.

My familiar danced back to my side. "Reach for it," he said. "Go ahead. Extend your senses."

Before I could protest, he took my hand and planted it on his shoulder. The magical strand between us flexed, and he opened his mirrored power. He was ready, waiting for me to draw on whatever reserves I needed.

I turned my head to look at David, fully expecting him to stop me from continuing. Instead, he jutted his chin toward the reeking mound. "You heard the man," he said. "Try it."

I closed my eyes and took a calming breath. My logical brain told me this was impossible. I'd taken classes on disasters in library school. I knew the impact of fire, of heat, of the water that followed after. I understood the vulnerability of parchment, of paper, of wood.

But no class in library school had discussed magical goods. And no disaster of this magnitude had ever taken into account a paranoid warder, a vault meant to keep out the most prying Coven Mother in the world, the most duplicitous Head Clerk of Hecate's Court who had ever served the world of witches.

I sent a tendril of my power through the ruins.

And I leaped back in immediate reflex. The stinking destruction I could sense with my nose and eyes was nothing compared to the perception I gained with my powers. With magic, I could see the precise path the harpy had taken through the house. I could detect each burning feather she'd shed, every bitter downsweep of her wings. My powers let me create a map that crossed from collapsed room to collapsed room, doubling back through the ruins countless times.

Neko whined, and I realized my curled fingers had dug in like a harpy's claws. I eased my grip on his shoulder, sending a whispered mental apology.

I braced myself, and I reached out again. This time, I consciously closed my mind to the route of the harpy's destruction. I blocked out the echoes of psychic distress from the night before, the horror of my students, my own stunned disbelief as my home kindled like a well-aged Christmas tree.

Instead, I focused on items I knew were part of the Osgood collection. The crystals were as good a place to start as any; stone had *some* chance of coming through fire.

I forced myself to think of my finest sample of amethyst, a single crystal almost as long as my thumb. The transparent purple was designed to raise spirits. I could use it to boost my hopefulness, now more than ever. I'd handled the amethyst countless times, tracing its facets with my fingers. I'd let it grow warm on my palm. Now, I concentrated on the crystal's weight, on its physical presence against my flesh.

Once that memory was fixed, I stretched to see if I could detect a ghost of the stone in the ruins. I cast my thoughts past the stinking wood, beyond the tangles of melted electrical wiring. I concentrated on the corner of the basement that we'd converted into a vault.

Tugging on the rope of power Neko offered, I allowed his fractal mirrors to amplify my own energy. I leaned forward, as if cutting the distance by a foot might make all the difference.

And there, beneath the harpy's wreckage, beneath the charred shingles, beneath burnt slabs that had once been kitchen counters, I felt the amethyst.

It gleamed like a tiny violet sun, bright and steady and confident.

I brushed against the other contents of the amethyst's box, automatically noting my other crystal treasures. The chalcedony had survived, the malachite and amber. All the stones had made it through the fire.

That knowledge gave me the courage to search more broadly. I envisioned the wands I owned, rowan and ash and oak. I felt their weight in my memory, recalling how they had balanced in my hand as I channeled energy through them.

And I found them, safe and secure where they'd been stashed in the vault.

The wands, the runes, the collection of cast iron cauldrons. Bells and chalices and three different athames, their blades untouched by the flames.

And, of course, there were the books. I could still sense the jumble, the crazy piles toppling into each other, haphazard stacks from when David had cleared my neat, orderly shelves. But every volume had survived, parchment and paper, leather-bound or not.

"Sweet Hecate," I breathed. As I spoke the words, I realized tears were streaming down my face. I was leaning on Neko, more heavily than I'd planned. My knees had somehow turned to water, and my heart was hammering in my chest.

But I was laughing, even as David stepped forward to close his hands over my forearms, offering up support I needed more than I dared admit. "It's there," I said. "It's all still there."

"And it will be tomorrow, when we can work out a way to retrieve it all safely."

"No!" I cried. "We have to get it now!"

"And how do you propose doing that? Even if you could make your way across what used to be the living room, there aren't any stairs to the basement. I'll talk to the firefighters."

"You can't tell them—"

"I'll talk to Rick." Emma's erstwhile boyfriend. Whether their relationship survived or not, he knew about witchcraft. He would understand the treasures we needed to salvage.

"Let's go," I said. "Now. Before—"

"You're not going anywhere," David said. "You offered up five Words of Display back at Blanton House. You can barely stand on your own two feet here."

I wanted to protest, but I found myself biting back a yawn that threatened to sever my jaw from my face. Instead of arguing, I turned to Neko. "Thank you," I said.

He offered up a little bow, apparently not caring if I was thanking him for calling me out to the farmhouse, for strengthening my exhausted powers as I reached out for the collection, or for simply being there when so much else was lost.

"Jane," David said, and I heard the warning note in his voice.

"All right," I agreed, because it really was taking every last ounce of my determination to stay on my feet. Neko stepped forward, tucking his body close to my side. David's arms settled around me, a comfortable, known weight. I closed my eyes, and I surrendered to being nothing.

Three days later, I stood in the Blanton House basement, beneath the section of the mansion that had served as Henry Blanton's personal home. As an architect, the man had maintained countless valuable documents, including blueprints for moguls' homes and the first skyscrapers ever erected in DC. He'd owned dozens of valuable paintings, a collection of Lalique jewels to adorn his mistress, and the first Faberge eggs imported into the United States. Blanton had been legendary for hoarding cash, enough to buy off the city's chief inspector, along with all the Congressmen he needed to guarantee unfettered operation in DC.

And all those riches had been stored in a vault three stories beneath Blanton's silk-hung bedroom.

The chamber wasn't like the modern one David had overseen at the farmhouse. Rather, Blanton's was constructed like a classic bank vault, with impenetrable metal plates set into the ceiling, floor, and walls. A trio of massive doors guarded the space, each equipped with its own massive wheel, with unbreachable tumblers forged out of solid Pennsylvania steel.

Blanton's vault had room for the entire Osgood collection, with space to spare. Rick Hanson had come through for us, working his private brand of firefighter magic, getting us access to the farmhouse vault. By dark of night, he'd helped us spirit away the arcane goods that would have been impossible to explain to a mundane insurance adjuster.

Here at Blanton, the books were still a librarian's nightmare. I'd completed some preliminary sorting, grouping volumes by topic, but there was no order within those tall stacks. Runes, though, went on one shelf, wands on another. A cache of silver flasks glinted beneath the old-fashioned overhead lights.

I was just shifting a massive beeswax candle when I heard the heavy tolling of the doorbell. The three bass notes told me I knew the person on the doorstep; David had set an impressive array of wards with specific allowances for our various allies.

I closed all three doors before I left the vault, spinning each heavy wheel. Having spared the Osgood collection from certain destruction at the farm, I wasn't about to get lazy in the city.

Melissa White was waiting on the doorstep. My best friend was bundled against a late November gale, her throat swaddled in a bulky scarf that trailed down her heavy winter coat. A gust of wind threatened to steal away the pasteboard box she gripped in one mittened hand.

"Welcome wagon!" she exclaimed as I urged her over the threshold.

"Come in!" I waved her back toward the kitchen. "I know I'm supposed to say 'you shouldn't have,' but I'm totally thrilled you did."

"'Sweets to the sweet', you know."

"Ugh," I said. "*Hamlet*. And I don't have to tell you the melancholy Dane was talking about funeral bouquets, not baked goods."

She laughed as I slipped my finger under the golden sticker that closed the box. I couldn't wait to see what she'd brought. "They're Turkey Day Temptations. I figured you're a close enough friend that I could assault you with day-olds."

"Assault me all you want," I said, reaching for a plate. I knew from past indulgence that the confections were addictive—spiced salty pumpkin seeds set in honey-based brittle. Each neat square had a decadent corner dipped into dark chocolate.

Melissa shook her head when I offered her some of her own fare. "I ate enough yesterday to last about five years. I still wish you guys had joined us for Thanksgiving."

I finished chewing my first Temptation before I opened the fridge. This was our inaugural night of Mojito Therapy in my new home. As I excavated limes, mint, and soda water from the cavernous refrigerator, I said to Melissa, "I really appreciated the invitation. More than you can know."

And I did. Each day of the past insane week had bled into the next, a constant series of meetings—insurance agents and fire inspectors and a stream of utility workers coming to Blanton House to turn on water, gas, and electricity. We'd outfitted rooms for all the witches, for their familiars and warders. We'd stocked three of the kitchens, leaving snacks and coffee in the other two. We'd turned two parlors into classrooms and cleared the largest basement space for group workings—for when we got back to those.

In short, we'd converted a luxury mansion into a school, in five short days.

I'd appreciated the invitation, but I'd pleaded exhaustion for Thanksgiving—both to Melissa and to Gran, who had invited us to join her and Uncle George, along with Clara and half the board of directors for Concert Opera Guild. David and I had treated ourselves to turkey sandwiches from a shop around the corner, splurging on kettle-cooked potato chips and a bottle of white burgundy that seemed to appear from some secret warder's stash. Neko had spent the day with Tony, meeting his boyfriend's family. He hadn't come back in the middle of the night, so I had to believe things had gone well.

However unconventional, my Thanksgiving had turned out perfect, the only one I could have handled under the circumstances.

Now, I put Melissa to work muddling mint leaves, while I started to juice half a dozen limes. I'd only sliced each fruit in half when the doorbell rang again—those same three sonorous notes. Someone else known to me was waiting on the steps. Someone deemed safe by David.

Wiping my hands on a towel, I headed back to the front door. Gran and Clara huddled on the front step, leaning against each other. Gran held the world's largest casserole dish in her gloved hands, and Clara balanced two canvas grocery store bags.

"What are you doing here?" I asked, ushering them in to keep from losing all the heat in the house.

"Half the fun of Thanksgiving is leftovers," Gran declared.

"So we brought the party to you," Clara added.

I wasn't getting choked up. No, my eyes were only watering because of the cold outside. Or maybe I'd rubbed a little mint in them by accident. "Melissa's here," I said. "Come back to the kitchen."

But Gran was glued to the hardwood floor in the foyer, gaping up at the heavy crown molding above the stairs. "This place is *stunning*, dear."

Clara's bags rustled as she set them on the floor, only to throw her head back like a silent screen diva, pasting the back of her hand to her forehead. "This is it, Jeanette! The perfect setting for the NWTA."

I'd say one thing for my mother—she was tenacious. Her plans for a crazy commune weren't going to fade away easily. "I'm not so sure, Clara. There isn't really a nucleus here. And only two tentacles—one long hallway in the attic, and another in the basement."

She clicked her tongue. "Oh no! You have it all backwards. The nucleus is the *common* space, the connected rooms at the top and the bottom. The tentacles are each individual bedroom, those private spaces where a witch can keep her secrets."

A shiver ratcheted down my spine.

Gran fussed at me. "Are you all right, dear? You look like you've seen a ghost."

Not a ghost. A harpy. A harpy and an orthros and a satyr.

The past week had been full of hard work, physical labor

to prepare Blanton House. But I hadn't needed to worry about my anonymous rogue student. Come Monday, my respite would be over. I'd be back in the thick of things, waiting for Pitt's inquest to pluck David from my side, parsing every last word uttered by my students as I tried to identify the traitor, all the while racing to beat whatever impossible new goals the Court mandated in their efforts to disband the Academy.

I wasn't ready. I didn't have a choice.

I forced myself to take a calming breath. "I'm fine," I said, but I knew my protest wasn't believable. "It was just the thought of tentacles wrapping around me—"

"There you are!" That was Melissa's voice behind me, cheerful and oblivious. "Mrs. Smythe! Clara! I didn't know you were coming over."

Gran shook her head. "And we didn't know you were here, dear." She kissed Melissa on the cheek. "We just wanted to see Jane's new home. We figured we'd bring by some Thanksgiving leftovers—"

"Here," Melissa said. "Let me take that." She collected the casserole dish from my grandmother, and I felt like an ungrateful fool for leaving her to hold it for so long. "Come back to the kitchen," Melissa said. "I just made a fresh pitcher of mojitos."

Well, that was why my best friend was in the hospitality business and I worked the witchcraft shift. She knew how to be nice to people. Even people with whacked out ideas about a nucleus and tentacles...

I followed everyone into the kitchen and set about stowing away an entire Thanksgiving feast into the refrigerator. I could only imagine how much Gran had cooked if this was what she'd set aside for me. I jockeyed things around, making room for the massive container of turkey, for the sweet potatoes and the mashed potatoes, for the corn pudding and green beans almandine, the oyster dressing and the sage dressing, whole berry cranberry sauce and an entire can's worth of the ridged jelly stuff, half a pumpkin pie, half an apple pie, and four ramekins that looked like they held homemade butterscotch pudding. Only then did I realize there was still a tote bag left on the counter.

"What's that?" I asked.

Gran's eyes gleamed with pride. "I told you I wanted to knit a little something for the wedding."

My first reaction was to wince. Hoping she hadn't noticed, I purposely amped up the excitement in my tone. "I can't wait!" Melissa gave me a strange look, so I brought it down about three notches. "I can't believe you had time to do this."

Gran reached into the bag, her chest swelling with pride. She pulled out three clumps of knitting, each more tangled than the last. I couldn't make out a top or a bottom for any of the pieces. I couldn't even figure out which was the front and which was the back. Each masterpiece, though, was made out of heavy acrylic yarn, a shade that might charitably be called Slaughterhouse Scarlet.

As I administered an emergency gulp of mojito, my grandmother spread her handiwork out on the marble countertop. "Wow," I finally managed. "These are…amazing."

Gran beamed.

"Um, why don't you tell me about them?" There it was—my librarian training, swooping to the rescue. In my last office job, my boss had required me to lead book groups for toddlers. I'd read the kids a story and ask them to draw illustrations. When I couldn't figure out if I was looking at the Mayflower or a garden flower, I'd use the exact same line on them.

And the kids always obliged, prattling on about their creations. Fortunately, Gran was just as forthcoming.

"Well, this one is a cummerbund, of course. I showed you the pattern that morning at brunch."

"Of course," I said. If I turned my head to the side and squinted hard, I could see how the tangle of yarn might stretch around the waist of tuxedo pants. I could even *begin* to imagine David wearing it. He'd never do anything to hurt Gran's feelings. But I was pretty sure Neko would have to be dead and stuffed before he'd loop the crimson disaster around his hips.

Gran sallied on, undeterred. "Once I saw how well the cummerbund turned out, I realized I *had* to do matching bow ties."

That explained the butterfly shaped monstrosity clumped on the counter. It might even work as neckwear, for some sort of massive cave troll. A man of ordinary human dimensions would have to double the thing up. At least. I said, "I've never seen anything like it."

"And this one is my own design," Gran said proudly, gesturing toward the last, and largest, mountain of yarn. "I've always preferred wrist corsages—there's no chance of tearing delicate fabric with a pin. The roses were a bit of a challenge, but making them twice the size really helped. This way, you won't have to worry about a bouquet for your matron of honor."

I caught a real look of terror in Melissa's eyes. She nearly reached for the bottle of rum, but she recovered enough to stick with her mojito. I braved a response. "That's incredible, Gran. And it's so…unusual."

My grandmother beamed. Melissa recovered first, pushing the plate of Turkey Day Temptations toward her. "Don't mind if I do," Gran said, picking out the largest one.

Clara nodded encouragingly. "This wedding of yours is certainly going to be unique," she said. "Now who did you say will be the celebrant?"

I was on firmer footing here. At least I could answer truthfully. "I haven't decided yet."

Clara's frown was offset by her understanding nod. "But you've chosen a venue."

"Not yet." I tried not to feel defensive.

"You've at least considered invitations, haven't you? Save the date cards? Have you even drawn up a guest list, Jeanette?"

Melissa earned her matron of honor title by interrupting before I could explode. "*Jane* has had a lot on her plate, Clara. With the move and everything, I'm sure she's been set back a few days."

A few days. Weeks. Months.

And part of my frustration—part of the reason I was digging my fingernails into my palms—was that I *wanted* to do all those things Clara had fired off. I was an organized person by nature; I liked to draw up checklists and spreadsheets. And more than anything, I wanted to be take care of my own wedding. I wanted to consider each and every task, evaluate all my options, make the most important day in my life *mine*. Well, mine and David's. Ours.

But it wasn't worth explaining all of that to Clara, turning her questions into a fight. She and Gran only wanted what was best for me. So I gave Melissa a grateful smile, and I answered my mother: "All those things are on my to-do list." In a flash of inspiration, I gathered up my grandmother's mutant yarn creations and added, "We should put these away so they don't get dirty!"

And then I picked up the pitcher and topped off everyone's glass. Because it was Friday night, and the Jane Madison Academy was on Thanksgiving break. And I was desperate for a little fun before serious business picked up again on Monday morning.

I raised my glass. "To ourselves!" I said.

It was an old toast, one we'd first shared more than three years ago, when these women had gathered to rescue me from a series of disasters, all stemming from my discovering I was a witch. From the smiles on their faces, they remembered that earlier toast, those earlier mistakes. "To ourselves!" they said, clinking glasses and laughing.

I made the next round of mojitos. They went perfectly with the leftover Thanksgiving feast we constructed when we raided the refrigerator.

It turned out, the serious business picked up well before Monday morning.

I was lying in bed on Saturday, listening to rain fall outside as I burrowed deeper under the comforting weight of a quilt. David had stirred hours earlier, taking Spot out for his morning walk. They'd gotten back more than an hour ago; at least, that's when the smell of coffee wound its way up the stairs.

I must have dozed off in the warm, lazy perfection of it all, because the next thing I knew, David was feathering a kiss on the side of my neck. "Mmm," I said, not opening my eyes. "This hotel has the best wake-up call."

I rolled over, ready to invite him to climb under the covers with me. Instead, I found him dressed in a severe grey suit, somber as a pallbearer. I sat up so fast, the quilt slipped to the floor. "Where are you going?"

"Hecate's Court. The inquest summoned me."

"It's the weekend!"

"Not for warders."

I threw my legs over the side of the bed. "Let me get dressed. I'm coming with you."

"You might as well wait here. It's a lot more comfortable. I don't know how long I'll be."

"But…" I trailed off. We'd had this argument already. There *wasn't* anything I could do, any way I could help him. Instead, he needed me to be strong. Steady. Confident. When he took the stand and admitted to his past mistakes, arguing for Pitt to be held accountable for his own misdeeds, David shouldn't have to worry about my falling apart at home.

"Be careful," I said, cupping his jaw in my hand.

"Always." He turned his face and kissed my palm.

I backed away first. I did that for him because I was his witch, and he was my warder, and that was what he needed. I stayed perfectly still while he left the room. I knew I wouldn't hear the front door open. He'd use warder's magic to reach the Court.

I scooped up the quilt and tossed it back on the bed. After pulling on jeans and a bulky cabled sweater, I went back to the quilt, taking an inordinate time to square up the corners, to make it perfect. I returned to my closet and went through the hangers, making sure they all faced the same way.

Everything in the house was too new, too orderly. With only a week under our belts, there wasn't enough to clean or straighten. Still restless, I headed down to the kitchen, and I wasn't surprised to find Neko sitting at the kitchen table. "Want a turkey sandwich?" I asked.

He shook his head.

I considered making a plate for myself, but the thought of food curdled my stomach. Better to distract myself with conversation. "How was Thanksgiving with Tony?"

"Fine."

"Was his family nice?"

"Yes."

"Did he come back with you?"

"No."

"Neko—"

He cut me off before I could scream my frustration. "Everything was wonderful—the people, the food, their home. Arizona is gorgeous this time of year. Tony will watch the football game with his father tomorrow, and then he'll be back to take care of Raven. I had a fantastic time, and I wish I was still there, and I can't believe the Court called David in for the inquest! I hate that they're doing this to him, and to you, and I want it all to be over."

I settled a hand on his shoulder. He was trembling, and I wondered if his insides ached as much as mine. "Let's go downstairs," I said. And I led the way to the vault.

The three massive wheels required physical strength to move them. I leaned in to the gears, stretching my legs. It felt good to push against something that couldn't be hurt.

I stepped back as the door swung outward. Neko peered around me to take in the half-sorted stacks of books. "Oh my," he said. "I *love* what you've done with the place."

His coy drawl was forced. The line wasn't all that funny. But we both started to laugh, giggles at first, that grew to guffaws, that expanded to full-blown gales of tension-relieving hysterics. I folded my arms around my belly and clutched my sides, trying unsuccessfully to draw a complete breath. That made me snort, and Neko tutted his disapproval, sending us both to the floor with renewed laughter.

Finally, I wiped away tears from beneath my eyes. I drew one full breath. Another. "Thank you," I said at last.

He inclined his head gracefully. We both turned back to

the books and started the meticulous task of alphabetizing.

In silent agreement, we took a break for lunch, and another for dinner. Neko watched as I finished off the Turkey Day Temptations. He helped himself to a cup of cream. We went back downstairs to organize more books.

And about fifteen minutes after the tall-case clock struck midnight, David walked into the vault. His face was grey. His hair stood on end, as if he'd tried to tug it out by the roots. Furrows creased beside his eyes, deep wrinkles of fatigue that I'd never seen before.

I caught a dozen questions against the back of my teeth, finally settling on, "Well?"

David shook his head. "I can't tell you."

"You can't tell the details! But you can give me a general idea of how it went!"

He rubbed a hand over his face, slowly pulling from his forehead to his chin. When he was through, he seemed to have reached some sort of resolution. "They went through everything," he said. "From the day I was sworn as a warder till this morning. They wanted to know about the Washington Coven. About my work as a clerk. About Pitt. They wanted to know a lot about Pitt."

"What did you tell them?"

"Everything I knew. Everything Pitt's done. And everything I've done." He swallowed hard, his throat rasping as if he were downing crushed glass. "Everything," he said.

That meant he'd divulged the documents he'd forged, the false path he'd laid in an unsuccessful attempt to frame Pitt before the Head Clerk could do some innocent witch lasting harm.

I wanted to ask more. I wanted to know how they'd reacted. I wanted to learn what they thought about the corruption in their own midst, about the man who'd endangered my students, endangered me, the clerk who'd worked so hard to destroy my magicarium.

But David couldn't tell me. And I couldn't torture him any more by asking. Not when he'd already told me, weeks before, exactly what could happen. They could take away his sword and melt down his ring. They could force me to choose another warder.

Instead, I asked, "Are you hungry?"

He shook his head.

I couldn't think of anything else to say, anything else to do. So I nodded to Neko, leaving him to place the last stack of books on the shelves.

I slipped my hand into David's, squeezing his fingers just enough to let him know I cared. I led him up the stairs to our perfect bed in our perfect bedroom in our perfect home. I helped him with his suit, with his tie and his shoes. I folded back the covers, and I tucked him beneath the sheets. And then I climbed in on my side and folded my arms around him and held him close, pressing against his unyielding back.

Some time in the night, in the darkest hours when the house was settled and silent, he turned to me. He slipped his arms around my waist, and we stayed like that, not moving, not speaking, just waiting for the sun to rise.

# Chapter 13

BY DAWN, SOMETHING had changed.

I'd lost all faith that the inquest could ever protect us. Clearly, they were intent on punishing David for his past wrongs. Try as I might, I couldn't make myself believe they were pursuing Pitt with equal vigor. Not if the Head Clerk had been given enough freedom throughout the proceeding to attack us with his monsters.

Maybe it was lack of sleep. Maybe it was the hangover from witnessing David's abject despair. But as the sun rose, I knew I had to take matters into my own hands. I needed to identify Pitt's mole *now*, root her out and destroy her, before the inquest concluded. If the Court wasn't going to protect me, I had to protect myself.

And that started with Raven and Emma. I'd told myself they had to be innocent. If one of them was conspiring against me, then horrific things would have happened before Mabon. They could have brought down my magicarium by dragging their feet through our first semester, and Norville Pitt would have had his victory without lifting a finger.

But I had to test them. I had to be sure.

I'd run through the math a hundred times—the sisters'

plane had landed at National Airport a few minutes after noon. They'd taken the subway into town. They had to walk eight long blocks to Logan Circle, to Blanton House.

"Relax," David said. "They might have stopped for something to eat." He sounded calm and soothing, nothing like a man who hadn't slept a wink the night before. I understood what he was doing. He couldn't control the inquest, so he was managing everything else.

Even though I knew he was right, I had to turn to Neko. "Did they? Can you sense anything from Kopek or Hani?"

My familiar wouldn't meet my eyes. He might have been my rock the day before, but now he was upset. He didn't approve of the rite I was about to perform. After all, Tony warded Raven.

Before I could force the issue, the doorbell rang, a four-note chime denoting a student. I ran my fingers through my hair and muttered a prayer to Hecate for clear sight. David glided to my side, even as Neko slinked closer to the stairs.

David opened the door to a jumble of conversation. Raven was juggling a Starbucks cup and shoving her cell phone down her bra, reaching for her suitcase and tossing some comment over her shoulder to Tony. Hani was talking to Caleb; they were in serious conversation about baseball winter meetings and trades that were expected to start in the next week. Kopek had his usual hang-dog look as he carried his witch's suitcase. And Emma brought up the rear, outfitted in a peacoat, like some British admiral looking over her domain from the deck of a ship.

Tumbling into the house, they stopped dead when they saw me. Tony flashed a quick glance at Neko before he said warily, "We weren't expecting a welcoming committee."

"Warders," I responded, including Caleb with a jut of my chin. The title made both men stand straighter. Tony's hand ghosted toward his waist, to the place a sword would hang if he'd been decked out in full regalia. "You may wait in the front room. Familiars, too."

I wasn't used to ordering warders and familiars about—not my own and certainly not other witches'. But I'd watched Teresa Alison Sidney conduct a coven meeting, so I knew how the game was played. I hit the necessary tone of command. I was the magistrix of the Jane Madison Academy, and I would not be crossed by anyone.

Of course, all four men checked with their witches before they acceded to my demand. Even then, they walked stiffly, one shade shy of outright rebellion. David followed, sweeping the double doors closed before things could get out of hand. He locked it with a warder's trick. I pretended not to worry as he turned back to me and my astonished students.

"We'll convene downstairs," I said. A mental nudge set Neko to lead the way, down the hall and through the kitchen, around the butler's pantry and down the stairs.

I'd spent the morning preparing for this confrontation. With Neko's reluctant help, I'd erected an altar in the center of the large basement room. We'd relied on wood this time, oak instead of marble, the better to separate this working from the disastrous one that had released the satyr at the farmhouse. I'd decorated it with pertinent symbols—a stylized figurine of Hecate carved out of yew, a palm-sized iron cauldron from the Osgood collection, a thick candle that breathed out the comforting scent of beeswax. A carved rowan box sat on the corner.

But that wasn't all that was on the altar. I'd also included a knot of piñon, the wood fragrant with sticky resin. At my telephoned request, Clara had brought it that morning, handing it over without a hint of her usual dramatics. I'd added one of my favorite wands, a slender length of ash.

The ritual was designed to harken back to Oak Canyon Coven traditions, to my students' home teachings. I'd traced a large pentagram of salt on the floor, centering the figure on my altar. A circle looped around the star, a line of salt that linked up the five tips of the figure, leaving open a single arc, a single passage in and out of the protected space.

"Join me, sisters," I said, and I crossed the room. I waited for David to take up a protective stance. His sword was bared now, flickering with silent promise. He'd argued about this, said Pitt's traitor was too dangerous for me to confront on my own. He's wanted me to bring in Clara and Gran, to have some astral reinforcements.

I'd told him, though, that they were too green to help. Neither my mother nor my grandmother had the power to fight off a monster. I could doom myself trying to rescue one of them.

No, we were better off isolating the potential traitors from the support of their warders, from the bolstering strength of their familiars. Raven and Emma would have only themselves to rely on, while I—the strongest witch in the Eastern Empire—had my familiar and my warder to assist me. And if they were innocent—as I prayed to Hecate they were—they could be my allies when I tested the newer students.

Setting my jaw, I plunged my hand into the rowan box and came up with a fistful of salt. Only after my witches had crossed the edge of my circle did I sprinkle the white grains, closing the gap and sealing us in.

I was breathing hard as Neko took his place beside me. I sensed his mistrust—not of me, per se, but of the action I was taking. Nevertheless, I intoned, "Well met, sisters."

And we *were* met well. Raven had deposited her coffee cup on the stairs, automatically fishing out her cell phone and leaving it behind. We'd come a long way from the testing that had marked our original relationship, her near-constant efforts to undermine me as her magistrix.

It was Emma, though, who answered first. "What's this all about, then? This is quite a bloody welcome home."

Raven settled her hands on her hips. "She thinks one of us summoned the harpy. The satyr and the orthros too. One of us is a traitor." She raised her chin, an action that automatically thrust her bosom toward me. "Or is it both of us you're looking at?"

Adrenaline thundered in my ears as I met her accusing gaze. "I'm testing everyone. You're the first two back from break."

"Jolly good," Emma said.

But Raven wasn't anywhere near as accommodating. "That piñon on the altar is from Oak Canyon. What do you have planned for us?" Well, she always had been attuned to the natural world, to green, growing things. Under any other circumstance, I'd praise her sensitivity, her ability to recognize wood from her original home. Now, I just felt nervous. Because if I'd misunderstood everything that had happened up till now... If I'd misestimated the devotion of my most senior students...

Instead of answering Raven's belligerent question, I stepped up to the altar. Staring directly at my statuette of Hecate, I touched my fingers to my forehead, my throat, and my heart. When I picked up the ash wand, the wood hummed with a residual power, a ripple of activated energy from the last time I'd used it. That frisson of potential was heightened when I palmed the piñon knot. I offered it toward each of the five points of my pentagram, and then I nestled it in the heart of the iron cauldron.

Using the wand to point toward the fragrant wood, I began to chant a spell. My concentrated force grew with each rhyming line.

"*Mother Hecate, wise and strong*
*To yourself I do belong.*
*Keep me safe, all danger bar,*
*Destroy all threats, both near and far.*
*As you shelter me 'neath your veil*
*My love for you will never fail.*"

As I spoke the last word, I pushed my energy through the amplifying ash. As expected, the energy snagged on the potential in the piñon, and the knot burst into flame. I gathered all of its power—heat and light together—and I wove my own native magic through that force, mixing my pure golden light with the orange-yellow glow of the burning pine.

Before Raven or Emma had a chance to react, I flung the mixed energy to the very limits of the protective circle I'd drawn in salt. At the same time, I called on Neko's augmenting power, turning his familiar's magic into a sort of spotlight that caught on every particle of power.

The effect was to encase Raven and Emma in a shimmering force field, layer after layer of tiny particles. The piñon's resin sank into their lungs. It coated their skin, their hair, every fiber of their beings, pulsing in time with their blood.

And because I'd charged the piñon with protecting me, those particles began to vibrate in time with my own magic, echoing my quest and amplifying my concerns. Wrapped in cocoons woven by me, Raven and Emma could not move, could not possibly break free. They were completely at my mercy.

I picked up the statuette of Hecate and folded my fingers around her soft curves. Walking to the eastern-most point of my circle, I traced the symbol for infinity above the salt border. As I closed the second loop, I chanted, "I call thee, watchers of the east, to guide me through the darkness and ensure my safety and the safety of my magicarium." I took three long steps, until I stood at the southern point. There, I traced another sign for infinity and repeated my summons: "I call thee, watchers of the south, to guide me through the darkness and ensure my safety and the safety of my magicarium." I repeated the invocation at the west and the north.

Returning to the altar, I passed the image of Hecate through the last of the smoke rising from the piñon. Clutching the statue with both hands, I chanted:

*"In our midst some evil hides,*
*Reaching out from many sides.*
*Send away the one who lies,*
*Banish them and cut all ties.*
*Keeping close those who mean well*
*Forever more with us they'll dwell."*

I picked up the ash wand and drew on the infinite power of the goddess, proclaiming, "So mote it be!"

When I touched the tip of the wand to Hecate's brow, there was a flash of darkness, a heartbeat of nothingness when the entire world fell away. I had no body. I could not see my students, could not smell the redolent pine in the iron cauldron. I could not hear my own heart pounding or my lungs gasping for breath.

And then I blinked hard, and the darkness fell away. I was a woman, standing in my basement. I was a witch, staring at an altar. I was a magistrix, gazing at my students, who were looking back in calm silence, still on their feet, untouched by Hecate, unharmed by my spell.

Raven and Emma were safe. They were good. They were not the ones who'd brought Pitt into our midst.

David lowered his sword by a handbreadth. Neko stared at me reproachfully, as if he'd always known my first students would pass with flying colors.

"Holy crap," Emma said, her voice flat with Midwestern vowels, her British affectation totally forgotten. "The other witches are going to have a heart attack when you do this to them."

"Especially one," Raven said, not bothering with her usual suggestive defiance. "Because someone is going to end up standing outside the circle."

I couldn't test each of my students the instant they returned from their Thanksgiving holiday. The protection spell I'd worked for Raven and Emma had required a huge amount of energy—more than I'd originally predicted. As soon as I'd wrapped up the working David had forced me into the kitchen, where he'd liberally administered turkey leftovers. Between exhaustion from our sleepless night, post-spell fatigue, and tryptophan, I nearly fell asleep at the kitchen table.

In fact, three days passed before David gave his approval for me to test another student. During the interim I protested, loudly and often, but he insisted that the risk of a traitor in our midst was less than the risk of my burning out my powers. Ordinarily, I would have appealed to Neko to help me out, but he wasn't in the mood to side with me. He was too busy spending time with Tony, making it perfectly clear that *he* had never mistrusted the warder, that *he'd* had nothing to do with the piñon spell in the basement.

It wasn't like David or Neko were the ones who had to change lesson plans. I worked hard to restructure all my magicarium classes. I certainly wasn't going to work on group exercises like the candle-lighting spell, not until I'd finally found out who had betrayed us. Even if I had Raven and Emma solidly in my corner, I didn't trust the three of us to be strong enough against an enemy who had outsmarted us so many times already.

Blanton House was too beautiful to burn to the ground. And I was pretty sure Teresa would hold me to our bargain—demanding David's services, even if the mansion was suddenly wiped off the face of the earth.

And so, I waited until Wednesday before I tested my first new student. We'd spent the day working on building rapport with each other's familiars. No overt spells were involved; instead, we concentrated on constructing communication bridges. I was surprised to find that I automatically changed my approach depending on the familiar I worked with. For Neko, of course, I could rely on the true bond between us; he *knew* my powers and managed always to be precisely where I needed him, astrally speaking.

With Hani, though, I reflexively took a more physical approach, leaning toward the brash man, increasing our physical proximity, even reaching out to touch him when I needed to draw him in. When I worked with Kopek, I unconsciously changed the pitch of my words. He was crestfallen so much of the time that I always felt I had to cheer him up. I manipulated the tone of my voice when I spoke to him, reaching out, bringing him into the circle of my working.

Once I became aware of the differences, I truly focused on them, and I encouraged my students to do the same. Some familiars needed visual stimulation—a hand woven through the air, a foot swinging rhythmically from a high stool. Others concentrated on sound—a hum deep in a witch's chest, a finger tapping against a table. Still others were deeply affected by mood, by the perceived emotions behind every request to communicate.

It was a fascinating discovery, something I longed to delve into in much more detail. But even as I put us through our paces, I constantly had a refrain running through my head: I needed to find the traitor. I needed to mark the witch. She'd rested quiet for three days, how much longer would she be patient? What was she going to destroy next? I needed to find the traitor...

Over and over again, I reviewed my plan. And on Wednesday evening, I dismissed class after a long session in the large basement room, telling everyone to brush up on energy spells for the next day. As my students headed away, I sought out David's eyes. He nodded once, a tight, controlled gesture, and then he looked up the stairs, toward the ground floor of the middle townhouse.

The door opened at the top of those stairs. Caleb and Tony came down, one behind the other. Each was dressed in black. They carried ceremonial swords, gleaming replacements for the one Caleb had broken while battling the orthros, for the one Tony had lost in the harpy's fire. At David's instruction, they moved to block the exits through the basement corridors.

"Alex," I called, even as Raven and Emma fell in by my side. "Could you hold up a minute?"

She stopped in her tracks, immediately wary. Seta, her familiar, dropped back too.

Turning slowly, Alex settled her weight evenly on the balls of her feet. The spikes in her dyed black hair seemed to stiffen as she stared me down, and the overhead light glinted dully off the tight steel hoops strung through the cartilage of her ears. Her charcoal-limned eyes were wary as she said, "Magistrix?"

"I just have a few questions for you," I said, purposely keeping my voice light.

For a moment, I thought she didn't react at all, but then I heard a door slam somewhere above us. Feet pounded on the stairs, missing more than a few. Heavy boots stomped across the floor above us, and someone tugged on the locked door at the top of the stairs.

Garth—because it had to be Alex's warder—didn't waste time pounding on the door or demanding to be allowed entrance. Instead, those same heavy boots clomped overhead again. I wondered if the warders had had the foresight to lock all five of the front doors, and the back ones too. It didn't matter. Eventually Garth would get into one of the other townhouses, and he'd make his way through the basement level to save his witch.

That meant someone—David or Tony or Caleb or Garth himself—would end up hurt if I didn't get a move on. I reached for a silver flask on a nearby table. It contained a tincture of angelica infused in pure rainwater that I'd collected on the night of a full moon. I'd poured the liquid over amber to heighten its protective value, and I'd added particles of my own golden energy when I filled the flask.

"We seek a traitor among us," I said.

"I'm not the one." Alex's eyes flashed fury. Despite the December weather outside, she wore a sleeveless T-shirt, the better to feel the magic, she'd told us just that afternoon. The deep V of the neck only emphasized the tattoos on her arms, the elaborate feathers that glinted blue and green and red.

Those feathers... I could not look at them without thinking of the harpy, of burning quills sweeping against curtains and walls and furniture, destroying so much that I held dear.

Her magic felt like feathers, too, like the hard edge of a quill. I'd known since the night the farmhouse burned that Alex was my first suspect, the student most likely to feel a kinship with that fiery bird-woman.

I raised the flask between us. "Then drink, and prove

your innocence."

But Alex didn't move. Instead, she cocked her head at a sound behind her—running feet, a wordless bellow. Caleb edged forward, slipping his weapon from its scabbard. As Garth tumbled into the basement room, Caleb called out, "Hold, Warder. You may not pass."

"You've got my witch in there!"

"Our magistrix is talking to a student."

"Get out of my way!"

Caleb repeated in a steady tone. "You may not pass."

I eyed Alex, trying to manage my rising tide of urgency. "Drink, before anyone is harmed."

She narrowed her eyes. "Anyone but me, you mean."

"If you aren't a threat, you won't be hurt."

"What's in it?"

I shook my head. "Drink first. If you aren't the one we seek, then I'll share all my knowledge with you."

"Don't do it, Alex!" Garth's growl was threaded with a bass note of command. But my student merely held my gaze. She obviously sent a silent message to Seta, though, because her familiar closed the distance between us. With a petulant snarl, Seta held out her hand. I considered holding fast, requiring Alex to come to me, but Garth's strangled cry convinced me not to stand on ceremony.

"Wait!" the warder hollered. "Let me taste it first!"

"The potion is not for warders," I said.

"Says who?" Garth cried, pushing forward until Caleb's blade lodged against his belly.

"Says your magistrix, man!" David's voice shot across the basement. I could imagine the brutal stare he'd be directing at Garth. I'd been the recipient of his disapproval more times than I cared to remember. I knew how intimidating he could be—and that was without a bared sword to back up his word.

"Drink, Alex," I commanded. "Drink and put an end to this."

She tossed her head like a high-strung racehorse refusing to submit to a bridle. But Seta edged backward, bringing her the flask. Alex unscrewed the silver cap. She brought the container under her nose, breathing cautiously at first, then more deeply as she tried to analyze the contents.

The muscles of her arms rippled as she raised up the silver vial. She must have spent hours pumping iron to get that sort of definition beneath her tattoos; each individual barbule seemed to move under its own power. She lifted the flask above her head, as if she was saluting me, as if she was making an offering to Hecate.

"No!" Garth roared as she lowered the container to her lips and tossed back the entire contents in three hearty swallows. When she was done, she dropped the metal to the floor, where it clattered loudly enough to wake the dead.

Neko was the first of us to break the spell; he leaped forward to keep the silver from rocking back and forth. Alex bared her teeth in a feral smile, turning her palms up to show she was innocent of anything we ever could have suspected. Caleb eased back a step, letting Garth bull past him.

Alex shrugged off her warder's attention. "Magistrix?" she asked, and her voice was the studied cool of a teen in a skateboard park, a kid smoking behind the 7-11 when she was supposed to be in school. "Anything else?"

She wasn't the traitor. My magic wasn't clashing with hers, carried on the arcane energy infused into the angelica, garnered from the amber. The elixir had to be spreading from her belly, into her veins, up to her heart, but she wasn't being bound by Hecate. She was unaffected by the strongest protective potion I'd ever devised.

"No," I said, shaking my head. "I'm sorry. I had to know."

"Of course," Alex said, and she flexed her arms again. The ripple of those feathers let me know she understood why I'd reached out to her, first of all the new students. For a moment, I thought I'd lost her; I thought she'd have no respect for me or my classes ever again. But then she folded her hands into fists. "And if you let me help you, I'll beat the crap out of whoever brought that harpy to us."

I nodded in silent acceptance, a little afraid of what Alex might actually do to the guilty party. "For now, the best help you can provide is to stay quiet. I need you to swear you won't let anyone know they'll be tested. You won't give them a hint of what's coming."

Alex licked her lips, letting her tongue stud click audibly against her teeth. "I don't have any problem with that."

I fished in my pocket, taking out the figure of Hecate I'd used in Raven and Emma's trial. "Do you solemnly swear, Alexandra Warner, that you shall not tell any living creature—witch or warder or familiar or mundane—about the trial you have faced in service of the Jane Madison Academy?"

She placed her right hand on the statue. "I solemnly swear."

I covered her fingers with my own. "And do you bind your warder and your familiar to this self-same oath, so they shall not speak of these events?"

"I do."

I pushed a golden wash of energy through my palm, into hers. She tightened her grip on the carving, bowing her head in reverence. I nodded and stepped away, returning Hecate to my pocket.

Now that the trial was over, I was weak in the knees. Raven and Emma gathered close, talking to Alex, telling her about their own testing. Tony crossed to Garth and leaned close to whisper something, clear instructions for him to forgive and forget if the glare he cast my way meant anything. Caleb ventured forward with an extended hand, ready to put everything behind him. Seta circled around Alex, keeping a jaundiced eye out for anyone else who might challenge her mistress.

I met David's gaze above the crowd. He shrugged, as if to say, *Nothing ventured, nothing gained.*

Before I could cross to him, though, there was a knock on the door at the top of the stairs. Someone tried the doorknob, and the knock turned to a pounding. "Jane?" I recognized Bree's voice. "Jane! We need you upstairs! *Now!*"

# Chapter 14

MY HEART POUNDED as I climbed the stairs to where Bree waited. My fingers still tingled in an aftermath of adrenaline from the confrontation in the basement, and I couldn't quite manage to draw a full breath. Behind me, David was still grappling with Garth, ordering the other warder to stand down, to let it go, to accept that everything was over now.

I fumbled with the lock on the basement door. From the expression on Bree's face, I knew I was in trouble. My sturdy Montana cowgirl looked like she was about to faint—not a comforting thought when I remembered how poised she'd remained in the face of a satyr, an orthros, and a harpy. She licked her lips and refused to meet my eyes. "I'm sorry," she muttered. "I didn't want to interrupt. But... You'd better see for yourself."

I followed her into the foyer to find an awkward young man, complete with smudged glasses, an over-large suit jacket, and a briefcase that looked so new I expected to see a price tag still dangling from its handle.

"May I help you?" I asked.

"Jane Madison?" he responded, and his voice actually broke on my first name.

"Yes." I fought not to laugh out loud as my relief fizzed

through my bloodstream.

"You're served," he said, and he whipped a packet of papers out of his breast pocket, slapping the blue backing against my palm.

I was so startled that I dropped the document on the ground. I gaped as he turned on his heel and helped himself out the front door. I shouted after him, "You can't serve me! I'm not picking that up! Come back here! You! Don't take one more step!"

But he did take one more step, and another and another, until he disappeared around the corner, presumably heading to the subway, because I wasn't certain he was old enough to drive.

I whirled back to Bree. "Why didn't you warn me?"

"He told me I couldn't. He said I had to get you, but that Hecate's Court forbade me to say who was waiting."

Muttering to myself, I bent down and picked up the document. I barely noticed when Bree hurried upstairs. Her bedroom wasn't even in this townhouse. She just wanted to get away from me.

I studied the paper I held in my hand. "Subpoena" proclaimed the light blue cover sheet, in a Ye Olde English font that made it difficult for me to pick out the individual letters. I folded back the top page and read the very formal, very intimidating document beneath.

"In the Matter of Norville J. Pitt," said the heading, along with a case number. "Subpoena to Appear and Testify at a Hearing before Hecate's Court,"

David came up behind me, his body warm against my back. That was just as well, because every cell in my body froze as I read the legalese: "To Jane Madison. You are commanded to appear before Hecate's Court at the time, date, and place set forth below to testify at an inquest before

Hecate's Court. When you arrive, you must remain at the court until the judge or a court officer allows you to leave. You must also bring with you the following documents, electronically stored information, or objects." There followed a long listing of materials: any and all documents relating to the formation, chartering, and operation of the Jane Madison Academy, any and all documents relating to Norville J. Pitt, any and all documents relating to David L. Montrose..."

I looked up at David in shock. "Can they do this?"

"Of course they can."

"But don't I get a lawyer? Someone to get me out of this?"

He looked grim. "There aren't any lawyers. It's an inquest, not a trial. An internal administrative matter."

"But I don't know anything they haven't asked you already! Anything I talk about would be, what, hearsay?"

"Hecate's Court isn't like the mundane legal system. They don't recognize hearsay."

"So, they can ask me about things I don't know anything about?"

"If they want to."

"That's ridiculous. What if I don't show up?"

He shrugged. "You'll be in contempt of court. You can be locked up, and the magicarium can be shut down."

I bit back a moan of protest. "That isn't fair! Can I appeal?"

David shook his head. "Look on the bright side. You don't actually have a lot of documents on hand."

He was right. Any materials I'd owned had burned in the fire. I continued with a steadier tone. "So I just show up, answer a few questions, and get back here to work on what's really important?"

"You show up and answer a *lot* of questions. About Pitt."
He paused. "About me."

This was going to be a nightmare. I scanned back over
the subpoena again. The testimony date was Thursday, December 4. Tomorrow.

"What if I had other plans?"

"You'd cancel them." David sighed and took the subpoena out of my hand. "Try not to worry too much. I'll be
by your side the entire time."

I stared at him. "You can do that? Why couldn't *I* be
with *you* when you testified?"

"Because you were still a potential witness. They didn't
want to skew your testimony. Besides, you're a witch. A
witch can always claim the protection of her warder."

He made the inquest sound easy. A little annoying. Maybe even uncomfortable. But nothing to be dreaded. I appreciated the effort he made for me, even though I remembered
how devastated he'd been upon his return.

Still, if he was pretending, I could too. I forced myself to
smile as I asked, "And what am I supposed to do between
now and then?"

"You have three more students to test," David said. "And
I recommend you move quickly—before the traitor strikes
again."

Skyler was up next. She'd taken up residence in the farthest
townhouse. Unlike the other witches, she'd chosen to share a
room with Siga. It was an old-fashioned arrangement, one
that treated a familiar like an object, almost like a slave. But
there wasn't anything technically wrong with her choice.
And Jeffrey, her warder, only had one room to watch over.

As I paused in front of Skyler's door, Neko pressed close
behind me. His lips curved into a nervous grin that showed

more skeleton than mirth, but he held up an ornately carved box and nodded. David stood a pace behind both of us, with Caleb and Tony farther down the hall.

We'd all made a silent pact to ignore the summons that had ended our last testing. No one had asked why I'd been needed at the door. We were all one big happy magicarium, pretending that nothing bad could ever happen to us.

I didn't want to knock, didn't want to confront another person. Instead, I longed to crawl into my bed, to pull my quilt over my head, shut my eyes, and rock myself to sleep. But a magistrix rarely got what she wanted. I knocked.

Siga was quick to answer. She rested her fleshy fists against her hips, filling the better part of the doorway. This close, her eyes looked too small for her face, an impression heightened by her habit of leaning back as she squinted for a better view. "Yes?" she asked.

"I'm here to speak with Skyler."

Without looking over her shoulder, she grunted, "Jane wants to see you, Skyler."

I resisted the urge to sigh in exasperation. The rooms here in Blanton House might be bigger than the old lodgings in the farmhouse garage, but Skyler had certainly heard every syllable we'd exchanged. She took her time coming to the door, though, leaving me gritting my teeth.

No. I was mistaken. Skyler did not come to the door at all.

Her warder, Jeffrey, took point as Siga stepped to the side. His ice eyes narrowed as his gaze met mine. I'd always thought of Jeffrey as a benevolent older man, sort of like an uncle who gave US bonds as birthday presents and delivered lectures on the value of compound interest.

There was nothing avuncular about Jeffrey now. He wasn't carrying any visible weapon, no sword, no edged blade stashed in a sheath. But like all warders, Jeffrey was trained in more martial arts than I could name. The mere fact that his fingers were flexing set off warning bells deep in my mind.

Those same bells obviously echoed down the hall. David closed the distance between us, shouldering Neko aside. He *did* wear his sword, and he didn't hesitate to let his hand fall meaningfully on the grip. Once he'd made his presence known, he eased back two paces—the better to clear his scabbard, if necessary.

I resisted the urge to wipe my palms against my thighs.

"Magistrix," Jeffrey said, as if no one had moved in the hallway. He inclined his head deeply, a semblance of perfect respect. He used the motion, though, turning his head to the side just enough to take stock of Caleb and Tony in the shadows. A blue vein in his temple began to pulse.

"Warder," I answered, lapsing into formality to match his age and tone. "We seek colloquy with the witch who calls herself Skyler Winthrop."

As soon as the words were out of my mouth, I regretted them. My stilted phrasing automatically sounded like an accusation. If I was challenging Skyler's very name, questioning whether she worked under an alias, I immediately sounded critical and cynical and suspicious.

Well, too late now. I'd just have to see if I could get this dance back on the right footing. And if I was right to sound mistrustful? If Skyler was my true enemy? Then tone and phrasing would be the least of my concern.

Jeffrey's tone was grave. "My witch is indisposed now, Magistrix. Perhaps if you were to return tomorrow?"

"Your witch is under my care, Warder. If she is ill, I am obligated to assist her."

I kept my words a simple declaration, avoiding too much

syrup, too much innuendo. I could see the counters ticking over in Jeffrey's mind, the re-evaluation of David's distance, a repeated tally of the known and suspected weapons ranged against him. I could not hear any movement behind the door, nothing that told me where Siga was standing, whether Skyler was even *in* the room.

"*Warder*," I said, giving full emphasis to his title. "You are in my house. Your witch is a student in my magicarium. Step aside."

Without a civil option, Jeffrey retreated from the doorway, but only enough to take up a vigilant stance beside Skyler. She stood in the center of the room, giving every impression of being a bored student interrupted in the middle of coursework. She was dressed in an ice-blue kimono, with the sash pulled viciously tight around her hips. Her long dirty-blond hair was piled on top of her head, secured by a single lacquered chopstick. Her feet were bare, and her toenails were coated with a glimmering shade that shifted between beige and crystalline blue. Everything about her looked painted, poised, as if she'd spent days planning for my arrival.

Siga shifted closer as Skyler stepped up, planting her feet and making it clear she was offering her powers to her mistress. I, of course, had no intention of giving that mistress the opportunity to work a dram of magic of her own. Instead, I began my inquisition, relying on the same formula I'd used with Alex.

"We seek a traitor among us," I said.

Skyler didn't waste time with denials or entreaties. Instead, she pulled herself up to her full height. Next to her, I felt lumpy and misshapen, a poor model that the gods might have used while they were designing the perfection that became Skyler. "You'll have better luck elsewhere," she said, with all the cool confidence of an old-time movie actress. I half expected her to whip out a cigarette holder from somewhere, to strike a pose with her chin up and her palm resting on one hip.

"We're searching here," I said. I gestured behind me, signaling Neko to approach. His steps were silent as he glided to my side. His eyes were wide, and I could see he was more than a little captivated by the ice princess in front of us. Nevertheless, he presented the oaken cask I had ordered him to take from the vault.

Jeffrey shouldered in front of Skyler as Neko presented the container. The warder raised his hands, curling his fingers into a defensive position. He looked equally ready to lunge at whatever we produced or to throw it back at us.

I nodded once, and Neko—ever the showman—flipped back the lid on the miniature trunk. I knew exactly what was inside; I could anticipate the reactions from Skyler, from Jeffrey, from Siga, if her flat face registered any emotion at all.

The cask was lined with black velvet, fitted to nestle a bottle. That receptacle was made out of cobalt blue glass, the color so deep it almost seemed black. The vial was about six inches high, rectangular in form, with the corners barely rubbed smooth. It was stoppered with a silver-topped cork.

As I lifted the bottle out of its velvet nest, I could feel the vibration of its contents. I'd made the elixir the week before, as soon as I'd decided to go forward with testing my students. It would have been stronger if I'd brewed it on the night of a full moon, but I hadn't been able to wait. Instead, I'd selected my clearest emerald, setting the stone in the bottom of a silver bowl. I'd poured water collected at a running stream over the crystal and left it to soak up what moonlight there was for seven long hours. I'd decanted the charged water into my glass bottle, topping off the magical infusion with a few stiff belts of Ketel One.

While a look of curiosity crossed Skyler's haughty face, Jeffrey seemed far more suspicious. "What is it?" he asked.

"A simple emerald elixir," I said evenly.

"For honesty?" Skyler choked out a scornful laugh.

"For honesty," I agreed. "For protection against lies." Emerald was a stone of great vision, of intuition.

Now, I plucked the vial from its velvet bed, and Neko hastened to stow away the oaken box. In its place, he produced a silver tasting cup, a simple bowl of hammered metal that shone from a recent polishing. When I nodded, he secured a matching flask from his pocket. He poured a decent measure into the cup.

"Pure rainwater," I said, and then I raised the cobalt glass bottle. "With three drops of the elixir."

"I won't drink," Skyler said.

"Then you'll leave the magicarium," I countered. Even though I kept my words even, my pulse quickened. What secret was Skyler hiding?

"Siga," Skyler ordered, not bothering to glance at her familiar. "Start packing my things."

"Siga," I interrupted. "Take one step away from your witch, and I'll turn you back into a statue."

I wasn't certain I could do that. I knew the technicalities, of course. I'd read them years ago in *On Awakyning and Bynding a Familiarus*. I understood the process of chanting the awakening spell backwards, of gathering a familiar's psychic energy and enclosing it in a confined space.

But I also knew that physical contact was necessary, direct touch for every word of the spell. And I was virtually certain Jeffrey would intervene before I could set a fingertip on Skyler's familiar. Jeffrey would intervene, and David would step up. Caleb and Tony would pour into the room, and I'd be a lot worse off than I was now, merely facing down a rebellious student.

I directed my next words to Skyler. "Go, if you must. But if you walk out of this house, know that my first call will be to the Boston Coven Mother. I'll tell her everything that's happened here, every spell this magicarium has worked. I'll let her know precisely what that satyr did, and the orthros, and the harpy. I'll tell her you refused to be questioned, and I'll let her draw her own conclusions."

I wasn't bluffing, not precisely. I *could* call the Boston Coven Mother, once I completed a bit of preliminary research and found out who she was. And she might even take my call. She might be scandalized by the behavior of one of her witches, of a scion in a family as old as the United States of America.

There was always the chance, though, that the Boston Coven Mother would laugh in my face. She might choose her Back Bay connections over any tales I brought to her doorstep. She might side with Skyler.

From the look on Skyler's face, though, I'd selected the right goad. Caught between the emerald elixir and being shamed in front of her Coven Mother, Skyler chose the magical drink.

She thrust her hand toward Neko, a rude command that he pass her the silver cup. He raised his eyebrows, clearly contemplating a sarcastic retort, but he was better trained than that. Instead, he kept his silence, watching intently as I added three drops from the dark glass bottle.

To the mundane eye, there was nothing special about those drops. They were as clear as the rainwater in the cup Skyler now held. The vodka couldn't be smelled.

But any witch with a modicum of training could sense the

energy dripped into that vessel. The emerald set up a strong vibration; I could feel it in my breastbone, in my heart. There was a purity there, a oneness, as if all the green of the natural world had been brought together and condensed into a single stone.

For all the calm dispassion on Skyler's face, she might have been holding a glass of mediocre Chardonnay. Jeffrey was more transparent. I saw the influence of the stone on his face, the softening, just a little, of the rugged line of his jaw. I watched the mere presence of the elixir relax his shoulders. What did he know that I didn't know?

Skyler's eyes were glaciers as she raised the cup to her lips. She paused a full minute, eyeing me over the rim. I felt Neko tighten in apprehension; I sensed David's growing alarm as she posed in the center of the room. Caleb and Tony had to be wondering out in the hall; they had to be concerned at the long silence, the perfect stillness.

And then she drank.

Three bobs of her throat, so smooth they seemed like satin flowing over her neck. Skyler drained the cup easily, flicking the tip of her tongue against her lips when she was through.

I waited for the intense harmony of the emerald's vibration to shift. I'd feel it as a tug on my heart if the stone was forced to battle Skyler's innate self. The elixir would burn like fire if it were consumed by a liar.

But nothing happened. Nothing at all. I took a deep breath, and the resonance of the elixir began to fade from my chest, exactly the way it would if the drink had been consumed in an ordinary magical working by ordinary honest witches.

"Magistrix." Skyler set my title between us, both an acknowledgment of the power I'd wielded over her and a challenge for me to take the next step.

"Thank you," I said, holding out my hand for her to return the tasting cup. "I'm sorry we had to do that, but you know the threat this magicarium faces."

She gave back the cup, but her gaze remained opaque. I saw no concession that my test had been necessary, no agreement that we faced a common enemy.

Suddenly, I was exhausted. I wanted nothing more than to crawl into the great king-size bed in the bedroom I shared with David. He could take care of me the way he had when I was first finding my way through my powers. He could slip off my shoes, ease a blanket over my shoulders, lie next to me until I drifted off into a healing, dreamless sleep.

But I didn't have that luxury. I was still the magistrix.

"Very well," I said, as if Skyler had agreed that the test was necessary. "There's one last matter—a vow from all three of you. Swear you will not speak of this meeting to any other students."

"I will not swear." Skyler's words were stones.

"It's necessary," I said. "I still have two students left to test, and they must not be alerted to what I'm doing."

"No."

"I'm not saying you'd betray us intentionally. All it would take is a glance, a wayward thought from Siga to one of the other familiars. Swear and bind her. Bind yourself."

Skyler's voice collected all the shards of ice at the North Pole. "I will never act at your command again, Magistrix. And that is the last time I call you by that title, because I'm leaving."

*You can't leave!*

I almost shouted the words aloud. She was my student. I'd *chosen* her. I'd felt her mental powers, the freezing touch of her workings, a perfect match to the cobalt energy of her magical abilities. She'd been tested. She was safe, an ally. She couldn't walk away now.

But she could. Every student was always free to leave a magicarium. Just as any witch could walk away from a coven. I'd done as much, and I couldn't require more from my student.

David found words before I could. "We'll watch you then. Until you step past the wards of this house."

Jeffrey nodded. I could not read his expression, whether he was pleased to leave Blanton House, or if he'd rather stay. Perhaps he though his mistress was being willful. Or maybe he believed she was well within her rights for leaving. In the end, it didn't matter. He was sworn to her, and he would do whatever she required.

Skyler barely glanced at her familiar. "You heard me," she said. "Start packing, Siga." The command was all the more dismissive because it was sheathed in ice. "I want to be out of here by midnight."

With that command, there was nothing left to say. David hastily cast wards about the room, cutting off the possibility of Skyler working magic to reach my remaining students. Tony was summarily delegated to keep watch while Siga packed. He took up a post just inside the door, his hand on the grip of his sword. His task was to make sure Skyler did not resort to more mundane methods of communication—phoning my other students, texting them, sending an email.

I headed out of the room, trying not to flinch before Jeffrey's glare. My search for the traitor had just cost the magicarium a skilled, if prickly, student. I'd destroyed any hope I had of building bridges with the Boston Coven, the oldest and most respected group of witches in the country. I'd uprooted whatever balance my students might have been learning, whatever comfort they'd taken in the communal work we'd begun to perform.

And I still had two students left to test. I still had a traitor loose in Blanton House.

# Chapter 15

EVEN WITH THE clock ticking on Skyler's silence, David insisted that I eat *something* before my next working. It was faster to give in than to protest. As night fell outside, I stood at the kitchen counter and bolted down a chicken sandwich, accompanying it with a cold glass of milk. Neko sneaked slices of meat from the cutting board.

I had two students left to confront. I actually only had to test one of them. If the witch I chose had betrayed me, then I could take the necessary steps to protect the magicarium. But if the next trial yielded nothing, then the last student was my enemy.

So who should it be? Bree or Cassie?

Bree was the stronger witch. Her sturdy russet power felt like sun-warmed granite in my mind; she was closely attuned to the element of Earth. Earth connoted stony ruins, the Greek sites that were the ancestral home of satyrs, of the orthros and the harpy.

Cassie presented an easier target for my testing. Her pale green magic manifested as fog, diffuse and hard to manage. Even if she hid the strength to summon monsters, it would take her precious seconds to coalesce her power, to wield it against me. Moreover, her warder, Zach, still had his arm

immobilized in a cast. It should be easier for David and
Caleb to manage a still-healing Zach than the able-bodied
Luke.

All logic pointed to Cassie as my next subject.

But Cassie had already been a victim. She'd nearly been
raped on our Samhain altar. The orthros had targeted her
too. No sane witch would have voluntarily placed herself in
such danger, much less cause physical harm to her sworn
warder. It felt too much like kicking a puppy to subject Cassie to the full force of my interrogation.

I took a determined breath. Bree, then. I'd test Bree next.

"All right," I said, planting my glass on the counter. "It's
time."

Caleb waited for us in the basement. We all made our
way to the fourth townhouse, where Bree had taken a room
on the top floor. She'd joked about it matching the altitude
of her favorite Montana mountains. Luke had obligingly
taken up residence across the hall, sharing the space with
Perd. I'd heard them call it the bunkhouse.

But we didn't need to climb all the way to the third floor.

"Looking for me?" Bree called as David passed the
ground floor parlor. I steeled myself and stepped forward.

She stood in the center of the room, dressed in her typi-
cal uniform of well-worn jeans and a man's flannel shirt.
Luke and Perd ranged behind her, flanking the fireplace.
Both men had their hands visible at their sides, an ostenta-
tious display of presumed innocence.

David gestured with his right hand. He put the motion to
double duty, waving Neko and me into the room as he swept
his sword from its scabbard. I didn't bother to note Caleb's
defensive position behind me. This late in the game, I trusted him to have my back. Literally.

"Bree," I said evenly. "I didn't expect to find you downstairs."

She crooked her lips in a wry smile. "I figured my bedroom would get a little crowded."

"How did you know I'd be coming?"

Bree laughed, a throaty sound of unabashed amusement. "You're mucking out the barn. Tracking down the witch who's raising those monsters. I reckon you talked to Raven and Emma first thing. They haven't said a word outside of class since we all got back. You did something with Alex today, before that kid arrived with the summons. And Skyler after that. You're almost out of time, with the inquest starting tomorrow, and you won't want to stress Cass for no good reason." She shrugged. "So here I am."

I liked her. I liked her directness, her honesty. I prayed to Hecate it *was* honesty and not the shrewd calculation of a spider luring a fly into the center of its web.

Bree shrugged, a motion that emphasized her empty, non-threatening hands. Maybe she was being *too* open, too free. I'd been debating whether to test her with spell or potion or elixir. As my heartbeat thudded in my ears, I decided to go with all three. All three avenues of magic exploration, backed by my familiar, by the two warders around me. I had no room for error.

"How do you want to do this?" Bree asked, before I could summon Neko to present the potion and elixir. "It's easiest if I just open my powers completely, right?"

With that, she sank to her knees. She moved with a rancher's ease, smooth enough to calm an edgy half-ton of horseflesh. At the same time that she knelt, her warder and familiar hit the ground. All three looked at me with utter complacency, holding their hands by their sides in absolute, earnest submission.

But that wasn't all. Bree opened her mind to me.

We'd already worked together. I knew the feel of her magic, its rich brown light, as if the most fertile earth in the world glowed from within. But this was more than weaving a spell, more than meshing our arcane forces into a single stream.

Bree let her consciousness expand between us, filling the astral space around her. Her awareness floated like dust in a sunbeam, each particle charged with her unique feel, with the warmth of sun-lit stone rubbed smooth by a lifetime of wind and rain.

If this was a trap, I could not see how she intended to spring it. She was completely vulnerable to me. If I chose, I could sweep her powers away entirely, obliterate her magical consciousness with a single swipe. Her astral awareness could be dispersed so thoroughly that it would take a lifetime, a hundred lifetimes to coalesce into anything resembling a modern witch's powers.

"Magistrix," Bree said, and there was a hint of strain in her voice, a whisper beneath the confidence that told me what her vulnerability cost.

I glanced at Luke. The warder's full attention was daggered to his witch. He was not watching to see what I would do, how David or Caleb would react. He was monitoring Bree's exposure, measuring the slow drift of her energy. He visibly fought his own impulse to stop her, to rein her in. His fingers curled into fists, only to open reluctantly, as if he remembered strict instructions. He ground his teeth, but he made no other movement.

Perd was equally restrained. The familiar tossed his head once, his only visible sign of distress. I flicked a snake of power toward him, testing his awareness, and I found that his magical energy, his capacity to reflect and expand his witch's abilities, was flayed open as thoroughly as Bree's.

Neko whined deep in his throat. He saw what was happening, and the strangeness frightened him.

Tentatively, I flexed my energy back to Bree. I concentrated on shaping my powers, on molding them into a single golden wand. I dipped the very edge of my awareness into the disparate sea of Bree's consciousness.

I was surrounded by her thoughts.

There—her decision to wait for us in the parlor, to confront us head-on instead of skulking like a villain. There—her realization that I could likely best her with spells and tools, that I could bind her to my will. There—her longing to resolve this matter once and for all, to muck out the barn, as she'd said.

She was tired of reeking suspicion, sick of throat-closing fear. She wanted the malefactor exposed so we could all get back to the reason she'd left her beloved mountain home. She longed to return to the business of witchcraft—free of monsters, free of traitors, free of the politics of the magical world around us.

All of it was there, displayed before me like supplies in a tack room. Thoughts hung on hooks, seemingly haphazard until I grew close enough to study them. Then I could see there was an order for everything, a *reason*. I could follow them logically, stepping deeper into the space of Bree's mind, traveling without limitation into the storage room of her astral self.

Now that I understood what I saw, I made short work of my investigation. There were her memories of everything she'd done at the magicarium. I slipped past her arrival at Blanton House, her setting up her new quarters to her liking. I saw her in the living room at the farmhouse, staring at the candle, struggling to find the balance with her fellow students, the power to work together to light the column of wax.

She'd been just as surprised by the harpy as I had been. She hadn't opened any door for the creature, had not worked a spell.

I skipped further back in time. It only took a moment to narrow in on our visit to the beach, to find the emergence of the orthros. Again, Bree had been astonished, taken completely unaware. I checked on our first working, on the satyr, confirming her innocence there as well.

I was deep in her mind, then, close to her magical core. I could reach out to private emotions, to her past with the Butte Coven, to any other aspect of her magical life.

But that would be unfair. That would be an abuse of my power—as a witch, as a magistrix.

I slipped out of Bree's memories. I stepped away from the diffuse edge of her consciousness, the warm, earthy feel of her powers, still welcoming me, still inviting me to do whatever I needed to do. "Thank you," I whispered.

Bree waited a moment, as if to see if I had any further demands. Then, she rocked back on her heels. The physical motion acted as a cue to her mental powers, gathering in her astral awareness like cows returning to a milking barn. Even as she swayed, Luke abandoned his humble pose and closed the distance between them, settling a calloused hand on the well-worn flannel between her shoulder blades.

Perd offered his own support, throwing off his own bridle. Rising to his feet, he came to stand beside Bree, letting her lean against his knees.

She took a single deep breath before she looked back at me. "Well," she said. "I suspect that was faster than whatever you had in mind."

I nodded, grateful for her common sense practicality.

But I was heartsick, too. Because now knew the truth:

Cassie was the traitor.

And if Bree had been clever enough to realize I was testing my students, Cassie would be just as aware. I needed to get her *now.*

"David," I said, turning to enlist his help. As I moved, I relaxed the tight grip I'd held on my powers, dissipating my golden wand. A few stray drops of power drifted away, merging with the faint residue of Bree's own display. The energy caught in an odd eddy, dragging *away* from us witches, toward the corner of the parlor.

In my mind's eye, it looked like water swirling down a drain, a miniature whirlwind spinning to the right. But that wasn't *water* draining out of the room. It was power. *My* power.

Someone had tapped into Blanton House and was stealing the remnants of my magic.

# Chapter 16

I LEAPED FORWARD, zeroing in on the disturbance before it could disappear. Even as I moved, the whirling power sank into nothingness. The drain had done its job.

At first glance, there was nothing to see in the corner. There certainly wasn't any physical sign of a vortex—no gaping hole, no break in the hardwood floor or the careful molding.

As I collected my senses, ready to reach out on the astral plane, David held up a commanding hand. He extended his warder's powers to cordon off the area, setting it behind the magical equivalent of yellow "crime scene" tape.

Luke joined him, muttering a curse under his breath. I glanced at Caleb, expecting him to step up as well, but Emma's warder pointedly hung back. He was guarding against anyone attacking us from behind. He was keeping an eye out for Cassie, for whatever havoc she might wreak while we investigated the anomaly in the corner.

"What the hell is it?" Bree asked, craning her neck to look around Luke's broad shoulders.

I eased a tentative mental probe past the warders' blockade. "I can sense Teresa Alison Sidney. But it's not really her…"

I trailed off, because I couldn't put my sensations into words. I *could* sense Teresa. But her signature was mixed with something else, blended into something completely different.

That combined energy had a kernel at its heart, a hard nugget of power. But there were streamers too, trailing strands of magic that siphoned toward the center, funneling into the core. The vortex was like...a sea anemone, waving fronds until an unwary fish ventured into its clutch.

That image chimed deep inside my mind, echoing another thought, a memory. The magical drain was like...

Clara's NWTA. Her Nucleus With Tentacles Attached.

The power-stealing vortex was a physical manifestation of the model Clara had been harping on from the moment she'd arrived at my school. "David," I said. "We need Clara. Now."

I don't know if he understood the course of my thoughts, if he actually knew why I wanted my mother. But he didn't hesitate to act. Taking a step back from his fellow warders, he slid his sword home with precision. After a single nod to Caleb and a slightly delayed glance at Luke, David crossed his arms over his chest. He lowered his chin, and he disappeared.

David's warder magic left behind a wispy steel-grey fog, a faint spray of masculine energy that sparkled in the air. As I watched, those tiny filings began a slow dance, wrapping into a loose spiral. They flowed toward the corner, toward the vortex, spinning faster and faster until they drained out of sight.

"It's like that urban legend," Bree said.

"Which one?"

"The guys who stole a million dollars from a bank. They wrote a program to skim off the partial cents from rounding transactions. They made a million bucks without taking a whole penny from anyone."

My magicarium would generate massive amounts of remnant energy when we functioned at full speed. We'd work hundreds of spells every day, as individuals, as groups. Each attempt would shed droplets of power, arcane fuel to be vacuumed up by the maw in the corner. Whoever had planted the device could be the magical equivalent of a millionaire in no time.

As I stared in horror, the air in front of me flickered and David's outline solidified into his body. Not just *his* body—his hands were planted firmly on Clara's shoulders.

"Jeanette!" she exclaimed. "What's going on? David said you need me."

I nodded grimly and extended a finger toward the corner where the steely remains from David's reappearance were swirling into nothingness. Now that I knew where to look, I couldn't imagine not seeing the vortex before, not being aware of it every single moment I'd spent in Blanton House.

But for everyday magic, I never worried about the drop or two of magic left over at the end. There was always *some* dusting of power left behind, part of the ordinary cost of a working.

And I certainly didn't keep my eyes open for magical signatures, for the unique appearance of anyone's magic. No witch did. Signatures didn't matter in standard witchcraft. Signatures hadn't mattered until I developed my own brand of communal magic.

To Clara's credit, she didn't waste time chatting. Instead, she pushed up the sleeves of her chartreuse and neon pink caftan. She rolled her head once clockwise, once counter-clockwise. And she extended her senses toward the device.

I watched the emerald glow of her astral energy as she

lobbed a gout of power toward the thing in the corner. She shuddered as her energy came in contact with the vortex's outer strands.

David's hand lashed out, ready to pull her back, but she shook off his attention. Catching the tip of her tongue between her teeth, she edged forward. I watched her pour out more of her power, purposely *feeding* the funnel.

I extended my own powers to taste the anomaly, to study how it worked. Growing fat with energy, the magical streamers reached farther into the room, centering on Clara. A pair of tentative strands stretched longer, thinner still, drifting toward my relatively minimal contribution of power.

With a terse nod, Clara reeled in her emerald stream. The tendrils responded, drawing back to their own center. Once again, I watched the device swirl away, chewing up the last fragments of energy left behind by Clara's exploration. My own debris followed, spinning into nothingness.

Clara stepped back and dusted off her palms. "Well she finally built it."

"Who's *she?*"

"Maria Hernandez," Clara said, as if she were stating the obvious.

"Who?"

"The Oak Canyon Coven Mother."

I shook my head. "What did she build?"

"A NWTA," Clara said.

As in so many conversations with my mother, I felt as if I'd entered somewhere in the middle. I tried to ease back a couple of steps. "I thought a NWTA was a living arrangement."

"It is," Clara agreed. "But it's intended to mirror a magical system. A way for sisters to share energy, to provide power to witches with limited resources."

"But how did Oak Canyon get involved?"

"I'm not sure. But it's not just Maria I sense there. Teresa Alison Sidney had something to do with this as well. And half a dozen others. It must take a lot of power to make these."

"*These?*" I seized on the plural.

"This one is part of a network. Can't you feel it?" Clara stepped back to peer at the ceiling. "There's one in the room above here." One of the empty bedrooms. "And a third directly above that."

Bree made a strangled noise. The third drain was in her own room.

Clara spread her hands in front of her. "There are dozens more, all through the house. Can't you feel them?"

I edged a finger of awareness into the empty room upstairs. Now that I knew what to look for, I *could* make out the presence of a drain. I started to extend my search, but that action generated a handful of sparks for the funnel in this room. I snapped off my power immediately, unwilling to feed my enemies.

Bree, though, purposely extended her hands over the device. With a steady determination, she sifted her magic over the thing, sprinkling awareness like a gardener passing dirt through a sieve. After a long moment, she pulled back, letting the rich brown remnants of her search spin into nothingness.

She shook her head. "I can feel the energy of the witches who made it. But my Coven Mother isn't there. Butte Coven isn't involved."

I turned to David. "These must have been placed here after we found the bugs."

He nodded. "Your Display Word would have shown them."

I finally understood why Teresa had bothered planting her obvious bugs in Blanton House. She'd counted on David and me growing over-confident after we found those devices. All the time her real goal had been planting the vortexes. And we'd waltzed into her trap.

"Then someone set these after we moved in…" I trailed off, because the answer was too obvious. Too terrifying. There was only one witch whose loyalty hadn't yet been tested.

"Cassie," David said.

Cassie had brought the NWTAs into Blanton House. She wasn't just working for Pitt, releasing monsters in our rituals. She was working for the Coven Mothers, too.

With a few sharp commands, David deployed the other warders. In seconds, Clara, Bree, and I were surrounded by a protective phalanx. Neko and Perd huddled close.

Like a trained army, we made our way out of the parlor. We took the stairs to the basement, and we marched to the last townhouse that comprised Blanton House. We surged up to the kitchen, into the foyer, up to the bedrooms on the second floor.

With each step, I recognized more facts about my enemy. Of course Cassie had set up residence in the fifth townhouse; it was the farthest from the rooms I shared with David. She could work mostly unobserved at this distance.

I found an energy drain in the basement corner of the fifth building, and another in the parlor. But there was none on the second floor. Cassie hadn't allowed her own power to be harvested.

Her bedroom door was open.

My heart galloped as we approached. I realized I was already picturing Cassie standing in a ray of lamplight, her braids picked out by the golden glow, her freckles highlighted on her pale cheeks. Even with everything I'd learned, I still thought of her as an innocent, as a child playing at being a witch.

"Zach?" she called as a floorboard squeaked. "Is that you?"

"No," I said, even as David led the charge into her room.

She gasped in shock, a strangled sound that was half a scream. Her wide eyes darted from David's sword—once again out of its sheath—to me, to the pair of silent warders who brought up the rear of our entourage. She edged into a corner, putting the upright of her four-poster bed between us.

Licking her lips, she darted her gaze toward the tall-boy dresser on the far wall. I wondered what magical tools she'd stowed there. I could see her fingers twitching to use them.

I stepped forward and raised my hands above my head, pointing at the traitor in our midst. "Cassandra Finch, I hereby summon you in the name of Hecate to answer charges of corruption against the magicarium known as the Jane Madison Academy."

"I—" Her first attempt at a reply was strident, but she immediately softened her tone. Her lips trembled as she said, "I don't know what you're talking about."

I loaded steel into my voice. "You have betrayed your sisters, Cassandra Finch. You have caused physical and emotional pain to the students of the Jane Madison Academy. You have sabotaged our workings. You have destroyed property, and you have threatened the destruction of the unique magical resource that is the Osgood collection."

She was crying now. Her fingers opened and closed in front of her, like a child trying to gather lost toys. "You're wrong, Magistrix. There must be some mistake."

Clara made a soft sound at the back of her throat, her

face softening as Cassie cowered behind the bed. The emotion wasn't lost on Cassie. My erstwhile student pleaded, "Please, Clara. You worked with us while we tried to light the candle. You know me. You know my powers. I would never do anything to hurt the magicarium."

"Address your words to me, Witch." I snapped out the command, as much to remind Clara of what was at stake as to discipline the traitor. "Tell me how you worked with Norville Pitt to destroy your sisters. Tell me how you worked with Teresa Alison Sidney."

"Please," Cassie sobbed. "Clara... Bree..." She turned her attention to the only other witch in the room. "We all worked together. You saw everything that happened. *Zach* was hurt when that...thing attacked us on the beach. *Zach's* arm was broken. *Zach* was injured, not Luke or David, not any of the others."

Bree was made of sterner stuff than Clara. She shook her head and said, "Crocodile tears, Cass." Before the traitor could wail a protest, Bree scuffed her toe against the floor. "Damn. Not even crocodile tears. You're not really crying."

And Bree was right. Cassie's cheeks were dry, no matter how hard her breath caught in her throat. The last shred of my doubt was destroyed. I was prepared to use my magistrix power to its utmost, to place Cassie under bond until Hecate's Court could hear the charges against her. I stiffened my wrists, the better to cascade my power as a net, as golden bonds to restrain Cassie until David's more mundane tools could complete the job. I took a single step back, to keep the angle right, to focus my power. I filled my lungs.

And a flash of darkness filled the corner.

My mind understood what was happening before my eyes could translate the scene. Cassie's words had not been idle; she had not merely been pleading her case. Each repetition of Zach's name had been a summons, a cry of witch to warder.

He'd used his own magical powers to travel into the room from across the hall, or wherever he'd been in Blanton House. He had his good arm wrapped around Tupa's neck, dragging the familiar even as he materialized next to Cassie. Tupa bleated in surprise when he saw everyone arrayed against his mistress; he reached out his tiny hands to offer aid to his witch.

Cassie grabbed onto those fingers, clutching them like a woman drowning in a well. Zach shifted his weight, pulling his casted arm around to offer some semblance of protection. He pulled witch and familiar closer to his chest, and then he nodded his head, triggering his warder's magic.

All three blinked out of existence.

David roared in frustration, leaping into the corner. Luke followed on his heels, immediately kneeling and spreading his palms to the floor. Caleb circled behind us witches, edgy and dangerous, even though no direct threat remained.

Luke started a steady stream of curses, each phrase more colorful than the last as he expanded the circle of his awareness. He ended with a speculation on Zach's heritage, a hell of a lot more exotic than the Greek monsters Cassie had summoned into our midst. Bree finally stepped forward, gentling her warder with a firm hand on his shoulder.

Heartsick, I led everyone downstairs. We crossed through the basement to the first townhouse, and we gathered in the parlor, collapsing onto the formal couches and chairs. Before I could figure out what to say, Tony strode into the room, his lips set in a grim line. "They're gone."

Skyler. He meant Skyler and Siga and Jeffrey had departed.

I closed my eyes as David filled him in on all that had

happened. Somewhere along the way, Alex and Garth came in. Neko must have reached out to Seta, summoning the group. Emma and Raven arrived too, their familiars in tow.

It didn't matter that they missed the beginning of the story. They heard the end. They knew Cassie had betrayed us. That she was gone. Safe beyond our reach.

Raven recovered first. "So? What do we do now?" she asked.

Before I could fashion an answer, the tall case clock began its slow toll of midnight. At the same time, chimes sounded in the foyer—the doorbell, in a five-note pattern. Someone who didn't belong inside the magicarium. Someone who David hadn't cleared as a friend.

Sick with dread, I followed my warder into the hall. No good guest arrived this late at night. As the entire magicarium gathered behind us, David raised his bare sword and nodded for Neko to open the door.

Ethan Beck stood on the doorstep. Teresa Alison Sidney's warder was immaculate in a navy pinstripe suit. A heavy sword hung low on his hips, suspended from a well-worn leather belt that somehow contrived to look normal. If Ethan was surprised by his armed reception, he gave no sign. Instead, he directed his gaze to David.

"David Montrose," he said. "By your bonds as a warder of Hecate, I summon you to fulfill your oath. Teresa Alison Sidney requires your attendance."

# Chapter 17

"NO!" I CRIED, clutching David's arm. "You can't go now!"

David's fingers were firm on mine. "I have no choice."

I turned to Ethan, already knowing my pleas were futile. "Let me talk to Teresa. Let me explain."

He didn't even bother to shake his head. "Your warder is bound, Magistrix." Of course he granted me my title. He was reminding me that Teresa had made possible the very continuation of the Jane Madison Academy. David had seen to that when he'd struck his obscene bargain.

One day—that was the deal David had brokered. Twenty-four hours.

We needed to track down Cassie. We needed to fight Teresa and Maria Hernandez, all the other Coven Mothers who had planted the NWTAs. I needed to testify before the inquest.

"All will be well," he'd said before he knelt in front of Teresa, his back to the harpy-spawned flames.

He'd lied.

Now David said to Ethan, "Let me change clothes, and we can be on our way."

"That won't be necessary."

Of course it wasn't necessary. Ethan was dressed as if

he'd stepped off the runway in Milan. David looked like he'd been cleaning gutters—he wore faded jeans and a black T-shirt, the better for handling his sword in close quarters. The contrast worked to Ethan's undisputed advantage. Without a visible sign of resignation, David reached for the buckle on his sword belt, ready to leave it behind.

"You can keep your weapon," Ethan said.

David froze. I looked from his startled face to Ethan's. All of us—the man on my porch and every last person crowding into the foyer behind me—knew Teresa Alison Sidney had been stealing power from my magicarium. She was our sworn enemy, had been from the moment I'd refused to join her prestigious coven.

It made no sense that David would be allowed to keep his weapon.

Ethan measured out his silence like a professional actor. When our tension was high enough to warp the very air we tried to breathe, he said, "Your sword will be bonded, of course."

David missed a full beat before he choked out, "Of course."

"If I may?" Ethan asked, gesturing toward the threshold.

David worked his hand in a complicated pattern, calling back the wards that shut off access to our home. As the energy shifted, I turned to Tony, the closest ally at hand. "What's he doing?" I hissed. "What is 'bonding?'"

Tony's face was grim. "David's weapon will be tied to Ethan's. David will lose free will to draw or to mount any attack Ethan doesn't permit. Any defense, either." I gathered my breath to protest, but Tony's fingers closed over my arm. "He's done it before," he said, the words so soft I barely heard them through my rage. "We all have. It's how boys are trained."

Ethan and David were proceeding as if no one else was present. David knelt on the Turkish kilim, holding his un- sheathed sword before him. Ethan matched the display with his own, standing tall as he settled his blade a scant six inch- es from David's.

Tony's grip tightened on my biceps.

The air shuddered between the weapons. My mind ex- pected to see light there, some manifestation of magic unique to Ethan. There was no light, though, no specially colored glow like a witch would have produced.

Instead, Ethan's power presented as a close-bound sphere of metal spikes, miniature iron caltrops. The jagged bits buzzed with energy, a low and vicious sound that pressed against my eardrums.

Ethan's grip tightened on his sword. He shifted his feet to a wider stance, the better to command the energy he'd gath- ered. At his silent order, a single tight nod of his head, the caltrops leaped to David's weapon, clinging as if it were magnetized. The buzzing rose in volume, vibrating all the air in the room, shaking my bones in their sockets.

David's arms trembled under the assault. The cords in his neck stood out as he labored to hold his own sword steady. I read determination in the planes of his face, but there was furious shame in his eyes, the awareness that he was being treated like child, mastered by an enemy.

I closed my eyes until the buzzing died.

When I opened them, Ethan was crooking one index fin- ger, inviting David to stand. When David had climbed to his feet, Ethan made a fine show of returning his own weapon to his sheath. David's blade followed the identical arc, sweep- ing into its own scabbard with the same secure snick. Ethan tightened his fingers on his grip for just a moment, forcing David to do the same, before he stepped back and rolled his shoulders like a hunting panther.

"Excellent," Ethan said after a silence settled over the foyer like a lead apron in a radiologist's office. "Let's not keep my mistress waiting."

David nodded once, in mute acceptance of the fate he'd brought on himself. Ethan raised a hand to my warder's neck, spreading his fingers wide for a secure grip. David's eyes were burned out coals as he stared straight ahead, not focusing on anything—me, my students, the walls of Blanton House that he'd traded for.

Ethan tightened his clasp on the man I loved and said, "Best of luck at the inquest, Magistrix."

"David!" I cried, but I was too late. Both men had winked out of existence.

Twelve hours later, I sat in a freezing hallway, flanked by two silent figures in pitch-black cloaks, wondering how things had come to this.

After Ethan had disappeared with David, I'd snapped orders to the others. Tony and Caleb were in charge of the search for Cassie. They could use whatever resources the magicarium had to offer. Ignoring my students' stricken gazes, I'd asked Luke to ferry Clara back to Gran's. Then I'd retreated to my bedroom, where I hadn't slept, hadn't even tried to close my eyes.

When the sun rose, Neko had come into my room. He'd laid out my clothes and applied my makeup. He'd shoved a purse in my hand, a tiny black bag that held lipstick and keys and a folded twenty-dollar bill.

As promised, the representatives of Hecate's Court had arrived at Blanton House promptly at eight. They'd transported me through an infinity of nothingness. And I'd spent the past four hours sitting in a corridor that could have been in any government building in any city anywhere in the world: beige floor and beige walls, fluorescent lights and an institutional clock.

The only thing that stood out was the pair of double doors immediately to my left. They were carved out of black poplar, a wood sacred to Hecate. Both doors were completed by polished silver knobs, spheres twice the size of my fist, each embossed with a sacred pentacle.

Another century or three creaked by. My guards were so still, I wondered if they'd been magically replaced by statues.

Just as I was ready to scream my frustration, Court decorum be damned, the doors opened. They swung on silent hinges, angling in like the entrance to a pharaoh's tomb. My hooded escorts sailed forward, taking up positions on either side of the gaping doorway as if I might not understand where I was supposed to walk.

I'd expected a courtroom, with a dais and a judge and a traditional witness box. I'd anticipated tables for lawyers, and seats for jurors, special seating for the members of Hecate's Court themselves. I'd thought there would be rows of benches for spectators.

I couldn't have been more wrong.

The room inside was much dimmer than the hallway. Actual torches flickered from cressets set into the walls. I felt as if I were marching into a dungeon as I entered the chamber.

A half circle of chairs greeted me, tall seats that looked like thrones. There were nine of them, three times three, the number sacred to Hecate.

"Come forward, Witch, and be heard by Hecate's Court," someone intoned.

The voice was ageless, sexless, and I could not tell which of the nine had spoken. I moved toward the semi-circle, trying not to wince as the heels of my shoes echoed on the marble floor. Marble for protection, like the doorstep we'd had at the farmhouse, like the centerstone that had done nothing to deter Pitt's satyr.

I stopped when I got to the perfect circle set in the focal point of the curve of thrones. Even in the flickering light, I knew I stood on a round of amethyst, a stone that had been used for millennia to ward off malevolent witchcraft, to protect against the evil eye.

A column of power rose around me. It acted like a force field, restricting my ability to move. My arms were free, my shoulders and head, but my feet and knees and hips were locked into place. I could not lunge for the Court, even if I'd been inclined to attack them.

One of the guards who had summoned me from Blanton House stepped to my side. He extended his arms, and a jasper collar materialized in his gloved hands. A frisson of energy sparked the exposed skin of my face.

"Set your palms upon the stone, Witch." The voice came from nowhere, from everywhere. I placed my hands on the mottled band, tightening my jaw against the jangled energy that shot through my palms and up my forearms. I stiffened my wrists and forced my fingers to stay on the black-veined stone.

"Repeat after me," intoned the Court member. "I, Jane Madison."

I repeated the words. "Do solemnly swear... Before Hecate and all the Guardians of Nature... That the testimony I shall give... Is the truth, the whole truth, and nothing but the truth... Or may my powers never be restored."

I repeated the last phrase, curling the words into a question because they broke the tradition of mundane courts, the recitation I'd heard a million times in movies and on TV.

Before I completed the word "restored," the collar beneath my palms turned into a swarm of stinging wasps.

It didn't change form, not really. But its malevolent force surged upward, raking over my hands, my arms, my entire body. It burned like an acid bath, and as its power receded, it peeled away every vestige of my supernatural powers. The essence of my magic drained into the stone like water into sand. I was blind and deaf and dumb, not through my mundane senses, but through my astral self.

This was what life had been like before I discovered my magic. This was how I'd lived before I found the Osgood collection, before I awakened Neko and came into my witchy inheritance. I'd forgotten what it was like to live as a mundane, to sense the world around me directly, without the sparkling veil of magic.

The guard settled the jasper torque around my neck, shifting it to weigh heavily on my collarbones. I closed my eyes to steady myself. I tried to think of what David would say if he were here, how he would calm me, how he would remind me that Hecate's Court was part of the natural order of the magical world, that everything happening to me was right and fair and proper.

But I could not hear David's voice. Teresa had him. I faced the Court without my warder, without my lover, without my friend.

"Miss Madison," a voice hissed, and my eyes flew open. I recognized the speaker even before I found him in the room, in the center of the half-circle of chairs.

Norville Pitt.

He had not dressed up for the court. In fact, he looked like the same rumpled bureaucrat he'd seemed to be the first time I met him. He wore wrinkled brown trousers that could have been fished out of a reject bin at Goodwill, and his short-sleeve dress shirt was yellowed under the armpits. Stretched-out suspenders arched over his cracked plastic pocket protector. He'd combed a few strands of hair sideways across his skull, but mostly he was bald. His top teeth worried at his lip, his overbite making him look like a fat Oestera rabbit.

But I wasn't fooled by appearances. Norville Pitt had countless resources at his command. And he was bent on destroying me, on destroying my magicarium—all because he hated David, hated what my warder had done to expose his excesses, his crimes.

I sucked in a deep breath and centered myself enough to say, "Mr. Pitt."

And without preamble, he launched into a series of questions. He fired off each interrogatory like a pistol shot, maneuvering me into one-word answers that I desperately wanted to explain.

Yes. I'd awakened my familiar on the night of the full moon. But I hadn't known the consequences of doing that; I hadn't realized I was breaching arcane tradition. I merely got out "but" before Pitt launched into his next query.

Yes. I'd rejected membership in the Washington Coven. But only after I'd been betrayed by one of its members, spied on and embarrassed and used for my own magical abilities. Another "but" before Pitt bulled past me.

Yes. I'd released an anima into Washington DC, resulting in a magic battle in public space. (But I'd controlled the damage, shielding our working so no ordinary citizens ever learned of the event.)

Yes. My warder was David Montrose who had been rejected by the Washington Coven. (But that had been years before I'd met him, and he'd suffered his own betrayal from those conniving witches.)

Yes. David had planted documents in Norville Pitt's office at the ministry. (But he'd been desperate to show that Pitt was abusing his power, taking bribes and stealing from the witches he'd sworn to protect.)

I gave up trying to slip in explanations. The Court could plainly see what Pitt was doing; they could hear him interrupt me. They clearly had no interest in the complete story, in the full truth. No one reined in Pitt; no one commanded him to stop. And so I answered, giving myself over to the process.

Yes. David had maintained an office on the grounds of the Jane Madison Academy.

Yes. David had ordered Pitt off Academy grounds even though Pitt arrived in his capacity as Head Clerk of Hecate's Court.

Yes. David had allowed his dog to snarl at Pitt.

Every admission twisted my belly. I was betraying David, offering him up like a sacrifice on a smoke-wreathed altar.

"Yes or no, Miss Madison. Did David Montrose steal records from Hecate's Court to build his alleged case against me?"

Those records had been vital to David's discovery that Pitt was extorting witches, that he was taking bribes, usurping money and goods and power that were never meant to be his. Pitt's question was too simple. He was ignoring the true facts, the important ones.

"Miss Madison," Pitt punched out my name. "Did David Montrose steal records from Hecate's Court?"

There wasn't a simple yes or no.

"Miss Madison!"

"If you ask that," I said, "then you have to ask what was in those documents. You have to ask how you took bribes from a dozen different covens. You have to ask how you joined forces with the Washington Coven Mother to destroy my magicarium. We put all the information in the Allen Cask! We presented evidence to this Court! We told the truth and now you're trying to—"

"Witch!"

One of the Court bellowed the single syllable, shattering my desperate reply. My head throbbed. My arms ached. My throat was raw, aching with tears I hadn't shed.

"Witch," the voice reverberated again. "You will answer the question put to you."

"Thank you," Pitt said to my hooded tormentors. Then, with a sickly smile: "Miss Madison, did David Montrose steal records from Hecate's Court?"

I bowed my head, and the jasper collar dug into the flesh at the back of my neck. "Yes," I whispered. The sound was amplified by some magic, made as loud as every question Pitt had shouted at me.

I waited for the next barrage, for the continuing cascade of dirty laundry, but Pitt held his fire. Instead, he settled more firmly on his feet, planting his hands on his hips as he breathed asthmatically through his open mouth. Sweat oozed down his temples, and the half-moons under his arms reeked.

"Honored Court," Pitt said. "At this time, I ask the Court to dismiss all charges against me."

"What?" I shouted, even though I knew I'd receive a bellowing "Witch!" from the Court. I wasn't disappointed.

Pitt merely pivoted on his crepe soles, squeaking as he completed a semi-circle. He stared at each member of the Court as if he could see inside their hoods, as if he knew the precise identity of each person he addressed.

Which, as Head Clerk of the Court, he certainly did.

He spread his hands wide. "The entire case against me

was built on theft. Montrose failed to honor his sacred vows to Hecate. He failed to serve as a faithful warder and an officer of this Court." Pitt looked straight at me and said, "Release me—and end this farce forever."

"You can't do this!" I fought against the amethyst disk, struggling to close the distance between Pitt and me. I didn't care if I didn't have my magic at my disposal. I'd sink my fingers into his fleshy throat and throttle him to death.

"Witch!" thundered the Court. "You have been warned!"

"Ask him what else he did!" I shouted. "Ask him about Cassandra Finch! Ask him how he planted an agent inside my magicarium, how he summoned a satyr to our Samhain working! He sent an orthros to kill us on the beach! That bastard conjured up a harpy to destroy my home and everything I—"

A bolt of power jolted through my body, snapping my jaws closed. It crackled through the top of my skull, burning as it paralyzed me. In a heartbeat, I was wrapped inside a violet cloud. I could not see, could not hear, could not even smell the acrid stench of Pitt's sweat.

Had they done this to David? Was this how the Court had broken him, sent him back to me cowed and meek?

I continued to fight, because I had no other choice. I tried to shout Pitt's crimes, and when I could not make myself heard, I resorted to *thinking* all my accusations, repeating them in order, in painstaking detail. I was determined to catalog every one of Pitt's sins, even if the Court never heard a word.

It might have been an hour before they freed me. It might have been ten. I'd lost all sense of time, of space, all perspective of up and down, of right and wrong. But in the end, the purple fog dissipated as quickly as it had snared me.

All nine members of the Court were standing before their thrones. Pitt was positioned in the precise center of the half-circle. The torches flickered, flared, then settled into a brighter light.

The same anonymous voice that had welcomed me into this farce of a courtroom intoned: "Let it be recorded that Hecate's Court opened this proceeding on the first day of the new year, hearing charges that Head Clerk Norville Pitt did abuse his position of trust. And let it be recorded that Warder David Montrose did steal documents from this Court to lay such claims against Pitt. Three times three times three witnesses did offer testimony about those charges, including Montrose's own witch, Jane Madison. Montrose did not refute those charges. Madison did not refute those charges, nor did she cast off Montrose when she learned the nature of his crimes. Now, therefore, to the glory of Hecate this court holds that Pitt cannot be held guilty when the proof of his crimes is built upon a foundation of stolen documents."

My belly sank through my toes. Pitt chortled, actually clapping his hands together in glee. But the Court wasn't done yet.

"For their roles in perpetuating a sham of justice before this body, Montrose and Madison are hereby cast out from Hecate's Court. No coven shall give them shelter. No magicarium shall offer them enlightenment. No witch or warder shall befriend them, offering counsel or succor, and no familiar shall be bound to their service from this day forward. Any who aid them shall be likewise cast from Hecate's grace, lest the true community of witches be corrupted ever more. So mote it be!"

There was a flash of darkness. The circle, the thrones, Pitt, and the torches—all of it disappeared. I felt the same wrench of *nothing* I associated with warder's magic, with David transporting me from one point to another.

And when I opened my eyes, I stood alone on the steps of Blanton House.

# Chapter 18

ALONE.

I was truly, utterly alone, standing in the darkness of a DC city street. If I entered Blanton House, I would condemn my students to my own sentence. I would sign their magical death warrants, banish them from their covens, bar them from the communities that had nurtured them since they were children. I couldn't even reach out to Neko, lest he be torn from the mysterious network of familiars forever.

My head pounded and my throat ached; my eyes felt like they'd been rolled in sand. I tried to swallow, but the jasper collar had shifted until it was crushing my larynx. I tugged at the stone, scraping it from my neck and tossing it into the bushes behind me.

A swarm of bees attacked my palms. White-hot acid flooded up my arms and down my spine, through my legs to my toes. This was the agony I'd felt in the courtroom, the jagged pain of the jasper draining away my powers.

But no, this attack was different. In its wake, my senses were *restored*. Everything shone more brightly. Every sound echoed in my ears. The cold December night was suddenly awash in fragrance—earth beneath my feet, crumpled leaves in the gutter.

I'd placed my powers on the line in that forsaken court-room, taking an oath to tell the truth. And I *had* told the truth, every bitter word. I'd recited facts that doomed me, that doomed David. I might be cast out from the society of witches forever, but the Court—or Hecate herself—still up-held one tiny corner of its bargain.

My magic was restored.

Eyes brimming, I looked up at the lighted windows of Blanton House. Everyone was gathered in the parlor of the first townhouse—my students, their warders, their familiars. Neko stood beside Tony. Gran and Clara sat next to each other, their own familiars gathered close.

I couldn't hear them, of course, but the entire group was talking earnestly. My heart clenched as I measured each fa-miliar gesture. I knew who would answer whom. I was cer-tain who would look to others for approval, who would press forward without hesitation. I understood the bonds between all of them, the friendships, the trust.

They were my magical family. We were all bound to-gether through the nucleus of the Jane Madison Academy, even as they remained individual people, separate tentacles of workmates, friends, lovers. They were the crazy NWTA Clara had proclaimed weeks before—not the thieving vortex of the Coven Mothers, but the good NWTA, the community that nurtured, that gave, that supported every individual member.

And they were lost to me forever, now that I'd been ex-communicated by the Court.

But no. I wasn't alone, not completely. Because David had been cast out too.

He likely didn't know it yet, still bound in his day's ser-vice to Teresa. But he would learn his fate soon enough.

And I had to be there when he learned just how much his life had changed.

Blindly, I dug in my purse, extracting my keys with numb fingers. Without my giving conscious commands, my feet began to shuffle—down the sidewalk, around the corner, and into the dimly lit alley.

The garage door slid easily on its well-oiled chains but I still cringed, glancing at the rear of the house. I couldn't let my students see me now, couldn't let them talk to me. I had no idea what the Court would consider "counsel or succor." A simple greeting might be enough to doom them forever.

David's Lexus hulked in the shadows. I eased open the driver's door, wincing as the dome light glowed. "If it were done when 'tis done, then 'twere well it were done quickly," I muttered. I imagined Melissa's wry voice quoting *Macbeth*.

Melissa. The Court couldn't steal her human friendship. When tonight was finally over, she would remain my friend.

Heartened a little, I started the car and eased out of the garage.

There was traffic, of course. There was always traffic in the city. But I made good time as I cut across town to the Key Bridge. It was easy enough to pick up the George Washington Parkway, and then I glided through the darkness, pulled forward by the car's powerful headlights. I knew the route, even though I'd never driven there myself.

I left the parkway, following narrower and narrower streets. The houses out here were set on acres; each had its own winding lane that spidered off the main road.

My palms were sweating as I turned into my destination. As always, the wrought-iron gate hung open, made for mundane show instead of magical protection. The driveway stretched beneath the oak trees. The house crowned its ridge, stone and wood seeming to grow organically out of the earth.

I slipped the massive car into Park and tugged the key from the ignition. I made my way toward the house. There was no warder lurking in the shadows, no gleaming sword forbidding me entrance. I felt only a whisper of dissipated power as I stepped across the remnants of an old magical circle, complete with its five-pointed star of protection.

Steeling myself, I took the slate path that led around the outside of the house. I knew the way; I had walked it once before. Teresa had reveled in the power of a new safehold for her coven, a refuge for her sisters to practice their magic. She'd used me to secure that base, to set the magical protections over the centerstone.

The path was exactly as I remembered it, and everything was different. Then, I had recited spells inside my head, jumbling words together in my excitement to offer myself up to the Washington Coven, to give and give and give so I might belong to that group for all the rest of my magical days.

Now, I was here to take.

I paused at the top of the garden, taking in the complete scene before me. The centerstone was set in a clearing at the far edge of the yard, in a circle of winter-dry grass framed by a creek that edged Teresa's property. The estate was secluded enough that no one was likely to stumble on any arcane events, but tall beech trees provided additional protection.

Nine robed figures, witches, stood within a circle of bleached stone, gathered close to a block of marble. Beside each crouched a dark body, a familiar lending strength to whatever working they employed. Squinting, I recognized Connie, Teresa's cowering familiar. It only took me a heartbeat longer to locate Tupa. Cassie's familiar looked lost inside that circle, dazed and alone, even though he was surrounded by others.

An iridescent shimmer capped the gathering, and I knew I'd find a powerful magical cordon in place if I stretched out my powers. Sure enough, eight warders stood watch, two at each cardinal point. One of each pair looked inward, toward the magical working in the circle, and the other looked out, toward any approaching threat. Toward me.

But that was not the only protection for the witches, for there were two more figures, standing in the clearing between the path and the cordon. One was clad in an elegant navy suit, so dark that the fabric would have disappeared in the night, if not for the pinstripes that caught the moonlight. That was Ethan, of course, Teresa's warder at his finest.

The other wore jeans and a T-shirt.

Those clothes weren't enough to keep David warm on this bitter winter night. They offered no protection, no barrier against the sharp breeze that had picked up from the north. I narrowed my eyes, certain Ethan must be playing with the elements, using his warder's magic to drive home his superiority.

He stood ten feet behind David. Both men had their feet planted solidly on the ground. Both held an unsheathed sword by the quillons, a wordless warning as I approached. Nevertheless, I came within a few yards of David before I stopped. I resented the fact that I needed to clear my throat before I could proclaim to David and Ethan both, "Let me pass, for I am Witch Jane Madison."

Witch—that was the only title I had left to me. I could not be magistrix of the Jane Madison Academy, because no sane student would ever commit to studying with me again.

I was staring at David, but I caught Ethan's motion out of the corner of my eye. Teresa's warder shifted his grip on his sword, easing his fingers around to grasp above the hilt.

As he moved, David followed suit, matching each tiny motion, tightening his forefinger, stroking his thumb against the pommel.

The bonded action was obscene.

Ethan moved with the leisurely ease of a grooming cat; he had clearly raised his sword in defense of his witch a thousand times. But David's parroting of the motion was anything but easy. Every tendon in his hand stood out. His knuckles blazed as white as bone. His wrist shuddered with the force of his grasp, as if he were desperate to throw the sword away.

"You may not pass, Witch," Ethan said. His voice was smooth, seasoned with just enough of a gloat that I was certain he understood the single title I had claimed. He knew I'd lost the battle at the inquest. He made sure David knew when he added, "You are outcast, Witch, you and yours. Be gone from our safehold."

"I've come to take back what is mine," I said, braving a step closer. I extended one hand, using more magic than I cared to admit to keep my fingers from shaking. "Come, David. Return to me."

I reinforced the command with a strand of power, a golden rope that I cast around the grip of David's sword. His eyes flared, but in the starlight, I could not tell if he was proud of my daring or if he was warning me away. I pushed energy into our bond, reminding him of all the strength I had at my disposal, of all the magic he had taught me to work.

Ethan's voice cut through the night. "David Montrose is sworn to another, Witch. He is not yours till midnight. For now, he wards the working of Teresa Alison Sidney."

Even though I knew Ethan intended me to do so, I had to look past him to Teresa's circle. All nine witches had pushed back the hoods on their jet-black cloaks. They were joined in a circle around the centerstone, fingertips resting in each other's palms. The cordon cut off sound from their working, but I saw Teresa's lips move, saw her throat work as she chanted something. It didn't take a witch to read the response from her acolytes: "So mote it be."

That was what the Court had taken from me. I would never again feel a surge of magic pass from another witch's fingers into mine. I would never share my powers, never feel the shimmering release as the arcane world became concrete, in glorious reification of Hecate.

A fog coalesced over Teresa's centerstone. The Coven Mother threw back her head, clearly reveling in the power she harvested from her sisters. The cords of her neck tightened, and she chanted more words. Her fingers stiffened, focusing all attention on the centerstone, and the assembled witches answered again: "So mote it be."

The vapor grew thicker, so dense I could not see the witches on the far side of the circle. Teresa raised her arms above her head as she shouted out another incantation. Eight pairs of lips moved in response. Eight witches allowed their own energy to be scraped into the Coven Mother's magic: "So mote it be."

The murk swirled about itself, circling into a vortex.

I recognized that tight spiral. I had seen it for the first time just that afternoon, in a corner of the Blanton House parlor. This was the evil side of Clara's NWTA, the nucleus with tentacles that damaged, that stole. The maws at Blanton had spun clockwise, drawing in power and energy with a positive force. But this one worked widdershins. It was an *unwinding* of magic, an *unworking* that traced an icy finger down my spine, more chilling than any winter wind commanded by Ethan Beck.

As I stared, Teresa bent her wrists, stiffening her fingers until they became iron rods. Energy channeled into the corkscrew on the centerstone, a flow of particles, a golden rivulet that cut through the dull fog generated by the other witches.

Golden power. *My* power. Teresa was feeding the vortex with energy she'd harvested from me.

Gold washed over the vortex, coating every fold, like oil spread over water. The swirling mouth tightened on itself. A bit of darkness appeared at the center, something soft, something shadowed. It spun with the vortex, bobbing against the gold-washed passage as if it were anchored somewhere far away.

Teresa clenched her fingers into two tight fists. The swirling gold drew tighter, more compact. The item in the center spun, froze, broke loose and spun again. I caught my breath.

And a leather sack burst through the vortex.

A leather sack that I recognized at once. A leather sack that was filled with jade runes. A leather sack that I had purchased, not one year earlier, choosing the exact color, the size and shape. A leather sack that had rested in the vault of Blanton House, secure in the basement with all the other supplies I used to teach my student witches.

Teresa Alison Sidney had stolen my runes.

My mind shrieked in protest. Teresa couldn't reach my collection. It was secure in its new vault, locked behind massive plates of steel.

But she hadn't tried to break through the walls of the vault. Instead, she was using sympathetic magic. She'd coated *her* vortex with *my* power.

Like called to like—that was a basic principle of the natural world. The Osgood collection knew my magic. I had handled every item countless times, cataloging them, shelving them, shifting them and shelving them again. I'd touched every single item not ten days before, when we'd settled the collection in its new, safe home.

Teresa had used one vortex to steal my magic. And now she used that pilfered magic and another swirling mouth to steal my goods.

Power pulsed in my fingertips, spiking high as rage drowned every conscious thought in my brain. "No!" I shouted, a verbal cry that ripped the back of my throat, even as I added a psychic scream orders of magnitude louder, stronger, more wracked with anguish.

Automatically, I offered up my thoughts, my voice, my heart. I was still sworn to Hecate; the Court had not broken that bond. I reached out to the goddess herself, to the strength she'd always given me, to the guidance she'd always shared. I stretched for the strongest spell I knew, for a Word of power, one forceful enough to freeze every witch, warder, and familiar within a dozen square miles. I took three steps toward the thieves in the safehold.

And I came up short as a gleaming sword was leveled against my belly.

David's hands shook on the hilt, trembling hard enough I heard his teeth rattle inside his skull. The blade itself was steady, though, utterly still in its deadly force.

That steadiness, that calm told me everything I needed to know. David would *never* raise a blade against me. Ethan controlled the weapon, managing it with the bond he'd imposed upon my warder.

I reached out for David's mind, for the bond we'd shared for five long years. I sent him an image of strength, of power. I bid him use *my* strength to break free from Ethan.

"No, Witch," Teresa's warder said equably. "That one is not yours to command." An iron sheet fell between David's mind and mine, Ethan cutting me off, exploiting his control over David yet again.

I growled in rage as David threw back his head, despair and remorse tightening every muscle in his body. He had brought us to this pass—his pride and his certainty, his determination to gain me Blanton House when my magicarium would have faltered. I lowered my hands to his trembling wrists.

"Release him," Ethan said, with the same casual tone he would use to tell me Mercury was in retrograde. He emphasized the command with a tightening of his right fist. David raised his sword higher. His hands were as hard as oak beneath mine. Ethan glided two steps back, forcing David from my touch.

I snarled at Ethan. "You call yourself a Warder of Hecate, but you raise a blade against a witch?"

"No true witch, you," Ethan said amiably. "Not any longer. Now you stand alone."

I glanced over his shoulder, at Teresa's group inside the cordon. They were leaning close to their vortex, hands raised in identical commanding gestures. A wand, rowan inlaid with ash, slipped out of the whirlpool. Teresa caught it with eager fingers, wasting no time in raising it above her head. She channeled more of my power through the ancient artifact, and the vortex doubled its speed, doubled its size.

My cry of fury had no words. All my years of hatred for Teresa crested to a rolling boil. She'd allowed others to betray me. She'd stolen my labor in setting her cornerstone. She'd paid Norville Pitt to attack my magicarium, and when I'd still gained my charter, she'd used my student to plant her thieving vortexes.

I clutched my powers tight around me, shrouding myself in a cloak of magic. I caught my breath, determined to force my way past David, past Ethan, past the shimmering cordon that protected my enemy. I tensed my muscles and ordered my legs to carry me forward, to ignore the threat of leveled steel.

One step.

Another.

And David's blade sliced deep into my veil of power, sending up a spray of steel-grey sparks.

# Chapter 19

THEY BURNED.

The sparks grew stronger as I leaned into David's sword, the fiery evidence of his warder's magic clashing against my protective shield. Each glint lasted longer than the one before, glaring brighter, carving a deeper channel into my own energy.

I recognized David's magic behind the flares—the familiar logic of his warder's mind, the rigid reason he'd used to guide me in all my witchy studies. This was the power he'd channeled when he'd first taught me spellwork, when he'd shown me how to use wands and runes and crystals. I'd always been aware of his power cast around me, over me, surrounding me to protect me from anyone who meant me ill.

I'd never once considered that his energy might be leveled against me.

I firmed my resolve, taking a tighter grasp on my powers. Beyond Ethan, I could see Teresa and her sisters pulling a book through their vortex. I had no idea which of my treasures they'd claimed—something in brown leather with gold lettering on its spine. As it emerged from the nucleus, it lengthened the tentacles of power even more. It *fed* the vortex that brought it into that circle.

I'd never asked to become a witch. I'd never asked to be in charge of the Osgood collection, to be responsible for those treasures. But they'd called to me from their basement stronghold; they'd beckoned me with their imposing sense of foreboding even before I lived in the garden cottage where they lurked. The collection had been primed with my attention. I'd organized it, learned with it, used it to teach others.

Even if I never spoke with another witch again, I needed to protect the Osgood cache.

Another glance at Teresa, another book pulled through the nucleus. The witches were working faster now, more in sync with each other, taking advantage of the larger, faster-spinning whirlwind in their midst. Every item they plundered super-charged their working. If they reached my massive box of crystals, all hope would be lost.

I had no choice. No matter what happened—if I broke David's sword, if he cut through my protective veil—I needed to try. I needed to fight for all I treasured.

I caught my lower lip between my teeth and stepped forward.

David's blade rose to meet me. This time, the sparks were a river of light, flowing from his sword, sizzling against my raiment. Each glint dug a trench in the protection I'd woven; every wave chewed away at my garb. The light show was matched with a horrific screeching, as if the harpy had returned, as if the foundation of the magical world was being sheared off its axis. My ears ached under the onslaught, my mind juddered, but I had no other option. I forced myself forward another inch.

I'd known David long enough that I could read the words Ethan did not let him say. I understood that his taut lips were ordering me to stop. The strained lines of his throat were commanding me to yield. Green flecks brightened the depths of his mahogany eyes, and I knew he was pleading with me, begging me to give up before Ethan forced him to destroy me.

"I can't," I whispered. "You know I can't."

He closed his eyes; Ethan gave him that much freedom. He even threw his head back. The other warder did not need him looking at me, did not need him concentrating on the sword that was wedged deep in my astral armor. I filled my lungs and tensed my belly, telling myself there was no other way. I could not let Teresa win without taking my last painful step.

My veil flared. Steel-grey sparks crashed against me like boulders. The sound of my shield shredding was a million cats stretched on a million racks.

It was suicide to push forward.

I stood down. Tears streaming down my face, breath snagging in my lungs like Velcro against silk, I forced myself to back away.

David's head slumped forward, his neck utterly slack in defeat. Ethan's victorious cry echoed across the lawn. Beyond him, Teresa and her cursed sisterhood dragged through a trio of silver flasks.

My knees started to buckle, and I closed my eyes so I would not have to see the rest. I wasn't strong enough to watch the destruction of everything I'd worked for. I wasn't brave enough to face my enemy in utter defeat. I'd pushed myself to my limits, and I was wanting. Teresa Alison Sidney had won.

Before I could hit the ground, a firm hand closed on my biceps.

I knew that grasp. My mind processed the touch even before my eyes bolted open. A strong shoulder was leaning in close to me. A warm body was standing beside me, giving far more support than he took.

Neko.

"No," I croaked through numb lips. "You can't. The Court—"

"Really?" he asked, cutting me off. "You awakened me on the night of a full moon. You gave me autonomy—twice. And you think I'm going to waste my freedom giving in to that desiccated group of pontificating bureaucrats?"

His fingers slipped through one of the rents in my gown of power, settling against the pulse point in my right wrist. He captured the remnants of my own flagging magic and mirrored it back to me, flooding me with sudden power. My mind cleared with every ripple, every reflection. My body calmed. My heart slowed, as if I were in the middle of deep meditation, and I took the time to focus on a series of breaths that cleared the last gasp of panic from my lungs.

Yes, I'd been cast out. Yes, I was poison to all witches who knew me, to my familiar. But that familiar was choosing me, choosing the crazy, patched-together life we'd built together, no matter the cost to himself.

"Excellent," Neko said. "But I'm not the only one who made a choice."

He tilted his head to the side with all the sly grace of a cat calculating its next pounce. My gaze followed him by reflex. A cry caught in my throat as I realized what I was looking at.

My magicarium was ranged in a circle around Teresa's cohort. There, at the east point, at the quarter devoted to the Guardians of Air, stood Raven. Kopek nestled at her side, his hangdog expression made no worse by the overwhelming surroundings. Tony stood behind the pair, his ceremonial sword raised.

Toward the south stood Alex, accompanied by Garth

and by Majom, Clara's familiar. Gran stood several strides away, her weathered hand resting on the forearm of Bree's familiar, Perd. A little farther off stood Emma, protected by Caleb and supported by Alex's Seta. Clara was next, her brilliant chartreuse caftan swirling around Raven's Hani. Bree was last, resting easy with Luke at her back and Nuri by her side.

"Ready?" Neko asked.

"I can't," I croaked. "Working with me will doom all of them."

"That's what David said, when he called me. When he warned the others away."

*When he warned...* That's what David had done, when he'd cast back his head. He could not speak with me; Ethan had seen to that. But the other warder had never thought to cut off David's communication with Neko. My warder and my familiar spoke on a channel nearly as well-worn as the ones they shared with me. Ethan had likely never imagined such a contact. Teresa's tethered familiar Connie certainly offered no such partnership.

"It's not fair," I said.

"Each of us made a choice," Neko answered. "Full and informed. Each witch. Each familiar. Each warder."

David had told them. They knew the cost. And still they'd chosen to stand with me, to preserve our community. I closed my eyes and I could feel it, the steady thrum of six willing witches, six willing familiars, all watched over willing warders. I saw the weaving we could make, the power we could raise.

"*Sisters,*" I sent, blazing into my students' consciousness with a power I'd never dared use before. "*Friends.*" I reached out to include their familiars.

Each responded to my unvoiced question with an offering. Raven rolled out a wave of violet power, an ocean of raw ability that sifted over and around us. Alex, Emma, and Bree dove under that astral blanket, buoying it up with their own signatures—indigo quills from Alex, silver water from Emma, rich brown earth from Bree. Gran and Clara were the last to chime in, rounding out the working with their familiar ruby and emerald strands.

As they poured in their energy, each of my allies shifted, physically moving to adjust their circle. Within a few strides, they'd expanded their boundaries, still enclosing Teresa and her companions within a ring that was large enough to reach me.

I laughed as I stepped into the circumference of their working. Golden light gathered in my chest, rippling to flow down my arms and through my fingertips. Neko bolstered the effect, tossing strands to Perd and Seta, to Hani and Kopek, Nuri and Majom. The other familiars responded as they'd learned to do, as my magicarium had taught them. They fed energy to their witches, reflecting back my students' innate power, charging it to become something new, something stronger.

Our magic sang as we wove our astral fabric above the cordon of Teresa's warders. I heard each individual note, a clarion call from every witch, amplified by every familiar. The ringing cloth sailed high into the air, increasing in strength, magnifying in intensity.

I saw Teresa sense our threat, measure out the danger we presented. I read her lips as she broke off another command to the vortex. Instead, she ordered her sisters to gather closer to the centerstone. She clutched at Connie's shoulder, the bones of her long fingers standing out white against the poor familiar's shirt. I *felt* Teresa's panicked draw on her magical lifeline, clutching at straws to boost her strength, even as she calculated the tremendous array against her.

With a mental nudge, my students and I lowered our weaving. Our cloth coruscated against the dome set by Teresa's warders. I fed more power into our strands, forced them lower, closer, tighter.

Of course those paired warders outside Teresa's glittering cordon did not stand idle. Individually, they poured their energy into their protective hemisphere. The iridescent surface bulged outward, issuing a series of noises like volcanoes splitting the earth. Empowered by their immediate success, the warders redoubled their efforts. The cordon pulsed again, stretching our weaving to the breaking point. Still more energy dripped into the dome, pulsing, pressing, ripping at our efforts.

We staggered.

As a group, we could not maintain our tension, could not continue the inexorable push down against the desperation of eight warders fighting to save the body and spirit of their witches.

Neko hissed beside me, the furious sound of a cat lashed into a corner. I gritted my teeth and tugged a little harder on the rope he offered me, on the strength that bound me to our joint working.

Slowly, painfully, we regained our collective footing. We pressed down on the others. We tightened our weaving, flaring our colored strands like the Northern Lights. Each of my witches renewed her bonds across the circle, reaching out for other familiars, relying on the community we'd built over the past six weeks.

We had a nucleus, a core of common power. But each of us remained independent, remained strong in separate ways. Alex lashed out with her angry urban energy, a wing of power as dark as midnight. Clara poured in her own crazy magic, a sage scented dreamcatcher that bolstered all our disparate strands. Bree and Emma, Raven and Gran, each maintained her own indomitable power.

I saw the look on Teresa's terrified face, and I drained the last power from my capillaries. My own tentacles were woven throughout our working, golden strands that reinforced a flagging edge of our work, that pressed down on the iridescent cordon, that shored up another swaying span.

Teresa's protection started to shudder. Spiderweb cracks opened and closed along the crest of her dome.

"No!" Ethan's bellow rang out beneath our woven canopy, echoing from ground to sky. The one word was filled with anguish, strapped tight against bitter command. He was a warrior who led other men. He was a warder who protected his witch.

Shoving David to his knees, Ethan grabbed for the sword that had been leveled against all my powers. He plucked the steel from David's fingers as easily as he might have taken cotton candy from a child. David was still bound, still enthralled. He could do nothing.

Ethan planted both swords—David's and his own—against the edge of the cordon. He channeled his iron energy through the forged steel, pouring out his power in double time. The angry buzz we'd heard as Ethan bonded David's weapon returned now, ten times louder, twenty.

The draw was too much to sustain. Ethan had to strip his focus from David. He loosened his grip on David's throat, allowing him to speak, to bellow wordless rage. Ethan gathered up the energy he'd spent on David's silence and fed it through the swords, bolstering the cordon still held by his men.

I leaned hard on Neko, crushing the mirrors of his reflective force. The splintering facets shone my power back at new angles. I harvested the dram of fresh power and stabilized our weaving.

Ethan peeled back more of his power from David, freeing my warder's arms. David reached toward me, grasping, desperate. Ethan poured the gleaned energy into Teresa's shimmering dome.

I countered again, reaching through Neko to the other familiars. I used stalwart Perd to excavate the depths of Gran's powers, scraping the last tendrils of her magic and adding them to our web. I clutched at Nuri, relying on my familiarity with the woman to deplete Bree. Majom was next, the mischievous little boy who'd joined our group so early. I carved out every bit of energy Alex could spare, leaving her barely enough to breathe, to swallow.

A sharp crack echoed between Teresa's cordon and my own. Her dome was breaking.

Ethan grunted in response. Sweat streaked his face, ruining the starched collar of his spotless cotton shirt. He pulled back the last of his power from David, yanking the final bonds free with a force that sent my warder staggering like a newborn colt. Ethan dumped his collection into his shimmering dome, shoving the last of his energy into the protection of his witch.

Everything rested in perfect balance. Our carefully woven net pressed against Teresa's cordon. Ethan's boost held our working at bay.

We had nothing left to give. Every witch in my community had poured out her utmost. Each familiar was channeling untold heights of power, weaving it, transmitting, keeping the entire impossible net charged. We were stretched to the outer limits of our capacity. Beyond.

Ethan drained his bond from David's sword. Iron caltrops leaped from the blade, falling against the iridescent dome. With each jagged spike, the structure swelled, pushing back against our net, becoming an opalescent shield that obscured the witches inside.

They were winning. We had offered up everything we had, every trick, every spell. We had nothing left to give. Teresa Alison Sidney and her eight compatriots were safe beneath their dome, secure to continue their working, to siphon off every last item in the Osgood collection.

Every last item, including Neko. He was part of the Osgood collection. When Teresa had stolen everything in Blanton House, she would come for my familiar. She would come for my friend.

My witches' power was stretched to the breaking point. Our familiars were drained.

But there was other magic in the world.

There were warders. Warders who bore their own magic. Warders who worked by their own rules, folding space, raising cordons, binding and releasing weapons.

How many times had I skated past David's astral strength, confident that it was offered to my benefit, for my protection, never caring more for what it did? How many times had I accepted a mysteriously found parking space, a full pantry to ground me after workings, a charm against rain or wind or cold?

David had been my first teacher, my only teacher. I had learned the shape of his powers by instinct, absorbing them at the same time I learned about my own.

Now he crouched beside me where Ethan had tossed him, head lowered to one knee as he reeled from the other warder's final blow. His lungs worked like bellows. He moaned, long and low, despair drawing out a single note into a dirge.

I settled my hand on his shoulder, fingertips reaching for

the pulse in his neck. "*Trust me,*" I thought, pushing the words deep, past his fury with Ethan, past his hurt, his exhaustion, his shame.

I pulled back a little of my power from the web I held with my students. Teresa's dome responded by bulging out, by expanding to capture another yard of earth.

Emma panicked; I felt her concentration shatter, and the cool silver of her powers began to leak out of our web. Everyone else did their best to dam the flow, and I took advantage of the shift to pull back another skein of gold.

In my mind, I shaped my magic into a vessel, a stemmed cup that shimmered in reflected light. Still counting out David's racing pulse, I extended my powers, pushing past our warder-witch bond.

At first, he resisted. His reflexes were trained to clamp down, to shut me out, to cut off any intruder. I shifted my hand on his shoulder, though, moving my palm to rest against the vulnerable side of his neck.

He fought back for a moment, warrior's body and mind refusing to yield. But then he relaxed beside me, issuing a conscious instruction to his clenched jaw, to his fisted fingers. I flashed a single burst of gratitude, and then I pushed deeper, past the dissipating walls of his conscious decisions, beyond the actions that made him the man I loved.

There. At the heart of his awareness. At the core of his being. The sphere was the size of my fist, the size of a human heart. It was steel grey and covered in spikes.

This was the heart of David's power. This was the steely authority I'd recognized the first night he came to my doorstep, borne on the wings of a storm, drawn by my reckless use of magic. This was his warder's energy, the steady stream of logic that he applied, sorting through threats, separating real from perceived. This was the masculine magic

David had focused on Norville Pitt, on maps and pins and strings, as he fought to save me, fought to save Hecate's Court, even when it didn't want to be saved.

I clutched my astral goblet, and touched gold to steel. I collected a trickle of pure warder's magic.

Discordant music jangled, an arpeggio played on the black keys of a piano, mysterious in its haunting familiarity. David poured off more of his power, filling my cup. I spun out the energy by reflex, twining gold and steel together into a single, solid thread.

Neko waited at the edge of my awareness. I passed the strand to him, bracing as he stumbled. He was startled by the weight, by the texture. Warder's magic might be manipulated like witch's magic, it might be gathered and spun and woven, but there was no disguising its masculine base, its solid, man-made core, so different from a witch's natural force.

Neko recovered faster than I thought he could. He braced himself and cast the gilded steel to Hani. *Of course*, a distant part of my mind calculated. *He knows Hani best, knows him through Tony, through the time he's spent with his lover.*

Hani nodded as he caught the astral stream. He hefted it in one hand before tossing it all the way across the circle, to Seta. David's steel began to seep into the net we'd already fashioned. It became a rib, a support for everything we'd already built. Seta handed off the energy to Nuri, and another brace was formed.

By then, Raven was reaching out for Tony. She rested his hand on her hip, the better to balance both of them. She tossed her hair and closed her eyes; I could only imagine the images she was receiving from Hani, the instructions Neko must be feeding all the familiars across their private, silent network.

Within a minute, Hani offered up a bronze bar accompanied by the a crash of thunder, both manifestations of the jagged energy I'd come to know as Tony's. This time, he threw his finding to Majom, an easy under-handed pass. The boy laughed and lobbed it to Perd.

Caleb's power entered the mix, a sleek pewter thread spun out with the crackle of a warming fire. Luke's was next, the easy coil of well-worked leather bound up with the cry of a hunting eagle. Garth was last of all, an uneven onyx strand. It broke once, twice, three times before it held, along with an acid chord on an electric guitar.

But those mishaps didn't matter. As we witches harvested our warders' energy, we fed it into our mix, bolstering our own innate power. Our web tightened. Our net sank over Teresa's dome, weighted down with warder's magic.

The Coven Mother managed one last push, one desperate effort to cast us off. But we renewed our power ten-fold, siphoning off warder's magic as if we'd worked with it for decades.

Leaving my right hand on David's throat, I raised my left, commanding the attention of every one of my allies. I counted off—one, two, three. And then I clenched my fingers into a tight fist. In that same instant, we all hauled back on our powers, tightening our net around the dome.

With a thunderous *crack*, the cordon shattered, exposing nine startled witches, nine panicked familiars, and nine hopeless, helpless enemy warders.

# Chapter 20

FOR ONE LINGERING MOMENT, I thought I'd been struck deaf.

Then, there was an explosion of sound. Teresa's witches gathered close around her, tugging at their familiars as if they were trying to rescue wayward children. Nine warders, Ethan included, circled around, clutching their weapons.

But it was hard to be intimidated by men who were afraid to set their feet flat upon the ground.

The warders could sense the magic that had been used against them, the different strands of steel and bronze, of pewter and leather and onyx. Even if they could not work out what my witches had done, how we'd cast our spell, they knew they'd been bested by a terrifying opponent, by their own breed of magic turned against them in ways they'd never seen before.

My own students gathered beside me. I heard Gran muttering to Clara, insisting she was all right, that she didn't need to sit down, that she was perfectly fit to stand on her own two feet. Bree took a quick inventory like a battlefield general, tallying up our injuries.

Emma stared at our assembled enemies, her face slack with disbelief. "Maria Hernandez," she whispered, not bothering to fake an English accent. I followed her gaze to one of Teresa's allies, a tall woman with angular cheekbones, with sweat-slicked black hair that fell straight down her back.

The name brought a scoff from Raven. Clara raised her voice across the safehold. "Why, Maria?"

The other woman sighed, expelling a weariness that seemed embedded in her bones. "The NWTA." She narrowed her eyes at me, a look that would have been a glare if she'd retained an ounce of strength. "I lost three good witches to that one. My nucleus was breaking up. If I didn't do something, I'd be left with nothing. Weak witches. Gutless followers. Tentacles alone."

Raven snorted in disgust. Maria's face hardened to stone, but she didn't try to explain further.

I used the heavy silence to look at Teresa's other allies. I recognized a couple of them from the case David had built against Pitt. Julie Harton, the Kansas City Coven Mother who had bribed Pitt for her title. Margery Shoreham, the Dallas Coven Mother who had paid off the conniving Pitt when he threatened to disclose her willingness to purchase a truckload of sham spellbooks.

Cassie, my former student. Her freckled face was stunned as she leaned against Zach. Tupa crouched between them, pressing against their knees.

"Why?" I asked her. "What did I ever do to you?"

"Nothing," she said. The single word was dull as sandstone.

"But why would you do this?" I gestured toward the centerstone, toward the jumble of objects stolen from the vault. I waved toward Zach's broken arm. "Why would you work for Pitt and Teresa?"

Cassie's hand fell to Tupa's head, and I wasn't sure she was aware of her action as she stroked his tight curls. She spoke to the ground beneath her feet. "Pitt said I had to." Her whisper was soft enough that I had to step closer to make out her words. "Otherwise he'd take away Zach. He'd take away my warder."

Zach's good hand closed on her shoulder. In that gesture, I saw the entire story, the one Cassie wasn't brave enough to tell. She'd fallen in love with her warder, against tradition, against the rules of Hecate's Court. She'd been too afraid to take a stand; they'd been too afraid together.

And Pitt had somehow learned about their indiscretion. He'd preyed on their fear. He'd forced one little action— applying to the Academy, no doubt. And then he'd demanded more. The satyr, whose brutal attack had only confirmed that Cassie was wrong for what she'd done, corrupt for loving her warder.

I couldn't help but look at David. He had also tried to follow the Court's strictures when we'd first met. He'd kissed me once, then pushed me away, told me that we could not follow through on our attraction. But we'd built on our bond, built on our trust. And we'd decided—together—that some things were worth defying authority. Love was worth taking a stand.

I shook my head as Cassie huddled in misery. "And Teresa?" I asked. "How did you come to work for her?"

"She found out what I did for Pitt. She sensed him when she helped you banish the satyr. He told her about me."

Cassie had caved to one blackmailer. It must have been easier to succumb to another. After all, Teresa hadn't threatened any witch's life. She'd only gone after *things*.

I turned to the Washington Coven Mother. "And you? What was Pitt holding over you?"

Teresa stared me down with chilly pride. "Nothing."

"But you joined forces with him a year ago. You did your

best to keep the Court from issuing the Academy's charter."

"Yes," she said, the single word perfectly toneless.

"You worked with Pitt to set impossible goals for my magicarium."

"Yes." She could have been testifying before the Court, for the bareness of her answers, for her refusal to explain, to justify.

"You conspired with Pitt to bring us down with monsters."

"No!" Teresa's sudden shout was full of anger. "I had nothing to do with the monsters. I told Pitt he went too far. The satyr, the orthros, the harpy—they were designed to maim, to kill. That might have been Pitt's plan, but I never wanted that. Never."

"What *did* you want?"

Teresa gaped at me, her face slack with astonishment. "You have to ask? After all these years? I wanted my property. I wanted the Osgood collection returned to me."

"You never had it!"

"The Osgood collection was squarely located in my territory for over a century. It should have belonged to my witches. It should have enriched *my* coven. But you stole it away the instant it was uncovered."

"The collection called *me*, Teresa. It summoned *me* to that cottage in Georgetown. It taught *me* to awaken Neko. Territory isn't ownership. You have no claim. You never did. You're just a liar and a fraud and a thief."

Her eyes narrowed, and I saw her brace to deliver her killing blow. "Call me whatever you want, Jane Madison. But *you* are outcast from Hecate forever. And you've destroyed every single witch you let work with you tonight."

But I had always told the truth. To Neko, when he appeared on this goddess-forsaken patch of lawn. To my students, through my trusted warder. The women and men who stood with me had known precisely what they paid to bring down Teresa Alison Sidney.

"We are not banished from Hecate," I said. "We are banished from the *Court* of Hecate. We are cast out from covens and magicaria, from institutions of magic so corrupt that we could never bear to stay within them."

As I spoke, I sent out a tendril to Neko, confirming that he'd regained some strength after our battle, that he could offer me a basic familiar's service. He shifted in the crowd behind me, just enough for me I could feel his arm brush against mine.

I reached out to David, too, tugging on our witch-warder bond to show him what I meant to do. I didn't ask his permission, didn't need his consent. But I was grateful, all the same, when he gave me the sparest nod.

Turning my attention back to Teresa, I saw a flicker of fear cross her face. She wasn't an idiot. Far from it—she was the shrewdest adversary I'd faced since I'd become a witch. She knew my momentary lapse in speech could not be an accident. She knew I was planning something.

But she seemed to have forgotten that I was the witch who had set her centerstone. I had poured my magic into the core of her safehold, relying on herbcraft and runes, on ancient knowledge and newly fashioned spells. I had longed for acceptance from Teresa, from the entire Washington Coven. I had been willing to invest anything to belong.

*Almost* anything. Not the Osgood collection. And not, in the end, my dignity.

I spun out a cord of energy, a golden rope long enough to encircle the centerstone. Before Teresa could measure my intention, before she could react, I tightened the cord, cinching it close about the marble.

"Teresa Alison Sidney, you accuse me of taking what you wish was yours. But you're the one who has taken. You stole my power and the power of my students. You plundered the Osgood collection. But your thieving vortexes weren't the first time you took what didn't belong to you. You harvested my magic under false pretenses the night you had me set your cornerstone."

As I uttered the last syllable—*stone*—I cinched my energy tighter, tugging with all the frustration of three long years, with the sorrow of a social outcast, with the shame of a woman betrayed. I drove my energy through the golden strands, reaching out to the spells I'd set inside the center-stone, to the magic that I'd used to secure the heart of the Washington Coven. Clutching at the power that suffused the marble, I broke it into countless shards.

Too late, Teresa cried out. But I had already used the backlash of my golden rope, spreading the power into a shimmering blanket. I gathered up my ancient rowan and ash wand, my bag of jade runes, a stack of leather-bound books that threatened to tumble to the dusty ground beneath the centerstone that was no more.

And when all the pilfered items were safe within my arms, I sent out one last lick of power, blazing toward the shrunken mouth of Teresa's swirling vortex. The stolen power of that whirlwind belonged to me. It broke apart the instant it sensed a command from its proper source.

As sparks flew across the clearing, David's hands settled on my shoulders. I leaned back into his competent, confident touch, and I let him carry me away from Teresa Alison Sidney and the Coven Mothers, and their broken familiars and warders, and everything they had done in their failed attempt to destroy me.

ᘛᘓᘔ

I blinked hard as I materialized back to physical existence.

I expected to find myself in the parlor at Blanton House, or maybe the basement, surrounded by my students and their supporters. But instead, we'd all emerged in an antiseptic hallway. A mottled linoleum floor stretched for miles beneath fluorescent lights. Portraits lined the walls, austere men and women in somber black robes.

"The Night Court of the Eastern Empire?" I asked David, squelching a chill. I'd spent too much time that day in a different courthouse, called before a judicial body that had betrayed me. But the Eastern Empire was separate from Hecate's Court. It was where David and I had come to find evidence of Pitt's crimes, to find records of his monsters terrorizing other supernatural creatures.

David nodded, but his answer was directed to everyone. "We're outcast now. Beyond the reach of Hecate's Court. We're fair game for any supernatural creature that wants our powers, our possessions. The best thing to do is file an Affidavit of Citizenship with the Empire."

I trusted him. I'd always trust him. But I had to ask, "Why? What does that do?"

"It transfers your allegiance from the world of witchcraft to the wider world of supernatural creatures. *All* supernatural creatures."

"Oh," Clara breathed. "Are there fairies?"

I rolled my eyes. Everyone knew there was no such thing as fairies.

"Yes," David said, raising a murmur among the others. "Fairies, gnomes, boggarts."

"Next you'll be saying there are vampires out there," Alex scoffed. Her eyeliner had run down her cheeks in the course of our battle, and she looked like a prisoner behind streaky black bars.

But I knew the truth. I'd seen vampires a year ago, when I'd first met the Night Court's clerk. "There *are* vampires," I said.

David rubbed a hand over his face. "You can read entire encyclopedias about the citizens of the Eastern Empire. And the bottom line is, joining the Empire means you might be sued by any of them. But not joining means any witch in the world can use Hecate's Court against you. From this day forward, you can't appear before Hecate's Court, ever. You'll forfeit any case brought against you there. But if you complete an Affidavit of Independence, any witch who wants to take action against you has to do it here. In the Night Court of the Eastern Empire."

Raven tossed her hair over one shoulder. "Where's the dotted line? I'm ready to sign." Somehow, even after a night of fighting, after the physical and emotional blows we'd all sustained, she still managed to make signing a document sound like an exotic sexual act.

David turned on his heel and led the way down the hall.

Sarah Anderson was actually working behind the counter as we poured into the clerk's office. She offered up her bright smile of recognition, sparing only the slightest glance of concern at the coterie that gathered behind us.

"Of course," she said when David told her what we needed. She disappeared into a back office for a moment, returning with a sheaf of papers. "You can take them down to the cafeteria to complete."

Like a horde of zombies, we shuffled to the cafeteria. I wondered if zombies really existed. If the Empire had jurisdiction over their legal claims. I hoped I never found out.

Collapsing at a cafeteria table, I stared at the rows of vending machines. The adrenaline from our battle was finally wearing off, and hunger was taking its place. I'd need to ground myself soon.

But for the meantime, I muttered a quick spell to banish my fatigue. It depleted the last of my reserves, but at least I'd stay on my feet for another hour or two. I'd pay for it tomorrow. For tomorrow, and the entire week to follow.

Shaking my head, I started to read through the legal jargon on the Affidavit. The requirements for joining the Eastern Empire were set forth in a series of bullet points. I had to be physically present in the Eastern Empire for at least thirty months before applying. Reasonably proficient in English or willing to pay for translation services. Willing to forsake all other loyalties, including but not limited to allegiance to Hecate's Court, Dionysus's Den, and Mercury's Council. Familiar with Empire history, government, and society.

"Just sign it," David said when he saw me hesitate over the last line. I was shocked to hear the sudden exhaustion in his voice. Exhaustion or something more, because he leaned close to whisper: "Sign it, and we'll get you some sort of astral protector tomorrow."

His words shocked me more than any affidavit requirement ever could. "*You're* my astral protector."

"I broke my warder's oath, Jane. I raised a weapon against my witch."

I laughed in disbelief. "That oath was sworn before a body that cast you out! Besides, you couldn't control your actions when you were bonded by Ethan."

"I placed myself under his control. I gambled for Blanton House, and I lost."

"No," I said, and now I was getting angry. "If you think I'm letting you walk away after everything that happened tonight, you're certifiably insane. Do you realize what we discovered out there? *Witches can tap into warder's magic.*"

"Jane—"

I silenced him the most effective way I knew, by pressing my lips against his. His pulse jumped, just as it had on the battlefield.

I knew I could reach out for his warder's power, for that steely sphere deep inside his consciousness. But I didn't want to work magic. I didn't want to burst through new astral frontiers. I just wanted to kiss the man I loved.

And so I did, ignoring everyone else in the room, ignoring the affidavit in front of us, ignoring all the things that were wrong in the world so I could focus on one thing that was very, very right: us.

And it *was* right, because David finally kissed me back.

"Marry me," I said when we came up for air. "Now. Tonight."

He laughed. "You've been planning our wedding for months. You can't toss all that away because you're hungry and exhausted and confused by everything that's changed."

"I'm hungry, yes. And I may need to sleep for a week. But I'm not confused, not by anything. I don't care about our wedding, about flowers and dresses and seating arrangements. And I definitely don't care about knitted cummerbunds and bowties and bouquets. That's just one day. I want all the days that come after. I want a *marriage*."

"Jane—"

I shook my head. "We're already going to be standing in front of a judge. We've got all the witnesses the Empire could ever require. Gran and Clara, too."

"But what about Melissa? She can't enter an Empire courtroom."

"I'll tell her we eloped. She did it herself. She'll understand."

David opened his mouth. Closed it again. Spread his

hands on the table and looked at them as if he'd never seen fingernails before.

"I think," Neko said, shouldering between the two of us, "the word you're looking for is 'Yes.'" He slapped a paper down on the table, another white sheet with bold black letters shouting from the top: Application for Marriage.

"You sign here," Neko said helpfully, pointing to David. "And you here," he said to me. He shoved a silver circlet in front of me. "Tony says you can use his warder's ring. He doesn't need it any more, not with Hecate's Court out of the picture." Neko cocked his head and waggled his fingers at David's own band. "You can give yours to Jane. She can get it sized later."

I signed my name, just like my familiar told me to. David followed suit.

I don't remember any of the details after that. Post-working exhaustion had set in completely, and I had no energy left for another fatigue-banishing spell. I know that Sarah Anderson laughed when Neko handed her the signed marriage form. And she stamped all our Affidavits of Citizenship, providing us each with a copy before she filed away the originals for safekeeping. And we all walked down the corridor to the courtroom, where Judge DuBois sat in his tall chair, steepling his fingers, and pursing his lips at our oddly timed request.

David and I pledged to love each other.

We swore to honor each other.

Neither of us even considered promising to obey the other.

The courtroom cheered when Judge DuBois intoned, "You may kiss to seal your bond." David's lips were soft against mine, gentle, the tail end of a promise he'd made the first night a windswept storm brought him to my doorstep.

We walked down the aisle hand in hand. Raven filmed us from the doorway, ignoring Judge DuBois's disapproving glare. Gran kissed my cheek first, then David's, stopping in between to wipe away her own straggling tears. Clara held me close, crushing the breath from my lungs in the first maternal embrace I could remember. My students pressed close, buoying us past courthouse security, into the bitter cold of a December night.

Caleb volunteered to spirit my mother and grandmother back to Gran's house, transporting each of them and their familiars through his waning stock of warder's magic. Garth hustled off Alex and Seta. Luke took care of Bree and Tupa. Tony brought Raven and Hani home, then came back to gather Neko. Caleb returned to guide Emma and Kopek to their own beds.

Finally, David and I were alone on the courthouse steps. His palms settled on my shoulders, and he leaned close to whisper in my ear. "To Blanton House?"

I nodded. "To home."

He pulled me to his chest, and I caught my breath, waiting for the world to drop away. Just before we swooped into the darkness, a clock began to toll midnight.

# ACKNOWLEDGMENTS

AS ALWAYS, I'M indebted to many people who helped make this new Jane Madison book a reality. Kirstin Olsen introduced me to the concept of a NWTA (the community type, not the magical device type) when we were in college, and she kindly agreed to let me borrow the concept for this novel. I am indebted to the hundreds of people on Facebook who answered spur-of-the-moment questions for me, helping me to choose all sorts of directions for Jane's life.

This book was created under the auspices of Book View Café, and I am indebted to my co-op's fine editors: Patricia Rice, Phyllis Irene Radford, and Jennifer Stevenson. Vonda N. McIntyre did yeoman's work with regard to format review and actually getting the book into the BVC bookstore.

My family continues to support my writing—from the nucleus of the Klaskys to all the tentacles attached. It's always a comfort to know that family has my back.

A special thank you goes to my husband, Mark. His patience, good humor, and constant tolerance keep me going, especially when I just need to spend one...more...night at the computer, helping Jane make her way in the world.

Of course, no writing career is complete without readers. I look forward to corresponding with you through my website: www.mindyklasky.com.

# ABOUT THE AUTHOR

MINDY KLASKY LEARNED to read when her parents shoved a book in her hands and told her she could travel anywhere in the world through stories. She never forgot that advice.

Mindy's travels took her through multiple careers – from litigator to librarian to full-time writer. Mindy's travels have also taken her through various literary genres for readers of all ages – from traditional fantasy to paranormal chick-lit to category romance, from middle-grade to young adult to adult. She is a *USA Today* bestselling author.

In her spare time, Mindy knits, quilts, and tries to tame her endless to-be-read shelf. Her husband and cats do their best to fill the left-over minutes. You can correspond with Mindy at her website: www.mindyklasky.com.

# ABOUT BOOK VIEW CAFÉ

BOOK VIEW CAFÉ is a professional authors' publishing cooperative offering books in multiple formats to readers around the world. With authors in a variety of genres including fantasy, romance, mystery, and science fiction, Book View Café has something for everyone.

Book View Café is good for readers because you can enjoy high-quality books from your favorite authors at reasonable prices.

Book View Café is good for writers because 95% of the profits goes directly to the book's author.

Book View Café authors include New York Times and USA Today bestsellers; Nebula, Hugo, Lambda, and Philip K. Dick Award winners; World Fantasy and Rita Award nominees; and winners and nominees of many other publishing awards.

www.bookviewcafe.com

CPSIA information can be obtained at www.ICGtesting.com
Printed in the USA
LVOW10s1045100116

469981LV00001B/184/P